The Per

J.M. Hewitt is a crime and psychological thriller author. Her work has also been published in three short story anthologies. Her writing combines the complexity of human behaviour with often enchanting settings. In contrast to the sometimes dark content of her books, she lives a very nice life in a seaside town in Suffolk with her dog, Marley.

Also by J.M. Hewitt

The Life She Wants
The Eight-Year Lie
The Other Son
The Crew
The Perfect Village

THE
PERFECT
VILLAGE

J.M.HEWITT

CANELO

First published in the United Kingdom in 2024 by

Canelo
Unit 9, 5th Floor
Cargo Works, 1-2 Hatfields
London SE1 9PG
United Kingdom

A CIP catalogue record for this book is available from the British Library.

Print ISBN 978 1 80436 507 6
Ebook ISBN 978 1 80436 508 3

This book is a work of fiction. Names, characters, businesses, organizations, places and events are either the product of the author's imagination or are used fictitiously. Any resemblance to actual persons, living or dead, events or locales is entirely coincidental.

Cover design by Head Design

Cover images © Shutterstock

Look for more great books at www.canelo.co

Printed and bound in Great Britain by Clays Ltd, Elcograf S.p.A.

1

For Dawson Dallas and Emma Rose

1

VIVACIA – NOW

The children appear on a Wednesday morning.

Rob Caver is the first to see them, and it is *him* that Vivacia sees first. Moving around the gated community, just before dawn. It is not unusual; Rob is often out walking at all hours. Today, though, he sports a large, military-style backpack. The same one that he was carrying when he arrived one year ago.

She hasn't seen him use it since.

Is he leaving?

Vivacia, staring out from the window of her house, averts her eyes. She is not here to look at him. Something else has caught her attention. Something she has been waiting for her whole adult life.

She shoves her bare feet into her trainers and races down the stairs. Yanking open the door, she hurries outside.

It is the start of summer, but the ground underneath her feet is sodden with rain that has been incessant for weeks. Fruitless blackberry bushes line the hedgerows, the first fences of the security-ridden place she's called home for her whole life.

Rob Caver is up ahead. She knows now that he *is* leaving. He is going early, purposefully, because once the sun is up, the residents appear. He knows them all now, is practically one of them. If they see him with all his worldly possessions on his back, she knows they will tempt him to stay.

Just one more cuppa, come on, fella, old Mr Bastille will cajole, his eyes watery and desperate.

In Mr Bastille's world, 'cuppa' means wines, beers or spirits. He is a not-so-secret alcoholic, a barely functioning man. Vivacia suspects he uses his dead wife's concealer to cover the tell-tale broken capillaries on his nose, and the yellowing skin around his eyes.

Sometimes, the guys at the golf club are there early, sinking a few holes and measuring their wealth against each other before turning in from the ninth for a breakfast at the bar. Rob occasionally joins them, which makes Vivacia like him a little less. All those men trapped by their lifestyles of working fourteen-hour days and having heart attacks at forty.

She tracks him at a distance as he heads down the main lane. Behind him is the tiny cluster of original cottages from a time when their residents – Vivacia included – owned all the land of Wolf's Pit. Now, he passes the new builds. McMansions, they call them in America. Here, in the UK, they are ostentatious, pretentious, a show of wealth. There is a very clear divide between the old and new, owners and homes alike.

Vivacia stares at them without slowing her step. They really are glorious, these homes. Stately, showy. Glamourous, like the shiny occupants who reside within them.

Within minutes, Rob reaches the large, double gates that are attached to the eight-foot-tall iron fence which Wolf's Pit is sequestered in. Vivacia pauses so as not to make her presence known to him and surveys the laughable security measure. The smaller, single gate beside the double ones is always propped open at this time of the day. It is an ongoing source of consternation for the residents. The newer ones, those in the McMansions, are constantly reporting the issue. The older ones, who lived here when there were no security measures and didn't even lock their own doors, ignore the cries from the helicopter parents who envision kidnappings and masked gunmen.

Rob slips out of the gate. Moments later, Vivacia follows and feels the band around her chest loosen. Just one step and she is in the countryside. Here, boundaries are natural, as they should be.

Thorny bush barricades, stinging nettle borders, sharp-leaved holly barriers.

Above, the sky is grey, turning from night into day. It will rain again soon. The sky has been emptying itself in an almost continuous torrent for the last five weeks.

Rob is now far ahead, and Vivacia concentrates on the reason she came out here and follows the road – the gated community on her left, the open land on her right.

A car goes past at speed, a big black monster of a vehicle. One of the golfers, no doubt, racing to the first hole, engine revving, twin exhaust shouting out, announcing the size of the driver's manhood to a neighbourhood whose opinion is divided. Half of them look with disdain at the golfing guys; the other ones, the newer guys, aspire to be them.

As if to prove her point, a curtain twitches in an older home behind the iron fencing.

Jackie Jenkins's white hand clutches the material. Her even paler face peers out, her mouth twisted at the sudden peace-shattering racket that the black car left in its wake. Jackie is the ultimate curtain-twitcher. At every noise, no matter how big or small, Jackie is at her window.

Vivacia tilts her head a fraction. A greeting of sorts. Jackie scowls and lets the curtain fall back into place.

Vivacia steps off the path into the copse of trees, half her mind on Jackie and the folk she's known for always.

The collective of strange locals: Bastille and Jackie, the Widow Ruth, Blind Iris. Living alongside people they despise, even though the sale of their land allowed them to remain in their original homes, many of which have been in their families for generations. They all got a huge profit, those landowners, Vivacia included. *We are really no different from the people we proclaim to dislike for their greed*, she thinks now. Pound signs dangled like a carrot, bursting big bank accounts, and then the reality of having an entirely different breed of people moving in next door.

Being somewhat in the middle, or on the outside, depending on the way one looks at it, Vivacia has observed both points of view, over the years. Sometimes it is fun. Mostly, she finds the atmosphere within the gated community depressing. She wouldn't blame Rob for leaving. She's amazed he stayed this long.

Vivacia could have – *should have* – escaped long ago. She's been waiting here, stagnant, a long time. For what, she didn't know until she saw it this morning.

He is at the edge of the wooded area now, she sees. Wolf's Pit behind him. Here is the invisible boundary of the strange little suburb.

Ahead and to their left, the sun is battling to rise through the low, grey, bloated clouds. An orange orb in amongst the silver haze. It is an amazing light, and she watches it shimmering for a moment, before a movement in her peripheral vision makes her look to the left.

Lady Well. Once a clearwater spring. Through last year's drought it was dry but is now probably swollen with water. It is disused and covered over, and hundreds of years old. As it stands now, it is just a haphazard row of bricks, more buried than unearthed, forming an almost semicircle in the woodland.

The new sun is casting beams onto it, and the cornfield dust creates fireflies. Orange and yellow and brown. The colours of autumn already in the blaze of a waterlogged summer that hasn't even started yet.

The husky motes aren't what catches Vivacia's eye. After all, they have been floating past her face and flaking to land in her hair all the damp season long.

Something… Something was there. She saw it, thought it might be a dream. Just now, and earlier, when she stood at her window.

She stays still for a while, watching Rob as he makes his way up the big hill, the one that her husband used to vanish beyond, night after night, day after day.

Nearing the top, Rob puts his hand to his chest. She recalls the morning when he came here, how hard his body was, how he could have heaved that bag on his back up this hill and not broken a sweat.

There is too much here for a single man on his own. The spinsters have fed him, leaving casseroles and the like on the red step of his rental home. The newer, Stepford wives-type have tried to counteract those offerings with protein shakes and bland seeds, which probably only served to make him reach for calorific cream and carbs. There have been pints with Mr Bastille, and breakfasts with the golf wankers. And espresso martinis from the women with thin, sharp-as-glass bodies.

Vivacia has given him nothing. Not even a second glance, despite her attempts at civility.

At the crest of the hill he stops, hands on knees, coughing and hacking away because of the cigarettes that the Widow Ruth is so fond of – small brown cheroots – that Vivacia had seen him accepting, probably so as not to appear rude, and then had become hooked on.

There is a sound of rustling from the well. Vivacia emerges from the undergrowth, no longer caring if Rob sees her, while also wondering what he sees if – when – he looks at her.

She keeps her breathing steady as she reaches the well and holds out her hands.

Obediently, they reach out their arms, a mimicry of Vivacia's own stance. They slip their small fingers into her own. As their flesh meets hers, she feels a burst of colour in an otherwise dreary world.

This is what she has been waiting for. They have returned to her, after all this time.

'Come on, Elizabeth, come on, Alex,' she murmurs, 'let's go home.'

–

On the walk back, the children's fingers curl around hers and it feels unnatural, like they don't really fit properly.

Like they're not used to holding someone else's hand.

She glances down at their heads. She hasn't seen them for four years.

She wiggles their hands in her own, filled with joy or madness — the two are so closely related — and they glance up at her curiously, then look away just as quickly.

She thinks about past foster children she had in her care, how when some of them arrived, they couldn't even look her in the face. How far they came, how much they grew in every way in her care. They had flourished, until… until they stopped coming.

Her grip tightens a little, maybe too much, because the boy flutters at her side. His sister darts a look at him. He settles, softening under her gaze.

The air has broken around them; it is no longer dawn, but daytime. Vivacia stops walking abruptly. This is Wolf's Pit gated community; anyone — *everyone* — could be watching. She already passed Jackie Jenkins, at her permanent sentry post.

Vivacia isn't supposed to have children in her care anymore, and there are enough busybodies here who would report her in an instant, just like they did the last time.

She jerks the children's hands, not roughly, but enough to let them know they are about to change direction.

'We'll go home now,' she says. 'Come on.'

She glances at them as they walk. Elizabeth is wearing a dress, a dark corduroy ensemble. Alex has on a shirt which once might have been his Sunday best but is now torn and ragged. His jeans are brown, but looking closer, she sees they may once have been classic denim blue. Both of their outfits are wet, soaked through from either the rain or the dewy grass.

She faces forward as she pulls them onwards. It is not the first time she's taken in a child who literally has arrived with nothing. Once, there was a child wrapped in a towel. It wasn't even a nice

6

towel, not one that had been tumble-dried to softness. Vivacia had ripped it off as soon as the social worker had handed her the child and dressed her in a brand-new pyjama set. Vivacia always has a stock of new clothes, in different sizes, for this very reason.

She hasn't had cause to use them lately, of course. She's no longer on the emergency list. She's no longer on any list.

But she never got rid of the clothes. She has known that one day there would be children in her life again.

She has prayed hard to a God she doesn't believe in for a day such as this.

On the main road Vivacia holds her breath. There is a back way through to her house, through the dented iron railings and the subsequent missing panel on her own fence that the rest of the community don't know or don't care about because it's far away from their own homes and therefore is not a blot on their pristine environment.

But she's not doing anything wrong, despite what happened before. It wasn't her fault. It was *his*.

Everything was his fault, but now he's no longer around to take responsibility for it.

She holds her chin a little higher, a bravado that she might regret later.

She has waited so long for this day.

Let them look, let them come.

She squeezes the small, cold hands in hers once more, slips in through the single gate that is still ajar, and takes the children home.

–

In the kitchen she deposits them at the table. The table is the heart of the home, so her mother said, and her mother's mother before her, when this was her house. For a while, Vivacia agreed with them, back when she had people to sit around the table. *He* had sat at this table, back when *he* was here, and the children.

Other people too. Friends, she had called them then; now they are simply neighbours. There had been tea and soft drinks, fizzy ones which she knew the kids loved, but she made sure to balance with healthier options.

Many children have passed through this house, but the last two, the final two – the two that have now returned – Vivacia had thought of as her own. There was nothing for them back home; their stay with her wasn't simply a respite for a struggling mother or father. For the first time she had dared to hope.

She'd done more than hope. She'd started looking into adoption.

Such a fine line between fostering and forever. That time, she'd dared to begin preparations for the latter.

Then everything had happened, and the children had been taken away. Then *he* had gone, and even though he wasn't here any longer, her own name was on some sort of blacklist.

No children allowed here.

As she leans against the butler sink, she feels a subtle thrill at what she has done today. She's brought children into the house again.

'Are you hungry?' she asks now, as she watches them looking at the chairs that she has pulled out for them. 'It's okay, you can sit down,' she adds.

They don't move. They stare balefully off into the distance, as though she isn't even there.

Here, in the full daylight that streams through the patio doors, she can see them properly. Their hair is long, both of them. It is brown, not a rich chestnut like her own hair, but stringy and dark, almost black in places.

Her stomach roils and tumbles. A sudden, unwelcome thought pierces through to the part of her that still houses some sanity.

These children are not Alex and Elizabeth. Even though they were so tiny when she last saw them, she knows deep down that the two currently seated at her table are not them.

8

She tries to calm herself. It is okay. It is still all right. These are still children. They have come to her.

They've *chosen* her.

Vivacia squints at them. She thinks that if – *when* – she washes their hair, there is a good chance they might be blonde. Their eyes are identical shades of green, emerald, bright, but marred by red lids and broken veins in the sclera. Alex and Elizabeth had piercing blue eyes. They were strawberry blonde – thin, wispy hair atop their heads – and Vivacia knew that, once grown, they would be full-blown redheads. She'd hoped to witness it. But…

She shakes her head to dispel the painful fragments of the past.

And, God, these children are thin. They're dirty, definitely malnourished; their eyes are dull, the lids heavy as though they're either near sleep or very recently woken.

And their skin…

It's… wrong. Something is very wrong with them.

As a former foster carer, she has seen it all. Babies arriving naked, pale, black and blue with aged bruises. Toddlers smeared in their own excrement, screaming with fear at nappies she had brandished; something they'd never seen before, never felt on their skin. Older children with big hollow eyes, sunken cheeks and a habit of flinching should she inadvertently move her hands too quickly. The older ones were the hardest, their shame at bed-soiling concealed with a learned aggression.

But these two, this… This skin thing. It's not bruising. It's an all-over sheen that is unnatural.

She thinks of Lady Well, and the old folk tales of the beings that appear atop of it from other places, other worlds, other universes.

She huffs out a nervous laugh.

Ghost stories.

Urban tales.

She takes a deep breath and addresses the girl. The hope of before refuses to be diminished so quickly. 'Are you… Is your name Elizabeth?'

9

She takes one step towards the table, towards them. The children rear back and their shoulders slide together, as if drawn by a magnetic force. Neither of them answers her.

In the ensuing silence, a knock at the front door forces a scream from Vivacia. She covers her mouth, apologises profusely at the same time as swearing silently at the person at the door. The children do nothing.

As if they didn't even hear either the knock or her subsequent shriek.

'Stay here,' she instructs.

She pulls the kitchen door closed behind her and hurries down the hall, muttering profanities to herself. She'd known people would be watching, but they have no shame. Not even five minutes have passed since she collected the children off Lady Well, and already they're hammering down her door.

Another, shocking thought: it is their parents waiting on the other side of the threshold.

She hisses out an expletive one second before she yanks the door open.

At the sight of the person standing there, she blinks.

'Oh,' she says, 'it's you.'

'Hello,' says Rob, the not-so-newcomer to the community.

She'd have bet money on it being one of the others. Not Jackie Jenkins, because she talks to nobody; she simply watches from afar. Not Mr Bastille, because he never rises before noon, but someone like Ruth or one of the other, newer ones, who have no shame and ask their nosy questions outright.

Those people, she can handle, because she's grown up with them and is now used to them, and she has a little bit of her mother and grandmother in her. Rob is... different.

He doesn't belong here, so he shouldn't really be so confident, even though people such as alcoholic Bastille and the golf-club knobs and even the rich new lot have welcomed him into their inner circles.

She's not exactly been friendly to him. She remembers that first time she met him. He'd asked if he could call her 'V'. She'd told him no, her name was Vivacia. Then, in a fug of coolness to disguise the sudden warmth that had crept over her, she'd informed him that there really wasn't any need for him to call her anything.

She looks at him now, but not directly, a little over his shoulder to avoid his uncomfortably direct stare.

'Are they okay?' he asks now.

'What?' she asks, fighting panic. 'Who?'

He gestures, seemingly impatient. 'Those kids. They were on Lady Well. I didn't realise what I was looking at, not at first.' He pauses for breath, leans over a little, as though he's run all the way here from the fields. 'Are they yours?'

It is such a loaded question. If he spent time with the villagers, which he has, he'd *know* they were not hers. If she says the wrong thing, it will get back to them, all those watchers. It is easier to say nothing.

'What do you want?' she asks, dodging the question altogether. The enormous backpack looms large. 'Are you moving on?'

Accidentally, she catches his gaze. She lowers her line of sight, but not before she sees the spark in his deep, violet eyes. Internally, she curses. It is the first question she's ever asked him, despite his many attempts at conversation.

Silence stretches so long that she dares to peep at him. His face is a curious mix of misery and hope.

'Probably, soon,' he says. His voice is heavy with resignation. 'Just wanted to stop by, see if they were okay.' He waves his hand towards the inside of her house.

Vivacia flinches, recovers and takes a step back.

'They're fine.' She nods at him, cool, calm, polite but offering nothing.

Rob doesn't move.

Vivacia feels herself deflate. She will have to give him something, anything, to make him leave.

'Thank you.' She smiles, though it has been so long since she smiled at a man that she's sure it simply looks like she's baring her teeth at him. 'Bye,' she adds, and closes the door swiftly.

The journey from door to kitchen takes seconds, but in the brief time it takes her, she is sure that the children will be gone. Vanished, just as swiftly as they appeared. Just like all the other children before these ones.

She throws open the door to the kitchen, and with something like sorrow, she realises they are as she left them. Children don't stay still as told, not normally. Not unless it has been drilled into them.

Beaten into them.

They haven't moved. Both boy and girl are sitting at the table, shoulder to shoulder. The boy stares at the oven. His eyes are big and round, and red-rimmed with tiredness. The girl sits beside him, but her gaze is narrowed, suspicious almost. Her eyes follow Vivacia as she makes her way around to the other side of the table, and pulls out a chair, sits down and observes them.

She would put them at five years old. They are dirty, unkempt and thin to the point of looking starved. Then there is the skin issue.

'Can you tell me your names?' she asks in a quiet voice.

There is no answer, no response, not a movement or a reaction.

She looks to the boy. 'Are you Alex?'

He stares at the oven.

'Do you have a mummy?' Vivacia holds her breath.

Even as she dares to hope, she knows it isn't the way it works. They are not stray cats whom she can feed and water, who will eventually move into her home and make themselves comfortable. She can't just find a pair of kids and keep them.

Can she?

Can I?

The desperate part of her thinks she can. They are clearly unloved, unwanted – look at them! If the mother came

12

searching for them now, Vivacia would fight before she handed them back.

Vivacia isn't a churchgoer. She hasn't set foot in a church since all those funerals four years ago. Unlike most of the villagers, and despite her constant prayers, she shuns God. He can't exist, not with all the awful things that happen in the world — that have happened right here in Wolf's Pit. But right now, she wonders if He is real, and whether He is presenting her with these two children.

It had been approaching sunup when Vivacia awoke this morning. The village was dark and quiet. The curtains were drawn, the bedroom relatively cool. She didn't know what had woken her, but something had prompted her to get out of bed and look out of the window. Not even her own bedroom window, but that of the spare room which looks out across the fields that lead to Lady Well.

There they were: two tiny figures crouched upon the spring. Like faeries or elves. Haloed in the strangest summer light she'd ever seen.

It had certainly seemed like a sign. A reward for a life she has tried, and mostly failed, to live correctly.

Her gaze wanders now to the window, to Lady Well beyond both her fence and the one that the community constructed.

Vivacia shivers.

God would not reward her. All she deserves is punishment.

She looks again to the children. The boy has moved even closer to the girl, is leaning against her. The girl sags under the slight weight of him. The boy's legs tremble, his fingers twitch. His eyelids are heavy.

They look… weak.

Vivacia stands suddenly. 'I'll get you food,' she says. 'You must be starving.'

Starving in the literal sense, she thinks as she whips bread out of the cupboard, butter from the fridge and pulls down all her home-made jams.

She works quickly, slicing, spreading, grabbing milk, sloshing it into glasses. She heaps the plate of bread on a tray, along with the milk. At the last minute she remembers the biscuits and snatches them up too.

Vivacia turns towards the table. There is nobody there.

There is a breeze at her knee, and an indistinguishable aroma, sudden and fierce, like a fruit that has rotted.

The children are here, at her legs, so close she can feel (and smell) them.

She jumps, squeaks; the milk slops over the side of one of the glasses. A biscuit rolls the width of the tray and slides over the edge.

'To the table,' Vivacia says. Her voice is breathless, high-pitched. She sounds fearful, she knows, and her heart is beating fast.

It is not a new phenomenon. For many years she experienced it. Only since *he's* been gone have the palpitations softened somewhat. Now they are back with a vengeance, taking her breath away.

It's because this is new, she tells herself. She's bound to be jumpy.

But the children don't move. The tray in front of her impedes her complete view of them, so she moves it to the left and peers down.

They look up at her, tiny things that they are. Eyes big but weary, as though they're a hundred years old. For a long moment, Vivacia is a soft, melting puddle. Then she looks again, lower this time. The boy is holding a knife. Her paring knife. She recognises it from the mother-of-pearl handle, a relic from when this was her grandmother's house. Vivacia keeps it sharp, well cared for, the blade deadly to attack fruit that isn't quite ripe.

The boy moves fast, drawing his hand back. His eyes change, the whites now red – wolf's eyes – as the blade whizzes through the air towards Vivacia.

2

VIVACIA – BEFORE

They married on an April morning. It rained all day. There were no photographs of them outside the town hall where the registry office was housed. The reception, organised by her mother and grandmother, was in The Bull, in the next village along.

Serafina Bastille presented Vivacia with a voucher for the food hall a few miles away and wished them luck.

Charles Lomax, Vivacia's new husband, took umbrage at that.

'Why would we need luck?' he asked.

His voice was cold. Vivacia hadn't heard that tone from him before, but somehow, perhaps instinctively, she knew what it meant.

She thanked Serafina profusely for the gift and led Charles to the bar. There, she attempted to allay his fury with spirits that they could ill afford and which he declined.

They could not have a honeymoon – there was no money – so Charles borrowed the car from Vivacia's grandmother, Kay. It had belonged to Steven, Vivacia's grandfather. He had been dead for five years, and the car, an old brown Ford estate, had barely been used in that time.

They got as far as Ixworth, a parish just six miles down the road, before the vehicle juddered to a halt.

Vivacia watched in the wing mirror as Charles kicked the side of the car.

Up ahead was a sign for a bed and breakfast. Vivacia dug in her purse, came up with fifty pounds that Blind Iris had given them as a wedding gift.

'We can stay there,' she said through the window to Charles, fanning the money at him. 'A romantic wedding night.'

He took the money, carefully folded it and put it in his pocket. 'You been keeping this from me, wife?' he asked.

Vivacia laughed. There was a nervous edge to it.

He booked them into the B&B. Vivacia hovered beside him, fingers gripping the reception desk.

Mr and Mrs Mark Mantel, he wrote on the booking slip.

'A bit of fun.' He winked at Vivacia. Then, to the receptionist, 'We won't be having breakfast.'

They didn't have dinner, either. With wedding-day nerves, Vivacia had barely eaten anything. Instead, she sat by the window, watching the rain slowly turn into sleet. Charles smiled at her, beckoned her to him.

This time, when he called her 'wife' again, he said it with a smile, and it changed his face into one that she recognised from when they were courting.

A taxi waited for them quite a distance down the lane the next morning. Charles hustled Vivacia out and gave the driver the address of their Wolf's Pit home. They drove past her grandfather's old brown Ford, still on the verge a half a mile from the B&B.

Later, as Vivacia put Charles's suit jacket in plastic for dry-cleaning, she found the fifty pounds that Iris had given them, still folded neatly.

She left the money on the telephone table in the hallway; she borrowed thirty pounds from her mother and promised twenty of it to the mechanic, Paul, if he managed to get Kay's car rescued from the side of the road in Ixworth, and a further ten pounds if he could fix the dent that Charles's kick had produced in the side panel.

A day later, the Ford was back in Kay's garage.

Iris's wedding gift of fifty pounds had vanished from the hallway table. Vivacia didn't mention it, and neither did Charles.

–

They lived in Kay's home. A set of six houses, built in the Twenties, five of them set in a row. Serafina and her husband Mr Bastille, Blind Iris, the Widow Ruth, and Jackie and Cally Jenkins on the end. Stephanie, Vivacia's mother, lived in a small cottage on the corner. When Charles announced his intention to marry Vivacia, Kay, frailer now – but only in body rather than mind – decided to accept Stephanie's long-standing invitation to move in with her. The newly-weds had a home in the place where Vivacia had spent all her childhood.

It was set way back from the other five homes, so they had no immediate neighbours. It was isolated, off the beaten track. Vivacia loved it.

Vivacia worked in a hotel on the outskirts of the village. Wolf's Pit was remote, visitors were scarce and she was the manager-cum-housekeeper-cum-receptionist-cum-occasional cook. She didn't have many friends, though there was Linda, who ran a book club in the evenings and always pestered Vivacia to attend. Sometimes she did, but the women there were on a different level to her. Cally Jenkins was Vivacia's best friend. They couldn't be more different from each other, but they'd grown up together. Their similarities made their friendship work. Both fatherless, both with strong, independent mothers. That, and the scarcity of other kids in the area.

Charles was a salesman. Of what depended on the week or the season or the month. All Vivacia knew was that their finances were never in great condition.

She walked to and from work, usually stopping at Stephanie's on the way home. Three generations, sipping tea, looking out over the land.

They couldn't be called gardens, even though the plots belonged to each home. An absurd number of fields. 'Wasted,' said Mr Bastille. Ruth said they could be used for housing developments. 'Probably will be, in years to come,' was Charles's input.

Sometimes Cally would sit with them, drinking wine instead of the tea that was offered to her. The older women enjoyed her adventures of nights out and weekends away. Kay, always too cool to be seen as a grandmother, would swap her own cuppa for a brandy.

'You enjoy it, girl,' she encouraged. 'You're only young once.'

Perhaps it was all in Vivacia's head, but she often thought all three of them gave her pitying glances, as though she was wasting the best years of her life in a marriage to a man that nobody seemed to connect with.

One Monday evening, while Vivacia was taking tea with her mother and grandmother, Kay pushed a fat envelope into her hands.

'Deeds,' she said. 'House and land. Yours.'

Vivacia was wide-eyed. She'd known that, eventually, the house she lived in would belong to her, but not for years. And, surely, shouldn't it go to Stephanie first, and then, many decades from now, pass to Vivacia?

'I've got my place,' said Stephanie, gesturing around the lovely conservatory in which they were presently seated.

'And I want to see you okay while I'm above ground,' added Kay, dark humour at its finest.

Stephanie, hands caked with clay, retreated with a smile back to her studio. Just the two of them, Kay leaned forward and tapped the envelope.

'Don't flash it about. There's no need for anyone to know you hold the deeds.' Her piercing blue eyes, which Vivacia had inherited, were sharp and clear. 'Just you, your mum and me. Got it, dear?'

Vivacia nodded. She loved this village, loved all the people who resided here, but she understood. Her grandmother, and folks like Mr Bastille and Iris and Ruth, were of another generation. They deplored nosiness at the same time as trying to root in their neighbours' business.

'Got it, Gran,' Vivacia said.

Kay insisted on escorting Vivacia the few hundred yards home. Vivacia held her arm, a support of sorts, but Kay was too independent, so Vivacia made it seem like they were walking arm-in-arm. Affection, rather than assistance.

'Perhaps I should keep the deeds at my place?' mused Kay as they walked the path to what was now officially Vivacia's front door.

'I'll keep them safe, Gran,' she replied.

A long moment of silence. 'When I say there's no need for anyone else to know that you're now the owner of this house, I mean...' Kay's eyes drifted up to the bedroom window where Vivacia and Charles now slept.

'Oh,' said Vivacia. 'Oh, okay.'

Kay patted Vivacia's arm and leaned in for a kiss, her skin papery and rough on Vivacia's cheek.

Charles had no boundaries. He liked to look at everything. One time, before Kay had officially changed her address, her bank statement had turned up at the house. He'd opened it, even though it was addressed to Kay, and read it, whistling over the figures until Vivacia took it away from him. Too ashamed to tell her grandmother that Charles had opened it, Vivacia shredded it into tiny pieces and burned it in the fireplace.

She decided to put the deeds in a suitcase, one of three that sat atop their wardrobe. There would be no holidays. There would be no money for holidays.

It softened the blow of what had so far been a little bit of a disappointment, she admitted to herself late one night, as she waited for Charles to come home. The secret knowledge of the deeds buoyed her, enabled her to carry on, walking to work, doing whatever was asked of her, returning home more and more often to an empty house, the place in darkness until her husband rolled in later and later each evening. He never offered an explanation as to where he had been, and Vivacia didn't like to ask.

Until a month in, when he didn't come home one night at all.

3

VIVACIA – NOW

At the sight of the swishing blade, Vivacia slings the tray laden with goodies on the table and darts away from the little paring knife.

A memory tries to push through. Someone hurling something, swinging a makeshift weapon. Vivacia buries it deep, like she's got so good at doing.

She reverses all the way around the table until she reaches the patio door. She grips the handle to slide it open and staggers outside. Door crashed to closed, scream emitted, hands over face.

Not even a second has passed before she hears a noise, a crashing, footsteps thumping up the alley and bursting through the gate.

That bloody Rob is here again.

He is expressing concern, like he always seems to. Vivacia doesn't know if she answers him or not. If she does, she is probably rude to him. She normally is. It is a novelty, to speak brusquely to someone, to ignore at times. Later, she almost always feels bad.

But not bad enough to apologise.

She turns her back on Rob and dares to peek through the window, dreading that the boy has changed the trajectory of that sharp, deadly blade onto his silent sister.

He still has the knife, but he also has another object in his small hands.

An apple.

They were behind her in the kitchen, she realises now, the basket of apples. That's what the boy was aiming for with his blade, not her.

She feels foolish. Idiotic. These are children. They don't hurt people.

Ignoring Rob, she slips back inside the house. The door slides closed behind her. She feels for the edge of the curtain. With an angled yank, she pulls it shut against Rob.

The children are upon the apple now. Literally falling upon it, both of them, like hungry foxes or wolves. The apple skin has fallen to the floor, an intact strip. The girl darts out a hand and snatches it up. Pushes the whole thing in her mouth. It is like they haven't eaten in months.

'Look,' says Vivacia, voice trembling. 'Bread, butter too. And biscuits.' She gestures to the tray again, on the table.

Carnage ensues.

Vivacia stumbles to sit on a chair and observes them. She doesn't notice that she's crying. Softly, silently, the way she used to.

–

The feast ends abruptly when the boy is sick. He slumps to the floor, head bent over, and purges everything he's just eaten into his lap.

Vivacia cries some more. She knows better than this. Malnourished kids need to eat gently, a little at a time, just like a dehydrated person needs to sip.

The girl leaps into action. She grabs the tea towel which is draped over the side of the sink and mops at him. All the while, she still reaches for the upended tray, picking up pieces of food without looking at it, shoving it into her mouth. Carefully, with a quick look at Vivacia, the girl picks up the knife and puts it on the tabletop, before resuming her feast.

She is the caregiver, Vivacia realises. She knows to look after him. How long has she been taking care of him? She wonders, has anyone ever taken care of *her*?

Somehow, she doesn't want to interrupt this tender but terrible scene in front of her. But, Vivacia reminds herself, *she* is the caregiver here. She needs to assert her role. She needs to let these two know that there is someone else to look after them now.

Someone else to *love* them now.

'Bath time!' she trills gaily. 'We'll get you both cleaned up, shall we?'

They turn their eyes on her at the sound of her voice but make no attempt to move.

'Bathroom!' she says. 'Come on, follow me.'

She moves past them, through the hallway to the stairs where she chances a glance back. To her surprise, they are following her. The girl leading, the boy clutching her hand. Behind them, the kitchen is a disaster. Vivacia studies it for a moment. The mess. It speaks of children in her home.

She smiles, gestures them in front of her, and together they trek up the stairs.

Even as the happiness floods through her, she worries.

Any second now there will be a knock at the door. Not irritating Rob, this time, but the police. She can imagine how it will play out.

They will brandish a photo, like they do in the movies. *Have you seen these children? They were last spotted in this area.*

Her breath catches. What will she say to them? What will her answer be?

She envisages it now. She will paint a mask of concern on her face as she peers at their photographs. *No*, she will say, *I haven't seen them.*

She will lie.

Happily and easily, she will lie to the authorities.

She leaves the children standing outside the bathroom as a thought strikes her, and she hurtles back downstairs. She slides open the patio door gently and peers outside. Rob is not in the garden anymore. She hurries back through to the front. The curtains are open wide in the living room. Her cottage is set out of the way of prying eyes, but only from the other homes. Any of the other residents could be taking their morning constitutional in front of her house.

What if the police see Rob, a rambler, and thrust the photo under his nose? What will *he* say to them?

She deflates a little. He will tell them the truth. What sane, normal person would lie about a pair of missing kids?

She yanks the curtains closed, races back upstairs to do the same to the front-bedroom windows and, without pausing to catch her breath, she hurries back to the bathroom.

The children are where she left them. They might not be here for long, but they are here right now. The least she can do is clean them up.

She flashes them a smile before filling the tub. Deftly, she removes their clothes as they stand compliant, unmoving, eyes fixed in a stare that goes beyond her.

She catches hold of Elizabeth's hands. Her nails are broken, jagged, caked in dirt.

Like she's dug herself out of somewhere.

Vivacia shudders and turns her attention to the rest of their bodies.

She tries not to stare too hard at their flesh.

Here, in the bright light of the bathroom, in all their naked glory, it is apparent once again that something is very, very wrong.

Their skin is green.

Like two tiny aliens in front of her. But Vivacia doesn't believe in things like that. Besides, she can clearly see beating hearts beneath their thin ribs. An allergy, perhaps, or a lack of some vital vitamin.

They are not other-worldly creatures. They are children, in desperate need of care.

24

They need to be checked over – medically, mentally, physically – by an expert. And there is the sticking point. Her former foster children had come into her care through the proper channels. Signed off, as it were. If she takes these two to a medical professional, there will be questions: who are they to you? What are their names? How old are they?

She wouldn't be able to answer a single one of their questions.

Why are they in your care?

She shudders: the worst question of all.

She tries to think of people who have some experience, who might help her, low-key. People she knows. She calls them that because she doesn't have friends, only mere acquaintances. The women of her age who live inside this community believe they are her friends. Vivacia is good at deceiving them. She goes to their homes, joins in their Pilates sessions and swaps recipes like a good little housewife.

Vivacia lets them believe they are pals. It is easier that way. But she'd never ask anything of them. Would never take them into her confidence.

There is another woman, Linda. She doesn't live in the community but she's local, in a nearby village that doesn't reside behind iron railings and constant scrutiny and locked gates. They used to be in the same book club, back when Vivacia had a life, years ago, when she was only just recently married. Then all that stuff happened with *him*, and the children and her family, and she had to start hiding away.

But she could drop Linda a line. The woman always seemed to *get* Vivacia. Nothing was ever said, but it was as though Linda knew anyway.

Her phone, the mobile she barely even switches on anymore, is in the drawer in her bedside table. She retrieves it now, pleased to see there is some charge in it. She hammers out a text to Linda:

She presses send. Realises belatedly she used no pleasantries at all in the message. It is as though she's forgotten how to interact with outsiders. Like she's feral. She glances at the children. Maybe that's why she was chosen for these two. Common ground and all that.

The bath is full now. Warm water, soap at the ready. 'In you get,' she says to the children.

They do so, again with no fuss. They sit down carefully, facing each other. The boy pats the surface of the water lightly. The girl stares at the tiled wall.

Vivacia's phone pings with an incoming message, making her jump. She snatches it up. It's from Linda.

Who is this?

Vivacia sighs. Skills rusty. She never even signed off her text message. She scribes one back.

It's Vivacia, I used to go to the book club. How are you, Linda?

She adds the last bit in a hasty, inexpert attempt at friendliness, before putting the phone on the floor and turning back to the children.

'Please, can you tell me your names?' Vivacia asks, her voice no more than a whisper, mingling in with the steam that rises from the tub.

The girl looks at her, eyes glinting but expressionless.

'My name is Vivacia,' she says.

The girl's eyes widen slightly, before she lifts a hand, water dripping, and points behind Vivacia. Vivacia turns. Behind her there are flowers, dried ones in a vase.

'You like the flowers?' Vivacia says, a little too eagerly perhaps, and scoots back to bring them to the side of the bath. Outside, the rain is now hammering down.

The little girl plucks out a dried rose and scrutinises it. The boy's eyes follow her movements.

'It's pretty, isn't it?' Vivacia says. 'Later, when you're clean, when it stops raining, we'll go in the garden. Lots of flowers out there. Real ones.' She pauses, locks eyes with the girl. 'Flowers that are alive.'

She pauses, reflecting on her words. She can take them outside, out the back, she reasons. Her home is secluded, set apart from the other homes. It isn't overlooked by any of the other houses – not the new, luxury ones, nor any of the original cottages.

She takes the plunge and scrubs at the children, lathering soap, gentle with their skin, trying not to shudder when her hands make contact with that strange, green hue.

The girl holds on to the flower, even when Vivacia pushes her carefully backwards and soaps shampoo first into her hair and then on the boy's head.

Vivacia studies them when they are clean. She was right in her initial thoughts; they are both blonde.

They are both beautiful.

They are still green.

She wonders where they came from. How they came to be here. It's not like this is a big city that's near to a shopping centre where a child can wander off. Let alone two children!

The thought comes again, hot with desperation. That these two *are* her missing babies, the ones who were taken away when they were tiny, fat, pink almost-newborns.

The love she gave them back then, the love she saturated them with, maybe it seeped into them. They remembered it. They returned for more of it.

'Alex,' she whispers. 'Elizabeth. My babies.'

They avert their eyes and look steadfastly at the wall.

She lets them stay in the bath for a while. They seem to enjoy the water, and judging from the filthy brown colour, she can only imagine how long it has been since they were cleaned. Carefully, she drains the bath, a little at a time, and refills it with warm water.

As she thinks of the other young ones she's had here, she feels a tug of sadness. The splashes, the shrieks, the screams, even the tears and tantrums. Back then, these two were happy in her care. What has happened to them in the intervening years?

Her phone goes off again. The boy starts at the sound. Vivacia pats him gently on his arm, wipes her hands and reads the new text from Linda.

> Are you coming back to the book club? We miss you! I wasn't a nurse, just a receptionist at the clinic. Ask that Rob about your skin complaint, he was a medic in a former life.

Vivacia dissects the message, line by line. She has no intention of returning to the book club. For a moment she thinks about those evenings. The escape they were, losing oneself in literature, be it a classic or a feel-good read. She generally skipped the crime fiction and horror weeks. Back then, she had enough of that in real life.

The other comment is a lie. They don't miss her. She doubts they even realised she'd stopped attending.

And what's this about Rob? Does Linda mean travelling Rob, sometimes referred to as the Newcomer? How does Linda, two villages to the south, know about him?

Somehow, the thought of him as a medic doesn't fit. He is simply a well-off man using his father's money to travel around the country, like an overgrown child on a gap year. That's what she presumes, anyway.

It's why he fits in so well with the Stepford wives and their husbands who reside here, and those idiots who race up and down the road beyond the fences to the golf course.

He does have nice hands, though. As though he takes care of them. A random thing to have noticed, but notice she did.

She looks down at her own hands. Red now, from the hot water. Tiny white scars criss-cross her palm, an injury from a night she'd rather forget but will never be able to.

Her phone beeps once more. Ever-helpful Linda, again.

> Here's Rob's number!

Something – envy? – prods at Vivacia. So, Book-Club Linda has Rob's number.

She puts the phone down again. Today has only just begun, but already she has spoken to far too many people.

The children are standing ankle-deep in the water when Vivacia pulls herself back to the present.

Vivacia is still not dressed. The children are clean, finally, and are now in tepid bathwater.

She grabs a bath towel off the rail and notices the boy is shivering.

Shit, shit, how could she have been so stupid?

Stupid. Mental. Crazy. Ugly. Worthless.

Vivacia draws a sharp breath. No. Those were not her words. They were someone else's. She isn't stupid, or worthless. She's a *mother*. Finally. And even the best mothers sometimes get it a little wrong, make silly mistakes. This is not a disaster. It is July; cold water will not hurt them.

So why is Alex shivering?

She scoops him out first, swaddles the towel around him, tucking the corner in so it stays put. She reaches for Elizabeth, who is still clutching the flower in her hand. The girl avoids her outstretched arms and clambers out herself.

Clothes! She remembers an earlier thought she had, all those bits and bobs left over from the children who have passed through over the years. There will be something in the airing cupboard that fits these two.

She pulls another bath towel off the side and wraps it around the girl.

'Wait here,' she instructs. Pushing herself up, she darts to the landing, wrenches open the door of the built-in cupboard and surveys the neat piles of freshly laundered kids' clothes.

She hasn't opened this cupboard for years. All these garments are a relic of a past lost to her.

The clothes in the cupboard are stored according to age and size. Neat, perhaps bordering on an obsessive nature. Not her doing, but again, *his*. He likes order.

Liked, she reminds herself.

She pulls out the piles for five-year-olds and closes the door to the past.

As she does so, she cannot ignore what science is telling her. Even though these children are little, and seemingly malnourished, their ages don't quite fit those of Alex and Elizabeth.

Her heart dips before rising again. It doesn't matter. They are still here, they have still come to her. Maybe they are not those two original babies.

Or maybe they are. Stranger things have happened.

Blue striped shorts and a navy-blue T-shirt for him, she decides as she rifles through. She pushes them onto his compliant little form. He stands, fully dressed in clothes appropriate for the season. The outfit is a little too big, but she doesn't want to open the cupboard again quite yet and have a barrage of further memories fall onto her.

Vivacia picks up the clothes she removed from them before their bath and holds them gingerly. She won't even wash them,·

she decides. They are stiff with dried, encrusted dirt, and far too heavy and bulky for this time of year.

She turns them inside out, sweeping hands through pockets on reflex. In the pocket of the girl's corduroy dress, her fingers close on something. She pulls it out. A piece of paper, typeset on both sides, a torn part of a page from a book.

Written across it, printed in heavy, black marker pen, is a name.

A name as familiar as her own.

The world spins dizzily before coming to a halt.

4

VIVACIA – BEFORE

In those early days of marriage, Vivacia thought of Cally, who lived two doors down.

Cally would never put up with a husband who stayed out all night.

On a rare day off, Vivacia knocked on her friend's door.

'Still sleeping,' said Cally's mother, Jackie, jerking her thumb towards the stairs.

Just the sight of Cally, in her bed, head under the covers, the room smelling of pot and vodka, cheered Vivacia. Cally was a constant, she would never change.

'I need your advice,' announced Vivacia when Cally's tousled blonde head emerged from the quilt.

'Ugh.' Cally passed a hand across her face. 'What the hell time is it?'

'Noon!' exclaimed Vivacia. 'Come on, up!'

While she waited for Cally to get dressed, Vivacia wondered how she found it so easy to order her friend around, when she dared not speak the same way to her husband.

'We're in a rut,' said Vivacia as they tramped the fields that were technically their gardens.

'Already?' Cally lit up a cigarette and blew smoke rings into the warm May air.

'I… I think maybe I'm not enough.' There, she'd said it. It was the first time she'd allowed the words to be spoken. It was hard enough even thinking them.

Cally scrutinised her through the fog of Marlboro Reds. 'How's the sex?' she asked.

Vivacia shrugged. 'Good.'

'For you or him?'

Vivacia reddened. 'Good for me.'

'Liar.' Cally lay back in the grass. Heavy exhausts rumbled like thunder as a fleet of sleek black cars passed through the lane. 'I think Charles wants to be one of those men.'

'Which men?'

'The sort that go down there every day.' Cally pointed down the road, where the golf course sat. 'Trophy wives at home, two-point-four kids, etc., etc. *Status*.' She emphasised the last word. 'He wants to be important. Someone other people look up to.'

Vivacia wondered how Cally knew what he aspired to be. It wasn't as though they spent a lot of time together. Charles and Cally, two of the most important people in Vivacia's life, disliked each other intensely.

She thought about the loneliness at home. The sad fact that Stephanie and Kay were always busy doing something. Stephanie in her studio, Kay trotting off to bridge nights and walking tours with the other older villagers. Cally, living twenty-four hours' worth of fun in a single night out. Charles, off selling, wheeler-dealing, schmoozing.

They could have a baby.

Their baby.

Her baby.

The sex was better now there was a point to it, she discovered. Charles seemed happier too.

'I knew you had it in you,' he remarked as he slapped her backside.

Vivacia didn't really understand his comment. She didn't like to enquire further.

—

33

The money tin was empty on the day Vivacia suspected she was pregnant. It was how her grandmother and her mother before her had managed the household. Money in the bank was not to be touched; it was there for the direct debits for the bills. Each month, cash was withdrawn for essential shopping and occasional treats. Vivacia monitored it carefully. She had no qualms about this; it all came from her small wage. She never enquired about Charles's money, even though they were married. They did not share a bank account – just one of the many things that as a couple they'd not yet got around to. She hadn't got around to changing her surname either. She wasn't sure she wanted to. She liked being a Williams, the third in a line of strong women, whose name was known and respected in the village. Even if she felt she didn't match up to her mother and grandmother's name.

She needed money for the bus fare on that particular Friday morning. She had a dentist appointment after work and would take the bus into town rather than walking home as she normally did. But the tin was empty – every note, every coin gone – even though it had only been two weeks since payday.

It wasn't a disaster. She would simply withdraw some from the cash machine.

At work that day, she felt a little like she'd failed. She'd never run out of money before payday. Then she thought of Cally, who blew all her wages on nightclubs and cigarettes and weed and alcohol, and was forever borrowing off her mother. That happened every month, and with that thought, Vivacia's mood lifted somewhat.

Until she inserted her bank card into the cash machine, and it swallowed it.

She enquired inside the branch. It was all gone, they said once she'd provided her identification, and they'd printed out her balance and recent transactions. All gone, the maximum amounts of cash withdrawn over the last couple of months at cash machines here, there and everywhere.

A couple of thousand pounds.

A new scheme, a business deal, Charles said later when he rolled in after midnight. It was why he'd been working so hard, such long hours, and besides, he'd *told* her, didn't she remember?

That had stumped her. She was certain he'd not asked to borrow two thousand pounds. She would have remembered that.

Charles had turned cold. 'I clearly recall telling you. You, on the other hand, were distracted, because she was here, your "friend".' He put inverted commas around the word, and Vivacia knew he was talking about Cally. He always did that when he mentioned her.

'You were both pissed out of your heads,' Charles went on.

Vivacia remembered the night. Cally had come for dinner when Charles had said he'd be working late. She generally only came to visit if he wasn't there.

Cally had a bottle of vodka, swiped from Jackie's drinks cabinet, and she'd ignored the lasagne Vivacia had made, smoking one cigarette after another, gossiping non-stop. Vivacia had run around the downstairs, opening windows, doors, flushing the tobacco smoke out before Charles came home and smelled it.

Eventually, she'd been defeated; she sat down and had a small glass of vodka mixed with some tonic.

He'd called them lushes when he returned. He'd made a show of getting the air freshener out of the cupboard and spraying it in such a quantity that Cally had started coughing pointedly.

'Too many fags,' he'd called after her as she'd ducked out of the door and gone back to Jackie's.

Vivacia recalled that night in full. She always did, with them two. Her husband and her best friend, dancing around each other, snide comments from Charles, sarcastic comebacks from Cally. Vivacia, in the middle, unsure of how to make amends or keep the peace or make them tolerate each other, even if they couldn't actually like each other.

She never recalled a request of money lending.

'Did it work?' she asked in a whisper. 'The business thing?'

Charles's lips worked, red and fleshy, as he seemed to choose his words. He withdrew his wallet, peeled out a wad of notes and flung them at her.

'Here you go, *wife*,' he said. He was smiling, but it wasn't an ordinary smile.

For the first time, Vivacia thought he looked ugly.

The notes in their bundles lay on the floor, beside and underneath the coffee table. Vivacia imagined herself on her knees, picking them up. She couldn't stand the image.

'I'll make some tea,' she murmured.

He stood there, downcast and sullen. Vivacia changed trajectory and ran to him, wrapped her arms around his lithe, trim waist. 'I'm sorry,' she said.

The money had been picked up from the floor the following morning. At work, she called the automated line to check her balance. It was still in minus figures. Charles came home earlier that night, bearing a bouquet of plastic-wrapped flowers with the price still on them.

'I don't deserve you,' he said. His eyes shone with unshed tears.

Just like with the deeds, she'd been keeping her own secret, holding it close like a precious thing. Now, she knew, it was time to release it.

She put her hand on her still-flat stomach. 'You do deserve *us*,' she said.

His response was odd. 'I suppose you think you're clever, do you?' he mused, putting his hands behind his head and leaning back in the kitchen chair.

She didn't respond, couldn't even think of how to reply to that.

'I made half of it,' he said. He brought a hand down and stroked his index finger from the underside of her breast to her underwear.

He left his finger there, jabbed it into her lower stomach.

'Yes,' she said. 'It's half of you.'

Her voice trembled, but she hoped he'd think she was simply emotional.

5

VIVACIA – NOW

Vivacia stares at the name on the piece of paper that was in the little girl's pocket until the letters blur and dance.

Carefully, she folds it in two and tucks it into the waistband of her pyjama shorts. Even though she can no longer see it, it lingers like a pungent aroma.

Out of sight, out of mind. Pushed far back into a deep, dark recess where she doesn't have to think about it. She's good at doing that.

First things first: the little girl who may or may not be Elizabeth needs to get dressed.

She surveys her and thinks of fantasies long gone. Pink dresses and flowery patterns. This girl is not that. Although she has not yet spoken, she is tough and feisty – the protector, the leader.

Vivacia thinks of another way.

'Come and choose,' she says, pointing at the piles of clothes on the floor next to her. 'What would you like to wear?'

Still swaddled in her towel, she pads over to Vivacia. With the flower clutched in her hand, she bends down and surveys the clothes.

Solemnly, she points to a blue checked, short-sleeved shirt. It is from the boys' clothes pile. Vivacia decides it doesn't matter. That small motion is in fact a milestone. Up to now, the girl has been willing and compliant, robotic almost, but now she has made a decision for herself.

'Good choice...' Vivacia says, softly. She manages to stop herself calling the girl Elizabeth, just in case.

The girl kneels and pulls out a flowery pair of shorts. They clash horribly with the shirt, but Vivacia nods.

The girl holds the shorts and pinches the flower pattern upon it, roses and lilies. Slowly, she locks eyes with Vivacia. With her other hand, the one still holding the flower, she points at her own chest.

'Yes, sweetie, it's yours. We can put them on you.'

A minute shake of the head, blonde tendrils of hair flicking droplets of water to her shoulders. With a little more force, and with her lips a straight line of concentration, she jabs her finger into her breastbone.

Vivacia looks more closely. As if the child has transferred her thoughts directly into Vivacia's mind, she knows what she is trying to say.

'Rose?' she whispers, fingering the material herself. The knowledge of her next words is deep within her. 'That's your name.'

It isn't a question, but she watches the girl for a reaction. A tiny, almost imperceptible nod is her reply.

'Rose!' Vivacia wants to draw the child to her but settles for hugging herself instead. 'What a beautiful name!'

It's not Elizabeth, and it stings, but not as much as she would have imagined. She leans back and regards Rose.

'Can you... Can you *say* your name?' Vivacia asks.

But Rose has moved away, clutching the clothes she has selected. Carefully, she pulls them on herself. Vivacia watches the boy. He remains in place, eyes lowered, standing stock-still. She is no closer to finding out his name. All she knows is that he isn't Alex.

'Rose,' she says, conversationally. 'What's your brother's name?'

She works as she speaks, doesn't want her own intense stare to mute the children further. If she talks to herself, as though it

39

is the most normal thing in the world, perhaps their own small voices will follow.

There is no reply from Rose; it is as if she didn't hear the question. As Vivacia straightens the shirt collar on the boy, she wonders about their silence.

Rose could be deaf; the pair of them could be. The only times she's had reactions is when she's been looking directly at them. Rose could be lip-reading. Or perhaps they are mute, or non-verbal. Maybe they have never spoken. And that's okay, Vivacia has had some dealings with that before. There are other ways of expression, and Vivacia has the patience for it all.

Rose has her back to Vivacia now, as she peers into the bathtub.

'Rose, please can you pull the plug out for me?' asks Vivacia, casually. She holds her breath.

Rose stills and then yanks the chain, going so far as to wrap it neatly around the tap.

'Jeeee-sus,' Vivacia whispers to herself. She isn't deaf, then.

Rose turns around.

Vivacia beams at her. 'Good job!' she says.

Vivacia pulls yesterday's jeans and shirt out of the laundry basket and puts them on. The paper flutters to the floor.

She picks it up, holding it gingerly. She could flush it down the toilet, she thinks.

But she's done a lot of things that are wrong, and she doesn't want to start off this new life with a bad action. She folds it in two, shoves it in the back pocket of her jeans.

–

Downstairs, and Vivacia had forgotten the vomiting that happened before bath time. Both children turn their eyes on her – soulful, doleful, slightly accusatory stares.

Vivacia leads them to the table. From the dresser she pulls out a pad and an old box of crayons. There from kids past, just like the clothes. *He* wanted to get rid of them, but Vivacia never did. As if she knew that, one day, *he* would be gone and the house would hold children again.

She puts the paper in front of them, tells them to draw her something lovely. 'Whatever you want,' she says.

She busies herself cleaning up, opening the patio doors, even though it is drizzling, to let the air into the house and take away the aroma of drying, cloying sickness.

She pauses as she dashes the mop around the floor and looks at the children. They have not removed any crayons from the box. Instead, they stare at the pads of paper. They are exchanging little glances with each other, she notices. No words are spoken, both silent still, but as she watches them, she sees Rose shake her head, as if her brother had asked a question.

Interesting.

Rose abandons the table, moving over to the bookcase. She moves with caution, eyes on Vivacia, as though at any moment she's going to tell the little girl, 'No.'

Vivacia loves this particular shelf. It houses books that she cherishes. Books that her mother read, that her grandmother Kay collected. Even Kay's own mother, a woman that Vivacia never knew, had some poetry collections that remain here.

Rose stares up at it.

'Do you read, sweetheart?' asks Vivacia. A tingle of excitement at a fifth generation's children's book being placed on this very shelf.

Rose turns to face Vivacia. Vivacia blanches at the look on Rose's face.

Pure fear.

At what, though, she has no idea.

The thought fades as she's struck again by that awful green hue that is Rose's skin.

She moves outside, just past the patio door, and looks out over the garden. Ruth's old home, now a holiday rental in which Newcomer Rob currently resides, is her closest neighbour. But it is at an angle, set up and away from Vivacia's place.

She has to move right to the furthest corner of her own garden just to catch a glimpse of his place.

She does this now, and glances over. It's not a house like hers, rather a chalet bungalow. No chance of nosiness from the living area.

She narrows her eyes. There is a tiny balcony that leads from the bedroom, and he is sitting out on it now, one leg up on the railing, mug of something steaming in his hand.

And he's staring straight at her.

Damn.

Feeling caught, she moves a couple of paces back towards the door, to her house. A quick glance tells her that the children have not moved. She peers closer. Is it her imagination or have they… wilted? They look tired, dazed, eyes glazed. From here, in the meagre light that has forced through the dark clouds at the back of the house, their skin looks… shocking.

Rob had said he was probably moving on. If so, it might be okay to ask his advice, and not just on this strange fleshy issue; he was apparently a medic, so he could give them an entire once-over. There would be no risk of the hospital or the doctor calling in the social and taking them away from her. And if Rob was leaving for pastures new, he wouldn't give her and the children another thought.

Vivacia takes a deep breath before stepping back into the corner of the garden.

He is there still, a half-smile on his face, his hand raised in a tentative greeting.

'Rob,' she calls. 'Would you be able to pop over, just for a minute?'

For several awkward seconds he doesn't respond. Vivacia feels her body curling in on itself. Is it possible she's misunderstood all his kindly gestures over the last year? Has she been – as someone once told her – her normal, stupid self?

Then he moves, using the iron railing to haul himself up.

'Come over?' he shouts back.

She winces at the volume of his voice and suppresses the urge to shush him.

'Please.' She tries not to gnash her teeth together and attempts a smile.

'Sure!' Rob says. 'Give me two minutes.'

He turns to leave, but she calls him again.

'Rob,' she says, 'come round the back, okay?'

He nods. 'Okay.'

She hears rather than sees the door close behind him. Vivacia stands in place, one eye on the back gate, shooting looks at the children, who are still at the table, paper unused and crayons unopened in front of them.

She clasps her hands together as sweat builds at her hairline and hopes that she hasn't just made the worst mistake of her life.

She is trusting Rob, someone she barely knows. And the last time Vivacia trusted someone, it ended very, very badly.

The steady drizzle has turned rapidly into the downpour they've all become accustomed to this year. He arrives swiftly, ducking through into her garden.

'Linda said you were a medic, is that right?' she asks before he's even closed the gate behind him.

She sounds breathless, even to herself, and she knows her eyes are alight in a way he's never seen them.

'Who is Linda?' he frowns, then grimaces as the heavens open once again.

Her excitement turns to frustration. 'From the book club,' she says.

'I don't go to a book club,' he replies, confused.

'It doesn't matter!' she says. 'Is it true?'

'Oh, wait... that woman with the sprained ankle? Ages ago!' Something in Vivacia's face makes him blanch and he reddens, slightly. 'I remember,' he says. 'And I was a medic.' He seems to snap back to the present. 'Are you okay?' he asks. 'You're... ill?'

She shakes her head. 'Not me. The children…' She trails off, intense stare searing into him before she hurriedly averts her eyes. 'My cousin's children are staying with me. She's not well – my cousin, I mean. I think they need… evaluating.'

It sounds like a lie. She is sure he knows it; she is aware that her eyes are darting around, left and right, anywhere but at him.

'What are your specific concerns? Are they sick, vomiting, hurt?' She can practically see his mind turn darker, suddenly reminded of things he might have seen in the past. *Abused? Beaten? Neglected?*

Vivacia leans back against the wall. Under the large fascia, she is sheltered from the rain shower. She chews at her lower lip. She is replaying his daily activities: his drinking sessions with Mr Bastille, his jokes with Blind Iris, his seemingly close friendships with all the residents of the community, apart from her because she's always acted coldly towards him.

'You haven't got anything to worry about. Doctor–patient confidentiality.' His jokey tone has her standing upright. There is nothing humorous here.

Vivacia pushes herself off the wall. She has decided.

'No questions,' she says as she opens the patio door and walks through it. 'It's delicate.'

She wonders what he makes of the scene in front of him. Two young children seated at a table which is strewn with pads and unopened boxes of crayons. They are clean; the aroma of recently used shampoo and soap is fragrant in the air. They are dressed in summer clothing, not the heavy, wintery attire of earlier. The boy looks neat, like a little sailor, and the girl is wearing a cute but mismatched outfit.

All normal, at first glance, she imagines he will think.

He steps inside next to Vivacia and walks around the table.

He stops short. His lips move then clamp closed, as though he has just about managed to restrain himself from uttering a curse word.

The next moment, he has recovered.

'Hi, guys!' His voice, when it finally emerges, is an embarrassing squeak. He coughs, reddens and attempts a smile. 'I'm Rob, I'm just going to check you guys over, if that's all right. What're your names, then?'

They stare at him, two caricatures of kids.

Vivacia clears her throat.

'This is Rose,' she says. 'And...' She hesitates. She has not yet worked out his name. 'This is Alex,' she finishes with the first name that comes to mind and raises her chin, daring him to call her out on it.

He turns back to the children, eyes roaming over their flesh.

Vivacia forces her shoulders to relax. Why would he call her out on the false name? He doesn't know it is a lie. He doesn't know the Alex that came before. The one she loved with all her heart.

The one that was taken away.

'Well?' prompts Vivacia.

He sighs. 'They'd be best being checked over at the hospital.'

'Is there... anything we can do? Here, I mean. Rather than... doing that?'

'They need tests.' His voice is firm.

'What do you think it is?' she asks.

He doesn't answer her question, but fixes her with a steely glare. 'What's wrong with your cousin?' he asks.

'What?' she asks, confused.

'Their mother,' he says. 'Your... cousin.'

She sees what he is thinking, clear as day on his face. All the things the original villagers say. That she's mental, has been since her husband left her, perhaps even before that.

He turns to face her full on, his back to the children. 'Did you steal these children?'

She has never seen Rob like that. Assertive. He's been... Well, he's been nothing to her, because she hasn't let him. But she had suspected he was rather soft and pliable.

He isn't.

It is a frightening realisation.

Her eyes flash, a mixture of anger and pain. 'I would *never* do that.'

He snorts, laughs loudly. 'Joke!' he says. 'I was joking.'

But it didn't sound like a joke. His expression is not one of humour.

A shuffling noise, someone approaching. Rose, whom Vivacia didn't even notice had left the table, is returning to the room.

The girl is carrying something – it's too big for her, but she struggles with it, nonetheless. It is a globe.

'Oh, sweetie, let me help you with that, it's heavy.' Vivacia comes around the table, arms outreached to take it.

Rob clears his throat as his phone vibrates in his hand. He holds it up. 'I'll just…' He gestures to the door.

Vivacia turns back to Rose. Let him leave. Asking him here was a mistake.

Together, they put the globe on the tabletop. Rose climbs back on her chair and carefully spins the globe around.

Vivacia wonders if she thinks it is a toy, before it becomes clear that she is actively seeking a specific part of the world.

The boy watches it in its lazy spin. His finger comes up to rest upon it, but Rose glares at him until he removes his hand.

Rose stops and rests her green forefinger on the sphere. Vivacia moves closer to her.

'America, darling,' she says.

Rose taps upon it – one, two, three times – then, with the same finger, she taps her brother's collarbone.

'Texas?' It is almost a shout from Vivacia. Guiltily, she looks over her shoulder, checking that Rob is still outside.

With one hand, Rose curls her small fingers around Vivacia's wrist and draws her closer. With the other hand, she touches her forefinger and thumb together then moves them apart.

'Zoom in,' murmurs Vivacia.

She understands the language of this strange little girl. The girl herself, although she seems like a being from another world, or another time, knows phones, has used one.

'Dallas.' Vivacia stands up, looks from Rose to the boy. With absolute, dead certainty, Vivacia repeats it again. 'Dallas. That's your brother's name.' Her voice doesn't rise in a lilt with a question at the end.

Rose nods, once, sternly almost, and sits back on the chair, hands primly in her lap.

6

THE CHILDREN

In the beginning, with Mother, they knew happiness and love. Tender touches and laughter. They couldn't say when things began to change.

There were others once upon a time. When Father was home, the others kneeled at his feet, fell over themselves to do anything they thought he might want or like.

The boy child and the girl child vaguely recalled a period when there were both spoken and written words, but the memories were long ago, and couldn't be pinned down to an age or time. Silence and absence replaced them. Sometimes, the girl child experimented with sounds and noises. The boy child was not as brave, and he remained mute.

Now, things have changed. The change had been coming for a while, and the girl believed she had been preparing for it. Just like Father taught them. When the change came, the boy would do what she told him to. He followed her always.

It was a matter of survival. The people who were once many were now zero, apart from Mother. They didn't count her, though, because although she was there in body, she had been gone a long, long time. Probably even before the others started leaving.

Father had been gone for longer than usual. So long that a red film had covered everything: the rooms in which they lived, Mother, even the very silence in which they existed.

The red film had such long-reaching tentacles, it even touched them.

Food was gone, a while ago now, and the doors didn't open anymore.

-

'Is there anything?' Mother's voice was a bleat, pitiful and husky.

Rose shook her head. 'No, nothing.'

Mother cried. Dallas sat in silence on Mother's bed. The bed wasn't a good bed. It wasn't really a bed at all, but a couch. But Mother had been sleeping on it for so long that it was referred to as her bed.

The bed/couch smelled really bad. The washing hadn't been done for longer than Rose could remember.

Many things were hard to recall now. In fact, it was only this morning she remembered her name was Rose.

R.O.S.E. She even remembered how to spell it. Mother taught her, along with many other things. The lessons stopped when Mother got too sad. Dallas didn't remember as much as Rose, or perhaps he just didn't feel the same sense of urgency that Rose did.

Or maybe, collectively, they'd all had that urgent notion, but they were frozen by it. Today was the first day that Mother sat up in bed. The first day she asked for food. It was called a *second wind*. Not to be confused with the second coming, which was what Father said he was.

But that slight breeze dropped eventually. Rose knew that there wouldn't be a third chance. Dallas never even got the second wind. He sat beside Mother, much the same way he had for the last however long. Eyes half-closed, fixed at a point on the caravan door.

Once upon a time, that door was always open. The voices, singing and laughing, would come into the caravan. Joyous, Father said it was.

The voices left over time, drifting away like the people they belonged to.

A creeping touch in her palm. She looked down at it, surprised. Dallas's hand. Small, soft, dirty; identical to her own. He jerked his head. She looked to the bed.

Mother was trying to sit up. She failed, fell back, head upon the dirty brown pillow. Her hand slipped from the bed, knuckles tapping a rhythm on the plastic floor.

Dallas curled up into Mother's back. Mother cried again, a whimper. Still, she tapped the floor, the tempo pulsing in Rose's head. It was the most noise she'd heard in days, and coupled with Mother's crying, it made her head hurt.

The movement changed. Mother was scratching now, fingertips plucking at the edge of the vinyl floor. One edge peeled back. A small amount, not even enough for a hiding place to be revealed. *But there is a hiding place there!* A memory came to Rose with such clarity it was like colours bursting in the sky, like fireworks. Rose remembered them too, a long time ago, back with the laughter and the joy, before the silence and sadness.

But the fireworks were not what Rose needed to recall right now.

She squeezed her eyes closed, curled her small hands into fists and tried to remember.

–

The night that Father burned the books. He took them out of the caravan and threw them onto the bonfire. Mother, her face thin and deathly white in the moonlight, her mouth an 'O' of surprise. Father raged; those words in the pages were other people's ideas, not in keeping with Father's rules. 'Back to basics,' he had shouted.

Mother had pulled on Father's arms, her face glowing in the firelight. Father had pushed her. Mother sat for a while on the scorched grass before running back into the caravan.

Rose had watched the fire burn for a while longer, drawing Dallas to her side. She didn't like the smell of it, but the warmth was lovely, because the nights were cold.

Across the way, two shadows moved in the space where once upon a time there had been many caravans. She recognised them, Albert and Sasha. Albert saw her looking, raised his hand to his lips.

Rose understood; they were leaving. Just like all the others.

It made her sad, but she admitted to herself that if she were able, she would rather like to leave too.

She nodded to Albert. But because they had been kind to her, Sasha especially, a single nod of her head didn't seem enough.

Rose stood up and waved. 'Goodbye!' she shouted. She gripped Dallas's arm, forced it to and fro, so he could wave as well.

A curse word carried on the wind from Albert. Father paused in his book burning and turned to see who Rose was waving at.

They ran then – Albert, dragging Sasha by her wrist – and Father took off too. Rose thought it was funny, adults chasing each other around like that. But then her smile faded. It wasn't the way she chased Dallas.

She pulled her brother to his feet and retreated to the safety of the caravan, and Mother. Dallas shook her hand from his arm. He crouched near to the door and watched the adults in their funny fight. He smiled, and licked his lips, and trembled the way he did when he was scared or excited.

While Father chased the people who were once his friends, Mother was busy inside the caravan.

She'd pulled back the horrid vinyl flooring to reveal a shallow hole. In it she tossed books, pens, pencils. A pack of biscuits, a pair of earrings and a silver bracelet.

Rose got it: these were Important Things.

Rose looked around for her Important Things that could fit inside the hole. But Rose was already wise beyond her years.

Mother and Dallas. They were important. Nothing else was, not really.

Not even Father.

Especially not Father.

This last was a thinking in a whisper because it was an Evil Thought.

Now, a long time after the bonfire, as Mother scratched at the floor, at the secret hole, Rose understood it was time for the Important Things to reappear.

Mother's fingers were bloody, red tracks, lines and swirls. They looked like they were hurting, so Rose crouched down to help, pausing only to poke Dallas and make him follow her lead.

He did what she told him, as always.

They worked in silence, a little family of three, bound by the blood that mixed on the floor.

7

VIVACIA – BEFORE

The baby didn't stay inside Vivacia for long.

She didn't make it to the three-month mark, when it was supposedly safe to tell people. Only Charles knew, although it seemed to Vivacia that he'd forgotten.

Before it went away, Vivacia squirreled money out of the cashpoint once her account was back in the black, always making sure to keep her bank card with her now. She took lunch breaks, whereas she hadn't ever done before. She walked around the town, buying the smallest booties, soft wool blankets, and pink dresses and blue babygros. Dummies and nappies and teddies. It was still unknown to everyone, and she stored her purchases in her locker at work. When that became full, she stashed piles of baby things in the bottom drawer of her desk.

Some days she was sick, but she didn't mind the onslaught on her body. It was proof of life inside her. She embraced it. Searched her face in the mirror, seeking signs of the glow she'd heard so much about. She didn't find it, but maybe it would come.

That night, they had dinner in a town a train ride away. They didn't go out much. When they did, it was to local, old-fashioned pubs like The Bull, where two-for-one meal deals were on during the week, and the pints were cheaper than in establishments in the neighbouring town centres.

Vivacia had on jeans, wanting to get all the wear out of them while they still fit her. Charles came downstairs in a suit. It was

53

his best one, his only one. A kind of shiny, almost silver, grey. The suit he'd worn to marry her a few months before.

He said nothing about her outfit, but he raked his eyes from her head to her feet.

'I can change,' she said. It was almost a plea. She'd not known they were going somewhere that warranted a suit.

He glanced at his watch. 'We really don't have time.' His face was a painting of disappointment.

She found an old scarlet lipstick in the bottom of her purse. Not hers – it must have been one that Cally left on a now-rare visit to the house, or an even rarer night out years back. She slashed it on her lips, using the window as a mirror.

'Oh Christ, really?' Charles looked to be in extreme pain as he regarded her face. 'Please, don't try and be someone that you're not.'

She was reminded of another time when she couldn't quite work out what his remark meant. Nonetheless, she scrabbled around for a tissue, finding none and resorting to wiping it off her lips with the back of her hand.

The red remained like a burn. Charles grimaced and turned away.

–

'Can we afford this?' she asked once they were seated, wide-eyed at the price of a simple eight-ounce. This was a fancy place, where events were held, like weddings and posh work dos. The steaks cost thirty pounds a head, the sides and fries extra.

His lips folded into a straight line. 'Great way to make me feel inadequate, *wife*,' he said, softly.

She would learn, in time, that when he called her 'wife', it was usually the starting signal of his displeasure.

She chose the cheapest meal, and then, in an attempt to make him feel the adequacy he craved so, she switched her choice to the filet, adding three sides and additional sauces.

The food came. Charles said, 'You'd think she was eating for two, wouldn't you,' to the server.

Vivacia laughed, thought it was a private joke, seeing as they hadn't told anyone else yet. The waiter's face was blank.

He leaned across and pinched her stomach. 'Piggy,' he said.

He told her on the walk back to the train station that the evening had been a little embarrassing, and they would have to learn in the future how to conduct themselves at places like that.

'I'm going places, Vivacia, so we need to act like we belong in the places where I want to be. Smart clothes, appropriate make-up, hair, and all that.' He clenched his fists and shoved them, balled up, in his pockets. 'And I think we need to eat better portions, in the correct manner. After all,' he forced out a laugh, 'we're not in Kay's kitchen, are we?'

He included himself as he spoke, but Vivacia knew he only meant her.

'I would have put a dress on, if I'd known we were coming somewhere nice,' she said, quietly.

Silence, filled with a terrible rushing in her head. She had chosen the wrong words. It would have been better to say nothing, to make no attempt to either defend herself or placate him.

There were football crowds at the station, a sea of blue funnelling down the streets, through the double doors and spreading along the platform.

As they waited for the train to come in, Charles said, 'Why would you assume we were not going somewhere nice?'

She didn't know how to answer without sounding ungrateful for all the other meals and evenings out, so she said nothing, just stared ahead until the train could be heard in the distance.

He stood beside her, one hand on the small of her back as the glow of the train's light appeared.

Vivacia started to sweat. The thought of his strength, that heavy, heavy hand. Just a barely-there flick of his wrist was all it would take.

She shuddered. He looked at her, cold as ice, and removed his hand.

Later that night, the baby went away. The physical pain was horrible. The mental aspect of it was worse, as she cradled her hands underneath her and tried to keep the remains inside.

Charles was dutiful, comforting, soothing in his actions as he wiped her brow with a cool flannel.

As the sun rose on a new day of emptiness, he murmured in her ear.

'You mustn't feel like a failure, my love.'

She hadn't until he said that.

8

VIVACIA – NOW

As if the task of providing them with Dallas's name was too much of an overexertion, Rose has fallen asleep at the table. Moments after her chin drops to her chest, Dallas follows suit.

Rob comes clattering back inside.

'Sorry about that,' he says. Once more, his voice is loud, and she puts a hand to her lips and beckons him into the lounge.

The curtains are still drawn. She recalls yanking them closed this morning, after she'd brought the children indoors, keeping out prying eyes.

She doesn't open the curtains. The room remains gloomy and, as if the children's exhaustion is catching, Vivacia sinks onto the sofa.

She thinks hard how she should play this. Why did she bring Rob into this? Why didn't she drive to a clinic, one in the city, or across the border? Why couldn't this be America, where she could pay a consultation fee in cash and give a false name? Why hadn't she done the most obvious of things, and googled their strange skin symptoms?

Why had she asked *him*? Why had she invited a stranger into her home? Why hadn't she learned the lesson, dealt to her in years past, that you can't trust *anyone*?

She glares at him now, but as if sensing her stare, he meets her gaze. Steadily, she stands up and wills herself to be assertive.

'Rose and Dallas are my cousin's kids—'

'Dallas?' A frown crosses his face.

'Dallas is his preferred name. Alex is his birth name. They don't talk much, their mother is… unwell. Their dad isn't in the picture. They're staying with me. It might become permanent.' The lies trip easily off her tongue. Too easily, she realises. Almost as though she's practised for this moment.

Which she has, she realises, but only in her dreams.

'I'm a foster carer, you know,' she blurts, desperate to salvage something. 'I would never take another person's child away from them without using the proper channels.'

He puts his phone down and gazes through the doorway at the sleeping pair. 'You need to tell me everything, Vivacia.'

She most certainly does not, she thinks. She called him here for a medical opinion. Belatedly, she realises she hasn't even got that.

Briefly, it all seems like too much. Her hand flutters around her eyes. The skin around them feels tight, taut, just like the rest of her body.

'They're staying with me.' Her voice is tiny, meek, small. A year ago, she'd roared as she made a promise to herself that she would never speak that way again. Here she is, twelve months on, and her old mannerisms and all those things that drove her husband away are back again.

She slaps her hands down to her sides and gives a quick glance to the children, still slumbering at the table.

She won't be that person. She won't regress.

'They are with me because I'm going to care for them *in an official capacity*. You will not take them from me. God help you if you try.'

She falls to sit on the sofa, breathless at the venom, exhilarated. *That's better, Vivacia. That's my girl.* Her grandmother's voice, urging her on.

She dares to look at his face, dead in the eye. It feels uncomfortable. It's been years since she did that.

'Vivacia. I would never try to take them from you. What are you even talking about? I'm simply saying they are not very well. Anyone can see that. You can see that: you called me here because of my medical background. They need professional care, a hospital, at the very least a doctor.'

She opens her mouth to protest and he holds his hand up to cut her off. 'I understand you are protecting your cousin, but this is bigger than loyalty. You're not the kind of person to do the wrong thing.'

She wants to laugh at that. She wants to tell him that he has no idea of the sort of person she is. He has no idea of the wicked things she has done.

Or the kind of punishment that she deserves.

There is nothing for a while. Quiet descends over the house, the only sound the gentle wheeze of the sleeping children.

Then, from beyond the confines of the gates, audible even over the now torrential downpour, comes a slow rumble. Vivacia raises her eyes. Here they come, right on time to hit the golf course. It's raining, so they'll go straight into the clubhouse. Those men, she thinks, who breed and breed and breed with not a second thought to the women at home and the mistresses elsewhere who will raise their offspring. Throwing money at any hiccup that comes their way, never going deeper into the whys or wherefores, never, ever facing the consequences of their actions.

It's harsh, Vivacia admits. She's sure there are some amongst the golfing crew who are normal, nice men. She's never met any of them, though.

The exhausts on their monster cars send a shudder through her very bones as they gun their engines the last few hundred yards to the course. The noise is extreme, unnecessary, another 'big dick' syndrome they all share.

'Knobs,' she says.

At the same time, Rob says, 'Wankers.'

They stare at each other as the sudden thunderstorm of the fleet of cars moves away to leave only the sound of the rain.

'I… I thought you liked them,' she says.

'I sink a few holes with them from time to time,' he replies. 'I don't like them.'

He has an amused look on his face. Possibly due to her name-calling. She'd never thought in all this time that he was of the same opinion.

He sighs. 'Anaemia.'

Vivacia jolts back to the present. 'What?'

'It looks like anaemia, as well as a vitamin deficiency.' He shoots her a look. 'I don't know their history, or that of your cousin. But they've obviously been put here for a reason.' He looks around the room, at the home that she hasn't built as such, but inherited from her family.

She looks too, seeing it through a stranger's eyes. It is old-fashioned, adorned with relics from her past. Inwardly, she cringes.

'The social obviously checked them before handing them over,' he says. 'What did they say?'

Vivacia swallows. 'They mentioned anaemia, too.'

He nods thoughtfully.

Vivacia stands up. 'I... I just wanted a second opinion. Thank you for looking at them.'

Her heart beats hard in her chest.

'I'm happy to keep an eye on them,' he offers.

She breathes deeply as he makes for the door.

He believes her story. The danger has passed.

For now.

–

She sees Rob out, hastily closing the door behind him. She leans against it, the unwelcome thought racing through her mind.

What has she done?

She has taken in two children, literally picked them up and brought them to her home.

Someone is missing them.

Someone... local?

Wolf's Pit is in the middle of nowhere, a segregated village in the back of beyond.

She knows the kids, the grandkids, of everyone here, even though she's not been a real part of the community for a long time.

They don't belong to Ruth, or Blind Iris. Mr Bastille and his wife never had children. And like Vivacia, Jackie is on her own, and even less sociable.

She frowns as she thinks of Jackie and her self-imposed isolation. She wasn't always that way. Once upon a time, when Vivacia was a child, and her mother and grandmother were still around, Jackie was the queen of the village green. A regular at the church, on numerous committees, boards of this and that, nose in everything and eyes everywhere. It changed when Cally left home.

Vivacia still gets a pang when she thinks about Cally. Jackie's daughter was nothing like the original villagers. She was wild and free, brave and loud. Everything that Vivacia wasn't, yet wished she was.

They'd been pals since they were little. From primary school through high school, during the teenage and young adult years. Then Cally had left, on a whim one day. She lives abroad now, enjoying the high life. She doesn't keep in touch with those back here.

Jackie had been at first frantic and worried, and then embittered and sullen.

She thinks of Rob. The first visitor she's had inside her home in a long time.

He was suspicious at first, not entirely buying her explanation that the children are here in an official capacity.

Does he still doubt her? Will he call the police to report two missing, unidentified, children in this house, when she's not supposed to have any kids under her care? Even worse, somehow, will he mention them to the other residents of Wolf's Pit? Or is she simply being paranoid? Maybe he will continue to be kind and helpful.

But the bigger question remains. These children have parents, somewhere.

Missing kids are a huge deal. Splashed across the news, the internet, social media.

Vivacia's own personal longing and the knowledge that she needs to do the right thing are in a raging conflict within her.

She peers into the kitchen. Both still slumber on. She thinks about moving them, to the bed, to the couch, to some place cosier than the kitchen table. Because these two seem like they've not known creature comforts in a long time.

Her heart shatters at the thought.

The pieces repair in an instant, a fracture that mends and is a little bit stronger. Harder.

She will not return these kids to whatever hellhole they came from.

Regardless, she needs to be prepared.

She picks up her phone, plugs it in and scrolls to the local news site for any clue of where Rose and Dallas came from.

Rose and Dallas.

Not Alex and Elizabeth.

She swallows hard.

The fault line fractures again. A pitiful bleat escapes from her.

She scrolls for a long time, moving from local to national news. She finds plenty of missing children, a horrifying amount, but not two, not the ones who are currently in her home.

She imagines what would happen if she called the police.

Officers would come, social workers too. The children would be taken away while they searched for their family.

Vivacia begins to tremble at the thought of it. Of another set of children removed from her care.

She is holding her phone, the old mobile that she hardly ever has cause to use. Three presses of that digit are all it would take to *do the right thing.*

Instead, Vivacia turns the phone off entirely and shoves it between the sofa cushions.

Shaking more than ever now, she presses her hands to her lips. She has made her decision.

She will carry on with her lie and front it out for as long as possible. She will not hide Rose and Dallas. To do so would only increase suspicion. She glances at them again.

But God, their *skin*. She can't parade them in the outside world like that, not with the air of confidence she's determined she will somehow fake.

Another worry comes back full circle at her. What if Rob mentions the children to the other residents of Wolf's Pit? The younger ones, the new ones, would be okay. They don't know her family tree. They don't know she doesn't have a cousin.

The other ones, though: Ruth, Bastille, Iris... They know everything about her.

She stands still, deep in thought, seeking but finding no answers to her quandary.

The community is quiet now, that mid-morning lull when the men have gone to work, the women are doing their HIIT workouts or mixing up their protein shakes, and the postman and the milkman have done their rounds. The golfers' cars are gone, not to return for a few hours. It is still raining, though. It's been raining for weeks and weeks. This year will be the wettest on record. She moves across the kitchen, slides the door silently open and steps outside. Just as she peers at the sky and wonders if the sun will ever break through, a jagged streak flashes across the field's horizon.

Immediately following it is not thunder, as she had expected, but a gut-wrenching scream.

Someone has been struck by lightning. It is her first thought upon hearing the scream.

But it was panicked, not pain-filled.

Perhaps the flash scared them, although this squall has been raging since sunup, and since the tail end of April, this weather has become the new normal.

Now the thunder does roar, a great clap in the clouds, right above the house.

Vivacia ducks her head inside the patio door to check that the children are not hiding under the table, but they are as she left them. Awake now, but not at all reactive, eyes still bleary, weary, like they've seen it all, done it all before.

The rain is sheeting down still, sideways on, landing in a splatter on the floor inside her house. She pulls the door to, almost closed, almost cutting off the scream that sounds again.

This time it goes on, a continuous wail. A shout joins it, male this time, a yell that tells Vivacia something bad has happened.

More voices, congregating now at the back of her house in that land beyond. Expletives, rarely heard within the cages of Wolf's Pit, the residents far too refined. Shouts of, *God, oh my God, no!*

It is enough to galvanise her out into the pouring rain. She runs down to the bottom of her garden at a clip and wraps her hands around the bowed railing.

The Widow Ruth is there, alongside one of the newer residents' private chefs, Colum or Calum or Colin. They stand a person's width apart, beside the half-buried bricks that denote the site of Lady Well. The place where Vivacia was only hours earlier, where the children had been curled up like sleeping kittens.

For a moment her heart stops. An absurd thought, that there are more children, a half-dozen siblings of Rose and Dallas. Greed interspersed with madness overwhelms her, a flash forward of the future, all the rooms in her once lonely house filled with them.

Lightning forks down, clearing both her mind and her vision.

Lady Well has flooded.

It has happened before, but not in Vivacia's lifetime, or not that she can remember.

When this was her grandmother's home, there was a river running alongside the rear of the property. Over time the riverbed dried up, and subsequently Lady Well became disused, a legendary feature rather than anything that actually had a use or a purpose. The council came, put a lid on it.

Now, the lid has not simply shifted, but it has burst right off the top of the well. It lies to one side, upended, rusty and decaying. Water flows over the edge of the well, streaming down the incline towards the iron railings of Wolf's Pit.

The new river is not the source of the screams, though.

The dead body that has erupted from the well is.

9

VIVACIA – BEFORE

Even though the baby went away, the want and the need remained.

The scars of that night also stayed with her. Memories were in flashes. Trying to keep it inside of her, trying to put it *back* inside. An abnormal thing to have done, madness caused by grief.

The house was so empty, and so was Vivacia. She began to think about other options.

'Fostering.' Charles repeated the word so blankly that Vivacia couldn't tell whether he was disgusted or interested.

'You get paid,' she said.

She felt dirty for using it as a selling point. The desire to help a child in need should be all that was required. But Vivacia knew money was so much to her husband.

'How much?'

She showed him the leaflets she'd gathered, the printouts from the library.

'And it's temporary?' he asked. 'They come and go?'

She nodded. 'Sometimes it's just like respite, for the parents. Just like being a carer, really.'

'You'd give up your job?'

She nodded.

'You'd just be here. Not working yourself to the bone for minimum wage.' He looked directly into her eyes. 'They take advantage of you, at that place. You let them mess with you. Do you see anyone trying to mess with me?'

'Oh. Well, I suppose—'

'You allow it, that's the worst of it.'

He opened the newspaper as he sipped at his tea.

The discussion was over. She wasn't sure if it had been a yes or a no.

Bravely, she emptied the locker and the drawer at work of the baby items she'd purchased, and brought them home. She stacked them in the airing cupboard where they would be clearly seen when Charles opened the door.

He never mentioned them. Vivacia took it as a yes and began the process of application.

Interviews followed, and Charles amazed Vivacia. This was where he came into his own. He wooed them; he was attentive, clever and witty, and he successfully sold the home they shared as a potential haven.

The first foster child was a boy of fourteen. Vivacia ruefully pushed the baby clothes and cuddly teddy bears to the back of the cupboard, replacing them with footballs, tracksuits and T-shirts.

Alfie was so... easy. He was charming. He took a liking to Charles. Charles began taking him down to the golf club and the attached driving range. He purchased a set of clubs for the beginner, as well as some for himself. He borrowed Vivacia's bank card, telling her she could claim it back from the system.

She didn't tell him that she didn't think it worked that way.

'They're beginning to know me, down at the golf club,' said Charles, proudly, one evening. 'They're beginning to see that I'm someone to be reckoned with. Someone like them.'

He was puffed up with pride.

It was important to Charles, this thing about status. He wanted to be seen as a powerful man, or if not that, a well-off one. Cally had seen that. Vivacia wondered why she, his wife, hadn't.

She didn't know how to answer him, so she just squeezed his arm and smiled.

He shook her hand off, impatient, and gave her a withering look as though he'd spilled his secret wishes to her and had only just realised it.

Alfie stayed for six weeks, and aside from dinner times, when they would all eat together, Vivacia started to feel like a spare part.

Fostering had brought out a new side in Charles. He gave the boy direction, guidance, like a kind of mentor.

She tried not to mind when she walked in on them watching eighteen-rated horror films, and ignored the fact that they would begin laughing when she walked out of the room.

The cash in the money tin vanished and Vivacia stopped filling it up, instead keeping her shopping money in the envelope where the deeds were hidden, in the suitcase.

Autumn came. The villagers put on their harvest festival, an annual event in the fields which consisted of a bonfire, roasted chestnuts, food and drinks, and general merriment.

Cally was there, wearing ripped fishnets and gothic make-up. Jackie stood away from her daughter, shaking her head as Cally annihilated the mulled wine and cider.

As the day turned into evening, Jackie took an inebriated Cally aside.

'Look at Vivacia: she's a mother. You're the same age, but you act like the kids she's fostering.'

Jackie's speech was a strange mixture of compliments for Vivacia, scorn for her daughter and discrimination against those in the foster system.

'Leave her be,' said Charles after a little while, gesturing to where Cally danced amongst the recently shorn corn. 'She's just having fun.' He gave a pointed look at Vivacia. 'It's okay to have fun.'

Later, Vivacia overheard Charles speaking with Alfie. 'That wild cat is the perfect example of a woman who is good for one thing.'

Vivacia moved closer, unseen in the shadows of the bales of hay.

'She is good for fun. She is a perfect receptacle to empty your load in. A vessel if you will. Then, you go home to someone like my wife.'

Alfie hung on his every word.

Charles nudged Alfie and they wandered over to where Cally stood. Charles slung his hand over her shoulder. The three of them chatted and laughed.

Vivacia felt something like hope shiver inside her.

Mates, at last. Two of the most important people in her life. She hoped it wasn't just the festival atmosphere, and that from now on something had been forged between the two of them.

Vivacia went back to her house and slipped inside. She left the porch light on for when her husband and foster child chose to return home. She tried to focus on the happy scene she'd witnessed and to forget the way Charles had spoken to the impressionable young boy about how he viewed women, as opposed to how he looked at her.

–

Alfie went back to his home, with his mother and his stepfather. When he'd arrived, six weeks earlier, he'd given Vivacia a slight wave and had limply shaken Charles's hand.

Now, he hugged Vivacia goodbye, his hands moving from her shoulders, down her sides to rest on her hips. He kept eye contact with her, his fingers lingered on her and he gave her a wink.

He did a handshake with Charles where they clapped each other's backs and leaned in, shoulders touching.

Vivacia closed the door behind him.

She hoped for a girl next time, one that she could take the lead on. Then, she remembered Charles's comments about women in general and thought maybe it would be best if they had a child who was much, much younger. One who didn't speak yet, and one who didn't listen.

10

VIVACIA – NOW

Ruth's terror has brought the rest of the residents running.

The lower torso is still caught inside the well, with the arms out to either side, an imitation of a crucifixion pose. The head is splayed backwards to rest on the mossy, sodden grass of the hill.

The mouth is open, a mask of awfulness, stretched in a silent scream. The clothes are falling away even as Vivacia watches. Mingling with the water, bits of this long-dead person creep ever closer to the crowd that has gathered to watch this real-life horror unfold.

As the water continues to gush out of the well, a strange aroma escapes the hole in the ground. Vivacia gags. The smell is of infection and decay.

Portia's private chef gesticulates wildly. Ruth screams again.

Another resident arrives from the first McMansion in front of Vivacia's. Aster Gould's eyes are wide.

'Oh my God,' she squeals. And then, again, only louder, 'Oh my GOD!'

The body rises, the chest emerging from the stinking, foul water. The transition is smooth, silent.

The screams and shouts stop suddenly, even though more people have gathered. There is a gasp from each new person who arrives, and then a diluted silence amongst them all.

The arms stay outstretched, the weight pulling the body backwards.

The eyes are gone, the lips are gone; all that remains is that terrible tunnel of a mouth, teeth exposed to the root in a macabre grin.

Before, when the body was a person, it was wearing a red sweater. Now, from the upper part of the torso, the material slips away as though it is not wool or viscose or cotton, but simple food colouring or dye.

The skin slides away too, from the nose and the cheeks and the forehead. Liquid flesh littering a path from Lady Well towards the railings of the Wolf's Pit community.

The skin sets them all off again. Ruth, tough as anything, who has lived through wars and has lost husbands and children, parents, friends and siblings, sits heavily down on the hill. She passes a hand across her pale face and lies back on the grass. She is out cold, Vivacia realises.

In the strange, thin prison corridor constructed of railings, Vivacia sees she is not alone. Rob is there, fifty yards downwind of her.

She darts a look at him; his mouth is a circle of shock, eyes wide and staring, face almost grey. At the sight of her, he seems to reset.

'Are you okay?' he asks as he moves down towards her. 'Are the children… indoors?'

She nods dumbly.

'Don't want them seeing this.' He has stated the obvious, a fact evident from the look she shoots him.

Her toes are wet. She looks down, sees that the water is collecting here, in the trench between the boundaries, where they stand. She wonders if his stomach is roiling, the sight of that old, creamy-coloured flesh sliding over his Nikes. The smell – that awful scent of old body gases and the result of a torso coming apart – is growing stronger, more pungent with every passing moment.

Vivacia swallows back the vomit that threatens and wipes her mouth with the back of her hand.

Sirens wail in the distance.

Rob moves closer to Vivacia. 'Ruth passed out,' he says. He slips through the distended railing, immediately in the throng of people who stand motionless around the old woman lying prone on the wet ground.

The water has slowed to a trickle, the rain has stopped altogether, the body hasn't moved.

'I called the police,' says Portia's chef.

Rob touches his shoulder. 'Thanks, Clive,' he says.

Ruth is sitting up now, dazed, surrounded by women in their activewear, this scene having interrupted their morning workout. One of them, Chloe-Joy, is still holding a kettlebell.

Vivacia hadn't thought that Chloe-Joy, Portia, Aster and the others paid much attention to the older woman, no matter how hard Ruth had tried to insert herself into their lives. She assumed the newcomers only spoke to those who can be of use. Diet tips, the latest influencers, gym owners, restaurant goers, the latest trendsetters – people to use as ladders to climb are those that are important to the front runners of Wolf's Pit. But Vivacia was mistaken, she sees now, as they gather around Ruth. They have not lost their humanity. Here, they are normal people, with appropriate reactions where it matters.

'I called an ambulance,' says Chloe-Joy as she catches Vivacia's eye.

'I think he's past needing an ambulance.' Bastille has arrived. His tone is condescending as always, but his face betrays his emotional reality.

Chloe-Joy stands up and puts her free hand on her hip. 'For Ruth,' she snaps.

Mr Bastille looks away. 'Oh, right. Good,' he says.

Chloe-Joy, temper flare gone, cradles her kettlebell as though it is a baby.

There is nothing more to say. Nobody has any words left. Later, once the shock has passed, everyone will want to talk, to speculate, to share, to repeat over and over again their own stories of when a dead man burst from Lady Well.

73

A murmur starts up, the gathered group alert, staring down the edge of the field. Vivacia cranes to see.

Jackie Jenkins is running, arms flying, as though she's possessed. For a woman who has barely moved in recent years, it's a compelling sight.

She thinks it's Cally, realises Vivacia. She thinks this body that has risen from Lady Well is the daughter who left her for a world of glamour and excitement, and never contacted her again.

Vivacia darts forward to meet the woman who once was as close as family.

It is as though Jackie doesn't even see her. She smacks into Vivacia hard. Vivacia raises her arms, encircles the other woman. Instantly, she is transported back to another time, another day, when they were in this position.

Only, that time, it was Jackie holding Vivacia back.

Vivacia speaks the same words that Jackie said to her that night. 'You don't need to see.'

Jackie sags and sways. She peers over Vivacia's shoulder at the slippery mess that is puddled on the ground.

Not Cally. Despite the state of the corpse, that much is clear.

'Oh,' breathes Jackie. With that single word, she turns on her heel and trudges back along the field to her own home.

Vivacia watches her go. She tracks Jackie's progress all the way to the road, before she disappears.

The sirens have stopped now, but the blues are still flashing. Two police cars, parked on the lane outside the community. Four officers – three males, one female – coming at a run. Collectively, they all have their hands on the batons strapped to their hips, as though the gathering has forewarned them of a mutiny.

The smallest, youngest and probably newest officer strides ahead of his colleagues. Vivacia watches as he pushes through the Lycra-clad women, using such force that he almost steps straight into the open well.

Only then does he see the body, still liquifying, flesh still sliding away down the hill.

The officer wheels around so he is facing away from the well. His hand gropes for his radio. It crackles to life, someone on the other end awaiting a command or instruction or request. The officer brings it to his mouth but says nothing. From where Vivacia stands, between the boundaries, she sees the policeman's cheeks bulging, his throat working.

For a moment he seems to be regaining control of himself, but then vomit emerges from between his clamped lips in a spray. He staggers off diagonally, his face buried in his arm.

His colleagues arrive on the scene. Older, world-weary – still not used to seeing this mid-morning on a Wednesday, but having had some experience of horror. They break off, herding the onlookers backwards, reaching for their own radios, barking instructions, requesting back-up.

The female stoops and puts a hand on Ruth's arm. Ruth brushes it off, struggles to her feet and walks away in the direction of her own home.

'We'll need to speak to you,' the female officer calls after her.

Ruth doesn't acknowledge her.

The officer surveys the group – a dozen people, of varying ages, standing in clusters.

The divide is still there: the Stepford wives on one side with the fancy chef, and away from them, Bastille next to Blind Iris.

Rob is alone, in the forefront. The female officer turns to him.

'Do you know this man?' she demands.

He shakes his head.

The officer grabs the sleeve of her young colleague who lost his breakfast in his keenness to be the first on the scene.

She leans close to him, her voice low, so quiet that Vivacia only hears snatches of the instructions.

Forensics. Tent. Tape. Crime.

Vivacia takes a couple of steps back towards her fence, her feet sliding in the moist grass.

She doesn't want to look anymore. She glances into her garden. When this was her grandmother's house, it was a carefully curated plot of beauty. Wildflowers grew in abundance, sweet peas curled their tendrils up the fence and swallows would nest in the eaves of the old three-sided shed.

Later, Vivacia's mother modernised the garden, so upkeep was easier. Expensive patio furniture was artfully placed. Flowerpots neatly distributed, dead leaves or flowers plucked off immediately. Not so family-friendly, not like it was when Vivacia took over.

Ten years ago, Vivacia had constructed a vegetable patch in the easterly side of the sizeable patch. When there were children staying, it became an enjoyable group activity. It kept them busy, focused and outside in the fresh air, and it was suitable for all ages. Tiny potted seedlings that the smaller kids couldn't harm, physical digging and weeding for the teenagers.

No matter their age, they went to bed happy, fulfilled, and physically and mentally stimulated every night.

The vegetable patch is long gone now. Overgrown with dandelions, sticky goosegrass and bindweed.

As if to push against the awfulness happening on the other side of the fence, she turns her mind to the garden and pleasant thoughts. It would be a lot of labour, to fix up this old yard, but Vivacia has never shied away from heavy lifting. She peers at the small lawn area. There is prickly milk thistle sprouting up. Those will be the first to go, she decides as she thinks of the children's bare feet. Even now, she can spot a clump of stinging nettles growing near the gate.

Outside, in the lane, she knows that there's a patch of hogweed, and beside it, hemlock and foxgloves. It's another point of consternation between the new and the old residents. Those like Ruth and Mr Bastille know that they are there, know the dangers, and they simply avoid them because they want to conserve as much of the nature around here as possible.

The newer ones have fought them. *Think of the children! Think of the pets!*

Vivacia, as she always seems to, sits on the fence.

She blinks at this new, sudden realisation. That has always been her persona. It shouldn't be, having had Kay and Stephanie raising her – two strong, independent women. But there was Cally, in Vivacia's formative years, and she followed the leader that the girl proclaimed herself to be. Then came Charles, with his instructions and guiding hand and his put-downs.

What would have happened if Vivacia had protested, against either of them?

Or rather, what had she been *afraid* would have happened? That they would walk away?

So what, they're both gone now, aren't they?

A sudden gushing sound brings her back to the garden, back to the terrible present.

She feels a coolness nudging at her toes. The terrible stream has made its way through the railings, lapping over the edge of her lawn, creeping towards her.

She covers her mouth with her hand and spins to face her house. From here, she can just about make out the children still seated inside. Rose's chin is on her chest again. Dallas is awake. He stares, eyes glinting, at the crowd of people intent on the catastrophe on the other side of the fence. Vivacia feels herself trembling. If the officers happen to glance this way, they will see him.

She shakes her head in an attempt to chase the panic away.

It is not an extraordinary scene, that one indoors. She owns a family-sized home, there are children in it. There is nothing strange about that. What's strange is what is happening *outside* the fence, and all eyes are on *that* scene. The officers do not know Vivacia. Do not know that there are not supposed to be children inside.

The others know, however. What if they happen to look over? What if Mr Bastille sees them? She imagines him, his bellowing voice, pointing out that they shouldn't be there. Or the newcomers, Portia and Chloe-Joy and the others. They

77

wouldn't bark and bluster like he would; rather, they would pass judgement amongst themselves, sly words passed between lips that they'd cover with their hands.

Vivacia returns to stand in the gap in the fence, essentially blocking any view of her house. Silently, she watches them all, as they stare at the watery figure.

Finally, Vivacia forces herself to look once more at the inert form.

What was once a red woollen sweater is now a watered-down claret pool of moisture. The hands attached to thin, silvery-white arms. The only thing that seems to remain is a huge gold watch on the wrist, like those the golfers wear. It smacks of a grandiose life; an extravagance used as an outward sign of wealth and status.

Vivacia sucks in a deep breath, then another. She takes a moment to collect herself before emerging onto the site of the well to stand beside the female officer.

'I know who he is,' she says.

'You do?' The officer's tone is disbelieving, hoarse, seemingly incredulous that an identification will be made so quickly.

Vivacia stares at the man in the well.

'Yes.' She can't take her eyes off him now. 'That's Charles Lomax. He is my husband.'

11

THE CHILDREN

Mother slept. Her fingers stopped working a long time ago, but Rose carried on scraping at the old floor and, to a lesser extent, so did Dallas.

It had been a long time now since they were outside the caravan.

Rose had learned how to do normal time-telling, with a watch or a clock. But they had neither, so she went back to what came more naturally: the sky.

The moon had passed through a few cycles. The bars on the window didn't allow for much of a view, but the sky was something that had not been off limits, visually at least.

When the door closed behind Father that last time, Mother hammered on it. That was not unusual. She always did that. Sometimes she would bash her fists on other things: Father's chest, her own face. Never on Rose or Dallas, though.

Little red welts on Mother's white skin.

The toilet got backed up in the time it took for the moon to turn from a waxing crescent to a waning gibbous.

Mother clapped her hands. 'We need to prepare.'

Rose's heart lurched with hope. She hugged Dallas to her joyfully. Mother had been lost for a while. At least thirty-two moon phases. Maybe more, but thirty-two was the number that Rose confidently counted to.

Sometimes she thought that was why Father went away so often, to avoid Mother's phases.

Rose stood upright at Mother's declaration, as tall as she could make herself, in order to help with whatever Mother needed for these as-yet-unknown preparations. Energy from Mother was rare. She had to grab it before the window closed.

Mother looked around the small caravan, the smell of human excrement permeating from the busted toilet. Rose saw what Mother saw at the same time.

There was nothing to prepare. There was nothing to pack. And, more importantly, there was no way out.

Mother, previously momentarily galvanised, sank back to the couch.

She'd done it before. But this time, she didn't rise for a long, long time.

Technically, she still hadn't risen. She had attempted to sit up, barked something about the hole in the floor, and half-heartedly pawed at it for a while before losing both strength and will, and passing out again in a sob-ridden sleep.

The crying had stopped. Rose wondered if it wasn't just a nap that afflicted her mother now, but rather that longer sleep, the one that lasted for always.

But Rose wasn't ready to consider that, not just yet. The prize in the floor was greater than anything, and she told Dallas to dig harder, faster, and she slapped at his fingers when he slackened.

As she worked, Rose imagined what was in the hole, aside from the few bits she remembered. It would be like a treasure chest. She thought back to when they had books, and the stories they told. Gold coins, beautiful jewels all the colours of the rainbow. Fairy tales. Rose scoffed at her own childish thinking. Pretty things were worthless. In the hole in the floor, she would find Things That Matter. Bread, meat, milk and a key that opened the door.

Mother's shoe had fallen off her shrivelled foot. It was a summer shoe, not like the sort that wrapped all the way over like Dallas's did. Not one of those fancy, high-heeled ones that Mother wore many, many years ago either.

Rose picked it up and inserted the sole into the corner of the floor that they had so far managed to pull so it stood at an angle. The hard plastic worked better as a shovel than tender, child-sized fingers. That strange red film in her eyes got heavier, darker, as Rose put her all into it. Dallas had come to rest on his haunches in a crouch, thumb in mouth, watching his sister's progress. She slapped at Dallas with the shoe.

'Help me!' It came out as a whisper because her throat was dry. There was no water to drink because the taps didn't work. The toilet, once a useable drinking receptacle, was now filled to the brim with a foulness that Rose wouldn't even contemplate.

Food. Water. Help.

Rose knew that they were the things they all needed now, not necessarily in that order.

When Martin and Trinity came to live here, in the van next door, they had a phone. Trinity took great delight in showing Rose everything it could do.

The possibilities were endless. You could phone people, which was like talking to them, but they didn't have to be beside each other. The other person could be hundreds, even thousands, of miles away! It had a clock on it, but it was just numbers. Rose thought the sun and moon made much better sense for time-telling.

The phone had a torch, which beat the fire-on-a-stick that they normally used. You could also write little letters, which with a whoosh would fly off over the airwaves and land on a similar device to be read by friends. Again, they could be on the other side of the world.

'Or even on the moon?' Rose had asked, eyes wide with astonishment.

'Maybe,' Trinity had said.

She'd let Rose play with it for a while. Rose pressed a button, and it emitted a shrill shriek, sounding a little like the pigs did when Father despatched one of them to turn them into dinner.

Trinity had laughed as Rose jumped. 'Gee pee ess,' she'd said. 'So, with this, I'll never get lost, and someone always knows where I am.'

Father had come back just then, returning from his exciting travels that involved going out in the nice car that was so nice it was kept in an old barn when he was back home.

'What's that, Trinity?' he'd asked, ruffling Rose's hair as he passed by where they sat.

Trinity had snatched the phone out of Rose's hands. 'An old phone, I let Rose play with it.' Trinity's chin wobbled. 'It doesn't work.'

Father had made his lips go together in a very thin, straight line.

'Trinity.' He'd said her name, just once, and his voice was loaded with ever so much sadness.

Mother came out, looking between Father and Trinity.

'Leave it alone,' Mother whispered to Father. Her eyes were fixed on the phone, something funny in her gaze, like it was a precious thing.

Father shook his head and held his hand out for the phone. His eyes were sad and disappointed, but his lips were pressed together like he was cross.

Rose had stood up then, grabbed Dallas's hand and led him into their caravan home.

She didn't see Trinity ever again after that, nor the phone, nor Martin.

But the phone was what she was thinking of now, as she shovelled Mother's shoe into the cracked vinyl flooring.

'A phone,' she said to Dallas. 'And meat, milk, bread and a key will be in here.'

The moon had moved by the time the tile had been broken through. The sun was in its place, casting a dull, grey light into the room that was devoid of light, love, life.

Rose pulled the last piece of floor up and away, and stared into the magical hole.

She looked for a long time. The only sound in the caravan was Dallas's short, shallow breathing, and the slow drip-drip-drip of the blood that fell from Rose's fingers, into the hole in the floor.

12

VIVACIA – BEFORE

'I have to go away on business,' said Charles.

It was an announcement, his voice full of pride, his stance bloated with confidence, like a peacock, preening.

They were almost over the first year of their marriage. The paper anniversary loomed. Soon they would be past that, heading towards the two-year theme of cotton.

Vivacia was pleased. On Monday, she'd be getting a thirteen-year-old girl coming to stay.

There had been a handful of placements in the last year. Boys under ten, girls of toddler age, another teenage lad. No babies, not yet. But their feedback was good. Charles wooed the kids each and every time. He had surpassed Vivacia's expectations of him, and though there were bad days – comments that needled her, veiled compliments that turned out to be anything but – they were on an okay-ish even keel.

He stayed out more and more, often overnight, and sometimes Vivacia thought it might be why they'd settled into a semi-good home life.

While Charles gathered up papers and folders and books, Vivacia readied the spare room for the new foster child.

She tried to make the room special for each visitor. She knew next to nothing about them in advance, so she'd got good at gauging furnishings simply by age and sex. She stripped the duvet of moon and stars off, and refitted a nice, patchwork one of pale green and pink. Not too babyish, because thirteen was the age when children began to look to their future, more adult, selves.

She sat on the newly made bed and recalled herself at that age. She'd discovered books, proper adult ones, rather than the short stories which contained more pictures than words. She had tried her hand at poetry, and begun to take more of an interest in her mother's pottery and sculptures. Cally, at thirteen, had discovered boys, booze and cigarettes – not necessarily in that order. It was the first time that Jackie had said the words, *why can't you be more like Vivacia?* Jackie had been saying those words for more than a decade now. Vivacia wished she wouldn't.

The memory of her friend reminded Vivacia that she'd not seen Cally for a while. Cally would be good for a thirteen-year-old girl. On days when she wasn't acting like one herself, she had that cool-aunt vibe. Charles would be away, so Cally could come over as much as she wanted.

She let herself into Jackie's house, raising a hand in greeting as she went upstairs in search of Cally.

She was in her bedroom, surrounded by clothes that lay in untidy piles on her bed.

'I've got a foster child coming,' Vivacia announced. 'I thought maybe we could do something, the three of us. Charles will be away,' she added.

Cally looked at her through eyes smudged with last night's make-up and wrinkled her nose.

'Nah, come on, me and kids don't exactly gel.'

Vivacia felt the sting of rejection.

'She's not a kid, not really. She's a teenager.'

Cally drifted over to the window and stared in the direction of Vivacia's house. 'I'm so busy...' she started, turning to face Vivacia. Her expression softened. 'Oh, maybe, then. We'll see.'

'She's not here yet, but we'll arrange something when she arrives.' Vivacia hugged her friend. 'Thanks, Cally.'

Cally turned back to the window. 'Bye, Vivacia.'

Vivacia thought about Cally as she scattered some appropriate young-adult books on the dresser, purchased for a pittance at the charity shop.

She'd seemed sluggish today. More so than usual. Her mind had been elsewhere. Her initial refusal had hurt Vivacia. She'd had a heavy night, probably. Perhaps it was time for Cally to slow down, to grow up. After all, none of them were getting any younger.

As a last-minute detail for the new girl's room, she added a brand-new make-up set of neutral colours, designed for children looking to experiment with bolder looks. Job done; she went in search of Charles to see if he fancied an early lunch.

His clothes were on the bed, laid out: suits and ties, and a new, heavy wool coat she'd never seen before.

He stood beside the bed, hands on hips, studying the row of three suitcases on the top of the wardrobe.

A cold prickle ran the length of Vivacia's body.

The deeds that Kay had given her, almost a year ago, that she'd hidden there. The new hiding place where she kept her cash.

'How long is your business trip?' she asked, hoping he didn't hear the beat of desperation in her voice.

'One week.' He looked out of the window, his eyes faraway, almost dreamy. 'Maybe a bit longer.'

She dragged a chair over to the wardrobe and pulled down the case in the middle, setting it on the bed.

'This is the nicest one, the newest one. And a good size for a week away.'

He looked at it, looked at the remaining two. His mouth turned up at the sides.

'That one is better, I think,' he said, and he pointed at the one to the right.

Vivacia felt a trickle of sweat emerge from her hairline.

Charles patted the one she'd brought down. 'This one can go back up there.'

She wiped her brow, picked it up and slotted it carefully into the dusty gap.

Up there, hands flat on the top of the wardrobe, she began to fiddle with the case she put back, shoving it an inch to the left, to the right, stalling, hoping for the doorbell to ring or for Charles's mobile phone to chirrup with a message or an email – something that normally sent him speeding over to it.

The house, the village, the world were silent.

She glanced at him. Charles sighed, pointedly looked at his watch.

She pulled down the case that contained the deeds and passed it to him.

He flipped it on the bed, unzipped it with a cruel slowness, before flipping open the lid.

It was empty. Bare of anything except the silk lining.

Vivacia stared at it, looked back at the remaining two cases. She was sure she'd put the envelope in the case that now lay on the bed.

Charles hummed a tune as he folded his clothes. It turned into a whistle, and he smiled as he packed, never once looking her way.

–

The foster girl, Brittany, turned up a day early.

'I'm sorry,' said Claire, the social worker who handed her over. 'The situation has become untenable.'

'It's fine, everything's ready,' trilled Vivacia. Her voice was high and squeaky. Charles had not yet left, was hovering in the hall, his suitcase in the way as Brittany tried to come in. They danced around each other, man and child.

'It's like a relay!' Vivacia laughed to cover her panic.

Charles exchanged a sympathetic look with Claire; Brittany rolled her eyes.

Brittany was like a teenage Cally. Too-tight jeans, a crocheted, navel-skimming sweater, clunky gold chains, large hoop earrings, and eyes layered in mascara and liner.

'Perhaps I can catch the next train, help get our guest settled in,' said Charles.

He looked at Brittany as he spoke, not Claire nor Vivacia.

'We'll be fine, darling,' said Vivacia. She gave him a gentle push. 'I'll see you in a week.'

He turned to her, his eyes dark as he gazed at her. 'Okay, *wife*,' he said.

She saw them both off: Charles first, waving him down the drive as he wheeled the treacherous case behind him, then Claire half an hour later.

She went in search of Brittany, pleased it was now just the two of them.

Brittany was in her bedroom, door closed, and she answered no to all of Vivacia's enquiries as to whether she'd like a drink, a late lunch or an early dinner, or a walk around the fields before the sun went down.

Downstairs, suddenly alone, Vivacia went two doors down to Jackie's house.

'Is Cally here?' she asked when Jackie answered the door. 'I wondered if she'd like to come over tonight for a takeaway.'

Jackie's expression was weary, as it so often was these days. 'She's not here,' she replied. 'I don't know when she'll be back.'

Vivacia traipsed home, despondent.

Brittany said yes to a takeaway and, pleased that the girl had left her room, Vivacia offered her all the menus and let her choose.

After the Indian meal, Brittany went to bed, even though it wasn't yet eight o'clock. Vivacia got the air freshener out to dispel the aroma of curry before remembering that it didn't matter, that Charles wouldn't be back tonight.

She locked the front door and removed the key, hating that she suspected that Brittany might sneak out, but deciding to stick on the safe side. She tucked it in her dressing-gown pocket before retiring to her own room.

There, she pulled down the remaining two suitcases. Her head thudded with a sudden migraine at the emptiness inside them, worsening when she slid her hands in all the pockets and came up with nothing.

13

VIVACIA – NOW

She had felt strong, for that single moment in time when she proclaimed it to be Charles's body. Then, the questions came. Bullets shooting at her from every angle, each one punching her strength until she was once more fragile and scared.

This is your husband?

Are you serious?

That's not Lomax!

How do you know?

This last wasn't an unreasonable question from the officer, given the state of the corpse.

Vivacia lowers her eyes. 'I… I recognise his watch.'

With that, all pretence at courage vanishes. Vivacia crumples forward, hands wrapped around her stomach.

'You'll need to come with us.' The older male policeman is at her side now, hands out but hovering, as though afraid to touch her.

'Do you live here?' The third male is there now, gesticulating to the house behind her.

She thinks of Rose and Dallas, seated obediently at the kitchen table. Rose sleeping, Dallas watching.

Wildly, she looks for Rob, the only one who knows they are here. She finds, to no surprise, he is already beside her.

'Go with them,' he murmurs. 'I'll keep an eye on your house.'

There is no time to debate with her inner turmoil.

'Yes, please,' she whispers, even though it wasn't a question he'd asked.

A hand is on her arm now. The female officer. The older man has stationed himself close beside her.

'This way,' he says.

The other residents are there, staring at Vivacia now, rather than the dismantled, disembodied travesty that's exploded from the well. Mr Bastille's mouth is hanging limply open. Blind Iris looks confused. The other ones – the new, young women – stare with wide eyes. Chloe-Joy's kettlebell tumbles from her arms to land with a wet plop on the ground. She snatches it up and holds it at a distance, nose wrinkled.

The officers surround her, hands hovering within easy reach as if there is a danger that she may pass out like Ruth did. Vivacia draws her arms in and wraps them over her chest. She walks briskly alongside the officers. Surprised at the sudden speed, they too pick up their pace. They pass more authority figures on the way to the car. These ones are in a van; inside the back doors Vivacia catches a glimpse of white. She's seen enough television shows to know this vehicle will contain white shoes, white suits, white coverings and masks, and a white tent.

The officer, the female, leans close to her. 'I'm Detective Inspector Ola Demoski. I'll ride with you. Someone will speak to you when we get to the station.'

Vivacia catches the officer's arm. 'I thought he'd left me,' she says now, her voice high with delayed shock and disbelief. 'We had separated.'

Inspector Ola nods. 'We'll speak to you at the station,' she repeats and closes the back door of the car.

The ride to the police station passes in a blur. Fields and hedgerows make way to two-lane roads and cottages, followed by office blocks and shopping centres.

They treat her with an almost reverence when she arrives. She is given tea, hot and sweet. Kindly looks and reassuring taps on her shoulder.

She is introduced to Detective Inspector Andrews, who guides her through to a room, Inspector Ola alongside her.

He tells her that although she believes her identification to be correct, they will need to run tests.

What sort of tests, she wonders, can they do on that melting, watery body?

She doesn't ask them to clarify.

She starts to cry. Sobs wrack her body, resulting in hiccups. Inspector Ola gives her a tissue. Vivacia clutches it tight in her hand.

She wonders what Rose and Dallas are doing at home. What is Rob doing? She thinks of all the police at the back of her place, Rob watching them from her garden, or at the kitchen patio. Has he approached them? Beckoned to one of them for a quiet word?

She imagines the conversation.

I know you've got your hands full, but look, there's something you need to know. Furtive, backward glances towards the house, and the secret it contains within.

The new information would be relayed to the very police officers who are sitting across from her now. A double questioning: anything she knows about events leading up to her husband's death, and her statement on what would likely amount to child kidnapping.

She barks out a slightly hysterical laugh. The officer in front of her stops talking and gazes in astonishment at her.

Stay sane.

She runs a finger underneath her eyes. 'Sorry,' she says. 'This is all very shocking.'

Rob does not know she lied about the children.

DI Andrews begins his questions. *When did you last see Charles? What was his mood? Did you look for him?*

Vivacia takes a deep breath.

'I lost my mother, and my grandmother, they were both…' She trails off, swallows and shakes her head. 'Four years ago.

It… It destroyed me.' She lifts her chin and smiles bravely at the DI. 'I wasn't very much fun to be around. Even before that, Charles… wasn't there very much.'

DI Andrews nods his head. 'My condolences. I recall the incident, the victims. Tragic.'

Vivacia widens her eyes and stares at him. She doesn't remember him. Doesn't recall ever speaking to him about the night that took three lives away. Four, if you counted her own.

She doesn't remember anything about that time. Her memories of afterwards are bare and empty, too. Just flashes. A bedroom, for a long time. Lying there, her body refusing to stop breathing; her heart wouldn't stop beating. Being lonely in a grief-filled pit of anguish.

'He left me, after that,' she says now. 'He left me a year ago.'

DI Andrews tilts his head. 'Had he done that before? Left, I mean.'

Vivacia sniffs. Belatedly, she remembers the tissue and unfurls it to blow her nose.

'Yes,' she says, her voice barely a whisper.

There were more questions, more when, why, how. Vivacia answers them as best she can. She tries to concentrate on Andrews, but in her mind are Rose and Dallas.

The clock ticks on.

What are they doing? What is *Rob* doing?

They've been through trauma, those children. They need stability, routine, love, care.

They don't need a stranger babysitting them. They don't need police tramping around outside their new home. They don't need sirens beyond the windows. They don't need Vivacia – their new mother – leaving them for an entire day.

She puts her knuckles to her mouth and glances at the clock on the wall. 'All this time,' she moans.

'Pardon me?' Andrews's voice startles her.

Vivacia takes her hand from her lips. 'All this time,' she says. 'I can't believe he's been in the well all this time.'

'This…' Andrews checks his notes. 'This Lady's Well, it wasn't covered, it had no boundary?'

'Lady Well,' Vivacia automatically corrects him. 'It had a lid, a flimsy one, the kind you'd put on an old-fashioned dustbin. The council fitted it, but in high winds, bad weather…' She trails off. Her shoulders move up and down in a small shrug.

He carries on, DI Andrews, his questions peppered with further ones from his colleague.

Vivacia watches them as though she's viewing a tennis match, back and forth, replying as well as she can. Some things – the timeline, the days and weeks and months – are hard to remember.

Eventually, after what seems like days and days, they run out of questions.

Ola takes her home. For once, it's not raining. There is even a little bit of late-afternoon sunshine, hazy in the sky, hesitant, as though it's forgotten what to do up there.

'Have you got somebody at home?' Ola asks, as they make the turn for Wolf's Pit. 'I've got a family liaison officer en route. They'll remain with you, be of any assist—'

'Oh, no!' Vivacia fights to swallow down the panic. 'Honestly, I'm fine.' She nods as if to reassure herself. 'I'll be fine,' she says, slightly louder, forcing herself to maintain eye contact with the officer.

'It's standard procedure, and absolutely—'

'I'm fine.' Vivacia nods and attempts a smile. 'Thank you, but I've got someone at home.'

She thinks of Rob, the stranger, currently sitting in her home. His almost-aggressive stab at humour earlier, his about-turn and attempt at friendliness. His mild, unreciprocated flirting over the last year.

Instantly, she braces herself for a barrage of questions. Who and what are they to you and can I speak to them?

Thankfully, Ola just nods, and as she draws up to Vivacia's house, she gives her hand a pat. 'We'll be in touch. Take care, I'm very sorry for your loss,' she says.

The kindness of strangers.

'Thank you,' whispers Vivacia, her voice cracking.

She forces herself to wait while Ola does a three-point turn and drives back towards the gates. Once outside, the officer turns left, and Vivacia watches the flash of white as the police car drives up the lane, past Ruth's, Jackie's and Rob's, and comes to a halt to the right of the now-tented Lady Well.

Vivacia turns and runs to her front door.

Rob opens it and she spills inside, looking past him towards the kitchen.

'Where are they?' Panicked, she pushes him aside, striding past him, into the kitchen – clean and tidy now – and whirls around. No sight, nor sound, of the children.

'WHERE ARE THEY?' Her shout bounces off the walls.

He's given them away, handed them in like so much lost property. Called a police officer aside, awkwardly told him what she'd done, what she had here, what didn't belong to her. Social services have already been. She wonders if it was Claire, who Vivacia always liked, or if it was that terrible one who reminded her of Aunt Lydia.

She sees the knives in the block out of the corner of her eye, remembers Dallas holding one earlier, the paring knife, her misunderstanding that he was a threat, and the concentration on his face as he peeled the apple in one, long, curly strip. She wants to grab one of those knives now. She wants to aim it at *him* for giving away her children.

Rob comes at her again, his hands up in a gesture of surrender. Vivacia bites her lip to stop herself from screaming.

God help him, if he's given her children away, she will scream and she will shout and she will grab that paring knife—

'…the garden.'

She blinks again, has missed what Rob said.

'What?' she asks him, realising that she is almost panting.

'The children are in the garden. The rain stopped; they need to be in the air. I think they've been cooped up too—'

The garden! The bloody garden, with the gap in the railing and the crime scene right outside and all those roaming police officers.

Vivacia spins on her heel and shoves open the patio door.

There they are. Rose, climbing over some haphazard slabs, poking one finger into the earth of the cracks in between. Slightly behind her is Dallas. He watches his sister, studying her, mimicking her when she stoops down to pluck a stone or a flower from the wet grass.

Vivacia's body turns to jelly.

They are here. They are safe. They are seemingly happy.

But the crime scene!

She lets out a gasp as she snaps her eyes to the fence and sees… nothing of Lady Well or the officers who are still there.

A screen, like a fence panel, made from bamboo fills the gap.

She feels Rob as he comes to stand beside her.

'Where… Where did that come from?'

'Ruth had it behind her shed. I don't know what she originally planned to do with it, but I brought it over here. The children can be outside. They need fresh air, Vivacia. But they don't have to see what's going on over there.' He lets out a grimace. 'Not that there's much to see now; they took it away earlier.'

Took it away…

For a moment she can't think what he means, then it registers.

'Charles? He's gone?'

Rob nods. 'I kept them inside while they did that. There's just one police car now, and I think that will be gone soon.'

There are two police cars. Inspector Ola drove up there after dropping Vivacia off. She doesn't correct him.

'How… How did they…?' She stops. She doesn't want to know how they removed that watery mass that used to be her husband.

'The kids had some lunch, just sandwiches, juice.' Rob is still talking, and she forces herself to look at him.

She is remembering another time, another man, who walked into her house and took over her life.

'Thank you,' she says. 'I appreciate your help.'

She is dismissing him. She wants him gone now. She wants to sit with Rose and Dallas, play with them, talk to them, try to get them to talk to her. She wants to make their beds up, and spend the rest of the afternoon and evening just being.

Tomorrow she will plan; tomorrow she will probably have to speak to the police again. They will think of more questions, no doubt, and then she'll have to get a babysitter again.

The turmoil will begin all over again. Vivacia wonders if she has the strength for it.

She looks at Rose and Dallas, and knows she does.

'I can make some dinner, now. You need to eat.' Rob hovers, hands on hips, only serving to irritate her further.

Vivacia shakes her head. 'I'm good. I just need some quiet time.' She swallows hard and forces herself to look him in the eye. 'It's been a really long day.'

He doesn't argue like she thought he might. He simply throws a wave to the children, along with a 'see you later', and makes his way inside.

Vivacia follows him as far as the kitchen, standing at the midway point where she can still see the children and watch him leave.

He pauses as he opens the door. 'I'm sorry about your husband.'

'Thanks.' She exhales noisily as the door shuts behind him.

Back across the kitchen, darting outside into the far corner, not looking at the kids now, but up at his place, searching... for what? For him to go out on his own balcony and make a phone call to the police? Evidence of him not returning to the rental but sneaking around the lane to speak with the officers still at Lady Well?

She doesn't realise her fists are clenched until her knuckles start to cramp.

How she hates this, depending on someone, trusting someone. Not even anybody she really knows, like Ruth or Iris, or even Jackie, but a bloody stranger who could have any agenda on his mind.

Vivacia sits on the step of the patio and puts her face in her hands.

Rob will leave. He said that, when she asked him if he was leaving. *Probably*, he'd said. Before tomorrow, he will be gone. A moonlight flit in the middle of the night. How can he not? He doesn't actually live here; he was just passing through, looking for a breather in a seemingly nice, peaceful community.

He didn't sign up for any of this.

He'd be a fool to stay.

—

There is a knock at the door, later.

A dozen thoughts hammer through Vivacia's mind.

The police.

Rob.

A villager who has seen the children here.

The true parents of the children, come to stake their claim.

Rose and Dallas are on the sofa. A children's show pulses out of the television, colour and animation and noise. Rose and Dallas stare at the screen, their eyes blank.

'Stay here,' Vivacia instructs them as she darts out into the hall.

It has started to rain again, and Portia is standing on her doorstep.

She scuttles across the threshold and pulls Vivacia to her.

'I'm so sorry, sweetie,' she murmurs in Vivacia's ear. 'I'm so terribly sorry for your loss.'

Vivacia extracts herself. 'Thanks,' she says. 'It's… It's a shock.'

'You shouldn't be alone at a time like this.' A voice from behind Portia, and Aster Gould appears, coming up the step to stand just inside the door.

'Oh.' Vivacia is thrown.

They're being kind, neighbourly. This is what Ruth would have done, or Iris or Serafina Bastille, back in the day, had her grandmother Kay had some bad news.

It is what they did do, when Steven, Kay's husband, died; the neighbours rallied around her, brought food and support.

Vivacia hadn't thought anyone would do that for her.

They wouldn't if they knew the truth. And they're probably just here for gossip, anyway.

The thought is sudden and nasty, and Vivacia tries to come back to herself to concentrate on what the women in front of her are saying.

'…should be on their own, nights are the worst to be alone.' Aster is speaking in her normal, strict, authoritarian tones. 'We'll sit with you, have a natter. Yes.'

It's not a question, nor an offer, Vivacia realises belatedly. It's a plan already put into action.

'Me and the children baked some vegan banana and nut scones,' continues Aster, thrusting a Tupperware box at her.

Vivacia just catches Portia's smile before she smothers it. She winks, holds up a bottle of wine and says, 'And I'm sure we can do even better than that.'

Before Vivacia can respond, without waiting for permission, Aster and Portia are reaching for the door to the living room.

The room where the children are sitting, watching television.

The children that she's not supposed to have.

14

VIVACIA – BEFORE

The deeds were nowhere to be found in the house.

Even though he wasn't there, she could hear his voice ringing around the place.

You don't mess with me. You don't ever *mess with me.*

There had been money in the envelope, too, funds that she'd hidden from Charles, protection from his overspending.

With still no sign of Cally, she took Brittany over to her mother's. Stephanie was wonderful with the girl, taking her into her studio, letting her have a go on the potter's wheel. The teenager showed no creative talent, but Stephanie's booming laugh and Brittany's small, girlish giggle were heart-warming.

'Those deeds…' Vivacia began, sitting outside in front of Kay's chimenea, hands wrapped around mugs of hot chocolate. 'I… I mislaid them.'

Kay frowned. 'That's not like you, dear.'

Vivacia felt her face burning. It wasn't like her. She was ultra-organised. She'd had to be, growing up with her messy mother. It was either that or drown in the constant untidiness. A losing battle, with Cally always over too, but a fight Vivacia fought, nonetheless.

'Maybe they'll turn up,' Vivacia said, weakly.

Kay looked like she was about to say something but seemed to decide against it. Instead, she sat, deep in thought.

Vivacia's heart dragged downward. She had disappointed Kay. Such a lovely gesture, such an important thing that the older woman had entrusted to her, and now she'd lost it.

'I'm sorry,' said Vivacia eventually.

'Maybe Charles moved them. While tidying up, perhaps.' Kay looked away, over the fields to the distant grey clouds that had gathered. 'Maybe you should ask him, later.'

They both knew what was being left unsaid.

–

She was out when he returned home after three days, not a week as he'd said.

She'd been out with Brittany, a trip to town for tea and cake. When she opened the front door, the first thing she saw was his wallet on the telephone table in the hall.

Her heart did a strange jolt at the sight of the red leather, announcing that he was back.

He smelled funny, as though he'd put on an overwhelming amount of aftershave. He was prickly, annoyed, and he flounced into the lounge and slumped on the sofa.

Vivacia wondered if she should ask him how the business trip went.

He produced a brown package with a black ribbon. 'Happy paper anniversary,' he said.

The anniversary wasn't until the weekend. Upstairs, Vivacia had written a card and got him a voucher for a meal for two at the golf club.

She took the package and felt a genuine smile on her face.

She undid the ribbon then paused. 'Should I open it now?' she asked.

He shrugged. 'Well, you've already started, haven't you, *wife*?'

It didn't sound like a slight, despite his use of the word wife. She pulled the rest of the ribbon and unfurled the brown paper.

It was an envelope, plain white, no writing on it. Inside, Vivacia knew, were the deeds that Kay had presented her with last year.

She peered inside, to make sure, noting as she did so that the money that she'd hidden in there was gone.

Upstairs, Brittany's music thumped a beat through the ceiling. Silence hung heavy in the lounge. Vivacia stared and stared at the envelope in her lap.

When she dared to look up, Charles had left the room.

–

'I was saving it to show you,' she said when she found him.

He was in their bedroom, sitting on the bed, his leg twitching up and down.

'Liar,' he said.

She heard herself gasp and tried to swallow it back, wondering at the same time why the word had wounded her so.

It was the first time, she realised, that his nastiness hadn't been concealed beneath layers of something else.

Perhaps because this time it was clear, Vivacia answered him back.

'Kay gave the house to me.'

If she'd surprised him by her own retort, he didn't show it. 'You thought you could mess with me? You really thought you could mess with *me*?' He barked out a laugh. 'What's yours is mine. I'm your husband.'

'And it is yours, we live here together.'

'With it in your name only.'

They went back and forth, his voice getting louder, her own shrinking. Perhaps he was hoping she'd tire, show the submission that she always had. But this was important, and she pulled together all her bravery to make a stance.

He came at her eventually, his height looming over her, and he put his hands on her face, one on each cheek. He held them, as one may do to a baby. His touch was light, gentle, until he pinched her skin, tighter and tighter until a sharp cry burst out of her.

'You are so boring, wife. You are boring and beige, and you are very lucky that I'm still here.' His words dripped venom. His expression bordered on hatred.

Vivacia failed to blink back the tears that had risen. Her husband disliked her. The shame she felt was sharp, a dull pain, like the onset of a migraine.

Somewhere along the way, Brittany's music had stopped. Now, in the silence that followed Vivacia's wail, footsteps thundered down the stairs and the front door slammed.

Vivacia planted her hands on Charles's chest and pushed him away from her. Face stinging, she hurtled down the staircase, past the thin red wallet which seemed like a terrible omen whenever it was *in situ*. Out of the door she sped, stopping in the front garden to look left and right in the dark, across the fields, seeing nothing, hearing only the sound of the blood rushing in her ears.

Brittany was in foster care because of a series of violent fights between her parents. She'd started cutting herself. Vivacia had seen the scars, and each day that they faded a little, she felt a tiny glow of pride that *she* was the one who was healing this poor girl from the outside in.

She would never be allowed to take care of children again. Brittany would be forever damaged, thinking this was the way every couple acted. Vivacia ducked back inside, pulling a torch from the cupboard underneath the stairs. Charles appeared, put a hand towards her to comfort or calm, strike or restrain. She didn't know his intention, and she whacked his arm away with the torch.

'Get away,' she snarled.

He caught her arms, pinned them to her sides, pushed her against the wall. He breathed heavily. She felt his excitement at this new, unseen side of her through his smart greyish-silver suit trousers.

He released one of her arms. She heard a zip. All her fury was gone now; her regular, normal fear had returned. He noticed it too and deflated rapidly now she was back to her usual self.

She moved past him, outside, switched the torch on and swept it in large arcs across the fields, seeking a girl who was just as wounded, scared and panicked as Vivacia was.

15

VIVACIA – NOW

She lurches towards the door just as Aster grips the handle to enter the living room.

Then, there's a flurry of activity outside the still-open door.

Rob, darting up the step, bottle of wine in one hand and a Tupperware in the other. Vivacia stares at it, glances at the one Aster holds. She wonders if they've had some sort of Tupperware party, like her mother used to back in the day.

'She's not alone,' he says, greeting them with his normal, cheery smile. He rattles the box that he holds. 'Ruth's biscuits: a guaranteed cheerer-upper.'

'Oh!' Portia and Aster exclaim in unison.

Portia recovers first, a sly little smile playing around her perfectly plumped lips. She leans forward, air-kisses Vivacia.

Aster has a different expression on her face. One that Vivacia can't quite fathom.

'We wouldn't dream of disturbing. V, we'll see you soon. Let us know if you need *anything*,' says Portia.

With a lingering look at Rob, the two women make their way slowly outside. On the step under the covered porch, they hunch over, pulling up their hoods against the drizzle.

'Bye, and thanks!' Rob reaches for the handle of the living-room door and strides in.

Vivacia watches him, shocked by how at home he seems to be here. She asked him to leave earlier, told him she needed peace and quiet.

He hasn't listened to her. Has ignored her wishes. She feels at sea. Doesn't know how to handle this interloper.

But she thinks of the following day. Of the further police interviews that will no doubt be requested of her. She can't bring the police into this house, not with the children. She will need to go to the station. She will need an adult to sit with Rose and Dallas.

She drifts into the kitchen and makes him tea. While the kettle is boiling, she looks longingly at the drinks lined up on a high shelf in the kitchen. She could do with a nip of whisky.

She remembers the wine bottle Rob brought. She abandons the tea and takes two glasses off the shelf.

That's what Kay would have done had she been here. Poured a hefty glass. *For the shock*, she'd have said.

Cally would have pulled a joint out of her purse, or a neat little selection of pills.

Vivacia barks a laugh.

She needs to be more Kay, more Cally.

'All right, in there?' Rob's voice comes from the living room.

'Yes,' she replies, as friendly as she can make her voice while she prepares a tray.

Carrying it carefully to the lounge, she pauses in the doorway and surveys the scene in front of her. They could be a family, she thinks. If someone came in and casually observed, they'd think it was a father there, his feet up on the table, a child either side of him.

He's got a piece of paper on his lap, is squinting at it, poring over it. The children, however, are staring at the television screen. She thinks of the paper she found in Rose's pocket and panic blares, briefly, before she remembers it is safely tucked away her jean pocket, buried deep in the drawer upstairs.

'What's that?' she asks, brightly, as she sets the tray down on the table and glares purposefully at his feet.

'I think they've been drawing.' He seems to notice her expression and, with a wry smile, he takes his feet off the table. 'Sorry,' he says.

He doesn't look very sorry.

She takes the sheet of paper he hands her.

She did give Rose and Dallas reams of paper, and crayons, but as far as she'd seen, they'd used neither.

She looks at the scrawl now. That's all it is: a scrawl. Colours, shapes, squares and none of it actually equates to anything resembling an identifying feature. She frowns. Some of it is in pencil, pen. A thick black line looks suspiciously like eyeliner. The paper is old, damp, dirty. Was this with them when they arrived? If so, how did she miss it?

They stare up at her with blank eyes.

'Lovely,' she croons.

The rain is heavy on the windowpane, and Vivacia shudders to think of these two out in that. If she hadn't come along when she did...

They were wet when she found them on the well, their clothes clinging to their skin.

The memory has a visceral effect on her. To counteract it, she thinks of the beds upstairs, made up now with fresh linen. The thought is mildly soothing, but a hundred other problems crowd her mind.

The children's parents – are they looking for them?

The gruesome discovery that erupted from the well – how long will the authorities hang around?

She turns to Rob. 'Are the police still out there?'

He shakes his head. 'They've cordoned it off, but they're gone, so is the tent.' He gives her a curious look. 'What do you think happened?'

She exhales noisily. 'I don't know. That well, the lid they fit on it... It was never very good. It was a hazard for such a long time.'

Rob nods thoughtfully. 'They told me that. Said they'd complained so many times.'

Vivacia sits up. 'Who said that?' she demands.

'Aster, Ruth too, some of the others. They said the well was always exposed, a health and safety issue.'

Vivacia bites her lip. 'Did they tell the police that?'

'Yes. You can imagine them, up in arms about it.' He pauses. 'I'm so sorry, Vivacia. It must have been a horrible shock.'

She shudders. Like a monster emerging from the sewer. A shock is putting it mildly.

'When was the last time you saw him?' Rob asks.

Vivacia stands up. 'I've already been questioned,' she says.

He holds his hands up. 'Yes, of course. I'm sorry.' He pats the sofa. 'It was insensitive of me. Please, sit down.'

But Vivacia remains standing. 'We're okay now. Thank you for coming by.'

She doesn't like the way he is talking about what came from Lady Well, in front of the children. Doesn't like his entitled attitude tonight.

Thoughts of the need for a babysitter fly from her mind. All she wants for now, for tonight, is to be alone with the children.

For a moment it seems like he might argue. Instead, he drains his wine, his eyes lingering on the children.

Then, with a cheery goodbye in the direction of the kids, he leaves.

Vivacia sits down in the space he's vacated, a child either side.

–

Indeed, she spends the entire evening speaking to the children. Probing, gently, the way she used to when she had an anxious foster child *in situ*.

'Where is your mummy?' she asks. 'Where did you travel from to get here?'

She directs her questions to Rose, because even though she hasn't spoken yet, she seems to be the more alert of the pair, the more receptive one.

But there is no indication that the child has even heard her.

Vivacia takes a hold of Rose's hand. The little girl's fingers lie stiff and heavy in her own. 'Could you… Could you show me the way you came?'

Rose is quiet and still for a long time. Then, just as Vivacia is thinking of another question to ask, the child shuffles to the edge of the sofa and slips off it.

She stands facing Vivacia, still holding her hand.

Vivacia's heart thuds uncomfortably in her chest and she glances to the window.

Darkness has just about fallen now.

'I didn't mean tonight,' Vivacia says, hating herself a little.

Rose climbs back onto the sofa and sits stiffly by Vivacia's side.

'I think it's bedtime,' Vivacia decides. 'Let's get you both comfy so you get a good sleep.'

They follow her silently up the stairs, compliant, letting her lead the way into the third bedroom where there are two single beds set up.

She's found nightwear for them, soft, cotton pyjamas that are for children aged five. They swamp both Rose and Dallas, even though Vivacia thinks they may be older than that.

'Do you know how old you are, Rose?' she asks as she pulls off the girl's outfit.

Rose looks solemnly at Vivacia – such a direct stare that Vivacia can feel her heart rate getting higher and higher.

She doesn't think the girl will answer her. She's said nothing so far, so she proceeds with pulling back the duvet and giving the mattress an inviting pat, when Rose turns towards the window and reaches up to the ledge with small but determined hands.

There are miniatures up there. Relics left over from when this was Kay's home. Tiny mice, dogs, girls, jars. Knick-knacks that Vivacia has no time for but can't stand to throw away or even put in a cupboard.

Rose selects a few of them, seemingly at random, and places them on the rug beside the bed. Dallas goes into a crouch and studies them.

Vivacia looks at them, helplessly, and picks one up.

It's a pottery puppy, probably one of Stephanie's earlier works.

'You like the dog?' she asks Rose.

Rose's tiny lips pinch together in a straight line. A slight frown crosses her brow. She kneels next to her brother and with her forefinger, she taps each one in turn.

Vivacia feels a cool breeze at her neck. Icy fingers on her spine. Her heart has returned to normal. Just like when Rose managed to tell Vivacia her name, she feels calm and centred.

'Seven,' Vivacia states. 'You're seven years old.'

Vivacia feels inordinately pleased. There is a connection here, a strong one between her and Rose.

She looks at Dallas, still crouched on the floor, looking at the pieces that Rose picked out.

'Is Dallas also seven?' she asks.

She holds her breath, wanting a breakthrough, wanting Rose to say yes, he is – or even a nod or a shake of her head would be something. Instead, Rose touches the seven ornaments again, one by one. A non-verbal confirmation that, yes, her brother is also her twin.

Twins!

Vivacia had known it, anyway – their size, their features – it had been easy to guess. But to have it verified is thrilling. A perfect little ready-made family, one of each sex.

Just like before.

Only this time, *it will work out*.

She helps them into their beds, warmed by the fact they allow her to embrace them both. They don't return her hugs; their arms hang limply at their sides, but when she holds Dallas to her, he tilts his head, his little face nestling into her neck.

Vivacia holds on to him a moment longer. This precious boy.

Her precious boy.

She leaves the door halfway open and the landing light on.

As she settles in her own bed, she can't help her legs twitching. She should be exhausted after the trials that this day has brought. But she knows she won't sleep.

Outside, the rain is hammering against the windowpane and the wind swirls noisily. She thinks about her neighbours, sequestered in their homes. Mr Bastille, what is he doing in the darkest part of the night? Does he sit in his chair and listen to the downpour? Or is he still drinking all day, pushing away his pain until he passes out before sunset?

Today was the first time she'd seen him in forever. Tempted from his home by the uproar outside. She recalls his words: *that's not Lomax!* She thinks about Jackie, her frantic run, the look on her face when she realised that awful, watery mess was not her daughter.

Two people who were once extraordinarily loud voices here, before the fences went up, before everything went bad.

And now, they are all quiet, damaged by grief. Herself included.

Vivacia glances at the clock on her nightstand. It is well past midnight.

A new day. The second day of the children being here.

There has been no sound from their bedroom. She hopes it means they are sleeping soundly.

As soon as the thought pops into her head, she realises she is wrong. She'd thought it was the wind which had whipped up outside, but now she thinks about it…

It is the sound of whispering.

And it is not outside.

Vivacia throws back the cover and tiptoes along the landing to the spare room. The light that she left on spills into their room. She peers around the door. For a second, her heart thumps a raging beat at the sight of one empty bed.

Dallas's bed.

But no, there he is, in with Rose.

At first glance it seems they are sleeping. Face to face, noses almost touching. The girl's arms around her brother, a protective, loving grip.

But if it wasn't them whispering...

She lingers in the doorway, watching their deep, even breaths. There is a strange sensation inside her. A thought that she wants to throw cold water over.

Will they ever need me, as much as they need each other?

'*Yes*.' She speaks the word aloud as if to confirm it to herself.

Dallas opens his eyes into tiny little slits. His rosebud lips pout as he stares at Vivacia.

For one awful moment, Vivacia is terrified. The boy looks like a tiny demon. She wants to turn tail and flee, but this is her house.

These are her children.

Vivacia raises her chin as she tries to inject some authority into her stance.

'Go back to sleep.' She is pleased with her own voice. It doesn't waver. It holds none of the fear she feels. She sounds like a mother.

But Dallas doesn't close his eyes. He just stares.

'Sleep.' She says it once more.

The wobble is there now, and she clears her throat. Rose stirs but doesn't wake.

'See you in the morning,' Vivacia manages.

She pulls the door almost closed this time. She runs back along the landing. A child herself, frightened of what lurks in the dark.

16

THE CHILDREN

The hole in the floor was horribly empty. There was no milk, bread, meat, key or magical mobile phone. Rose let out a scream and stamped her feet. Dallas stared blankly at her, but in response to her daughter's shrill cry, her mother's fingers twitched, and a low moan escaped her.

'There's nothing in here!' The tantrum was building in Rose.

Strangely, though she was physically weaker than she'd ever been, a fire burned within her. The fury was life and survival. Rose, young as she was, knew this.

With a wisdom beyond her years, Rose regarded Mother.

'Do you love us, Mother?' she asked now.

Mother's eyelids flickered. After a long moment, she blinked at Rose.

Rose almost wished Mother's eyes had stayed closed. Father used to say Mother had pretty eyes. Delft blue. Clear as pools. Now, red lines zigzagged them. Rose remembered something from a long time ago, in a different place. It was called *car-tunes* and it was on a large, flat square that had moving pictures. They had eyes like Mother when something bad happened. When they got clunked on the head with mallets or got run over by fast-moving cars.

Rose peered at Mother's scalp. There were no lumps that suggested she had been hit. Plus, there was only the three of them here. Rose narrowed her eyes as she stared at her brother, before turning her attention back to Mother.

'The hole is empty.' Rose took Mother's limp hand and trailed it on the floor, sweeping her fingers through the hole.

Mother coughed. Rose despatched Dallas to the bathroom for water. There was none, she remembered belatedly. Hadn't been for days now, or was it weeks? But sometimes good things happen. Roofs cave in, rain falls through holes.

She knew this had not happened. They would have heard had the roof caved in.

Rose thought of the land below the caravan. She remembered it being patchy, yellow, brown and in places even black from oil that leaked from old car engines or campfires that happened in another time, another life. It would contain moisture, though, in some form.

The hole in the floor came to a natural end. There were four sides and a bottom, like a box. But clever Rose knew there was something else underneath the bottom. There was grass. Under that, there was soil. Further down still, water, an abundance of it, and clay and metals and core.

Rose didn't need all that. She just needed to get through the first bottom to where the grass was. There would be the vegetable patch to the south, the old rubbish store to the east, blank empty spaces west, where other people's homes in the form of vans and tents once were. North is where she once played with Dallas, in the tangle of low-growing hedges and sturdy-trunked magnolia trees.

Beyond all that were more things. Behind those tall fences were the places where Martin and Trinity and the others came from, and where they went back to.

She bet there would be water too, and food and mobile phones and people.

She thought about it for a long time. So long that her train of thought drifted and disappeared, *poof!* It refused to come back to her, lost in the airless caravan.

She would catch the thought again, though. It was there, floating somewhere. It couldn't escape, that thought, because the doors didn't open. It was somewhere in this room.

Dallas returned from the bathroom. He was empty-handed. Rose realised her fingers were bleeding. They did not hurt. She was past pain.

She sucked on her hands. They tasted like pennies. It was moist, like dew. She put her hands to Dallas's mouth. His lips were pale, white like his face in the patches where there was no dirt on it. The blood stained his mouth like blackberries on flesh.

Mother moved, jerking her arm back and forth against the hole that Rose had dug.

Rose rested, knees clasped to her chest, rocking in time with Mother's motion.

Soon, Rose noticed a line on Mother's arm. Grey skin marred by a deep, red, oozing slit. With it, she beckoned her children.

They pounced on her, mouths jostling for position, like blind kittens, fighting for the teat.

They sucked and sucked, taking the life blood out of her, putting it in themselves.

Mother gave it to them, willingly.

17

VIVACIA – BEFORE

Vivacia found Brittany on the Bastilles' front porch, sitting beside Serafina, rocking on the swing chair.

'I've been looking for you!' Vivacia said, hating the false joviality in her voice. 'Are you coming home?'

'It's not that late yet, stay and have some punch.' Serafina giggled as she poured. 'It's only the year's end of apples – we try to stay clear of the stronger drinks.' A shadow passed across Serafina's face, and Vivacia knew she was thinking of her husband's fondness for the hard stuff. She wondered about all the secrets they kept here in Wolf's Pit, which were so out in the open, but that everyone ignored to save face.

She wondered if, privately, Serafina and Mr Bastille shared thoughts and gossip about herself and Charles.

She accepted a glass and sat down underneath the porch light in a wicker chair. She felt Serafina's gaze on her face, and belatedly remembered her cheeks, and how Charles had squeezed them so hard. She imagined them, red, with little half-moon crescents left in her skin by her husband's nails.

She looked away, conscious not to stare herself at the scarf that covered Serafina's radiation-riddled scalp, and thought about what Charles had said to her. She was boring, beige.

The embarrassment of her own inadequacy washed over her again.

Later, back home, she muttered an apology to Brittany for the disturbance. The girl shrugged as though she was used to it, which she was.

None of them – not Vivacia, Charles or Brittany – mentioned the night to Claire the social worker.

None of them mentioned it to each other or, as far as Vivacia knew, anybody else at all.

–

Brittany went home eventually, without ever meeting Cally, who was more and more absent from Wolf's Pit.

There were no more children for a while. They needed a break, said Vivacia to Claire the social worker. Just for a little while, because Charles had a lot on with work, and Vivacia needed to support him while he found his feet in his new business venture. She prayed Claire wouldn't enquire about it, because Vivacia had no idea what it was. His ideas came and went, just like the money did.

'I spoke to Kay,' announced Charles, one Sunday morning. 'She is quite unmoving in her opinion that my name will never be on the deeds to this place.'

Even though, or perhaps because, he said the words so breezily, Vivacia felt a jolt of worry. It had become clear over the last year that Stephanie and Kay tolerated Charles to a certain extent. They didn't like him, though they'd never said as much to Vivacia. The whole thing about the title deeds was statement enough.

'What did you say to her?' Vivacia was embarrassed at the thought of the conversation that would have taken place. She could see it now: Charles wheedling, doing his best salesman pitch, Kay firm and clear on her stance. She was so strong, Kay. Vivacia wondered why those genes had bypassed her.

'It needs to remain in the Williams name,' he said. 'Those were her words. The Williams name.' He chuckled, as though it were all very funny, though his mirth didn't reach his eyes.

'My dad left us,' Vivacia said. 'Kay has trouble... trusting.'

He squeezed her shoulder. For once, it didn't hurt. 'I'll win them over.' He chucked her chin and laughed. 'I won you over, didn't I?'

She would never tell him the reason behind her acceptance of his proposal. Of when he'd arrived in the village, and Cally had sat up, and said, *he's so hot*, and *who is he?* And how Vivacia held the knowledge inside that she'd seen him the day before, and he'd smiled at her in The Bull, and bought her a glass of white wine. Of how, for once, Vivacia thought that perhaps she might like to be the one who got the man, and maybe have Cally as the third wheel, and how she'd so casually said, *oh, I had a date with him yesterday*, and the look on Cally's face, half-envy, half-joy for her friend who normally didn't have drinks, nor men, nor the possibility of a future.

He was worldly, she'd thought, and handsome and exciting and a proper, real man. He didn't come from the village – he was raised in the city, and he knew everything – and the flattery that he'd looked at her, even *after* he'd met Cally, was enough to say yes to him.

All the sins, wrapped up in a decision to later regret. Envy and gluttony, greed and lust and pride. Most recently, on that awful night with Brittany, there'd been wrath. Soon, especially because there were no children here, and therefore no purpose, there would be sloth.

She didn't say that. Instead, she lowered her head, the way she used to at the beginning, and told him that, yes, he had won her over. She placated him because she was already weary, and it was easier, and really, was he so bad anyway?

For a little while, things were different. Charles went away more and more. He never said when he was coming back. His homecoming would be announced by the sign of his red wallet on the table in the hall. Sometimes it was thin, almost flat. On occasion, it would be bulging, so much so it wouldn't close. Vivacia learned to gauge his moods in advance by the size of that wallet.

'A successful trip,' he'd say, fanning money at her. Belatedly, she remembered the vouchers for the golf club meal she'd got for their anniversary. She presented them to him, already planning what dress she'd wear, and how to do her hair to look respectable and not show him up. He pecked her on the cheek, and invited an investor, new to the area, to join him for a few holes and a dinner, instead of taking her.

'I'm going to make something of this place,' he told Vivacia as he straightened his tie, preparing for his meal. 'You mark my words. I'm going to be king of the pile.'

–

He had meant selling off the land.

The handful of homes in Wolf's Pit sat on a fair few acres. Somebody – maybe Charles – had floated the suggestion of the residents selling what were, effectively, their gardens to a developer.

'I could head up the committee,' he told Vivacia, that dreamy look back in his eyes.

He wanted in on it, probably because he couldn't own Kay's house, and he had a desperate need to own. To fit. *To be someone of importance.*

He didn't own any of the houses, nor the acres that went with them, but he could insert himself into the community by steering the development and therefore becoming a figure of notability.

The murmurs floated around the village again, of selling the land, the gardens, and committees began to crop up. Stephanie and Kay were opposed, Mr Bastille and the Widow Ruth filled with joy at the thought of the cash they'd have, and others undecided. Charles hovered in the middle, acting as mediator. Both sides came to rely on him, calling him into their meetings, nodding sagely at his calm tones and careful arguments for and against. Jackie seemed not to care one way or the other, all her time spent on trying to keep track of her errant daughter, who still didn't work, still partied, still went missing for days, sometimes weeks on end.

In the midst of marriage, and the foster children, and the potential land sale, Cally had slipped away from Vivacia.

Not so much slipped, Vivacia thought. Rather, her friend had detached herself, extracted herself away from Vivacia's new life.

Vivacia swore to make more of an effort and the opportunity presented itself a few days later, when Charles was away. It was early in the morning, the time of day that Cally usually never saw, but there she was, leaving Jackie's house.

Vivacia hurried from her house, skipping up to her friend, wrapping her in a hug.

'I've missed you,' she murmured. 'Where do you go all the time?'

She stepped back, saw that Cally had a small, wheeled suitcase that she was dragging behind her.

'Nowhere, just… out.' Cally lowered her head and slipped on a pair of huge sunglasses, even though it wasn't particularly sunny.

'Do you want to do something?' she asked.

Cally shrugged apologetically. 'I can't,' she said. 'Another time, maybe?'

Vivacia felt the now familiar pang of Cally's rejection. She stepped back to take in her friend's outfit. She wore a suit, a pencil skirt with a fitted jacket, high heels, and her hair was pulled back in a neat bun, face minimally made up.

'You look like a stranger,' joked Vivacia. 'Do you have a job interview?'

'Something like that.' Cally pulled Vivacia in for a hug, and for a moment was herself again. She leaned her head on Vivacia's shoulder, a tender embrace. 'You deserve to be happy,' she said. 'You're wonderful. You need to move on.'

One last squeeze and then, without a backward glance, Cally hurried off along the lane.

Cally was talking about the stalled children situation, Vivacia realised. There hadn't been any, not for a long time. She missed them, horribly, all of them that had come before.

She returned home, and got on the telephone to Claire, the social worker, and requested that she send more children, as soon as was feasible.

She kept an eye out for Cally. She wanted to thank her for pushing her back into doing the thing she loved, but weeks passed without seeing her friend.

18

VIVACIA – NOW

Instead of returning to bed, she moves through the dark, down the stairs, to the lounge. She sits on the sofa. Her body is stiff. She feels chilled but resists grabbing the blanket that is folded neatly on the back of the chair.

She doesn't want to fall asleep. She will spend the remainder of the night sitting here, keeping watch.

Waiting for the whispers to start up again, or for the sound of tiny feet padding down the stairs. For anything else that is chasing her, whether real or all in her head.

–

At daybreak, Vivacia stretches languidly. She didn't sleep. Not a wink. Every hour, she crept up the stairs to peer into the children's room. They didn't change positions at all. On the third visit, when she felt brave enough, Vivacia moved closer to the bed to look at their faces.

Rose's face was partially hidden; she had burrowed into her brother's chest. Dallas stayed in the same place all night. Those eyes… Vivacia wonders if he sleeps like a cat, eyes partially open.

She shuddered as she returned downstairs and wished hard for daylight to come.

Now it has arrived. A new day. Her first full day as a mother.

And as an official widow.

Vivacia opens the curtains.

Sunshine spills into the room, flooding it with a light so bright it makes Vivacia wince.

No rain! She can't remember the last time she woke up to bright sunlight rather than a torrential downpour of biblical proportions.

It's a sign, she thinks. A new, fresh start.

For all of them.

For the briefest moment, everything on Vivacia's mind is pushed away by the beaming sun. The sleepless night, the fact that her husband's body was discovered the day before. The people who were, prior to yesterday, women she lived alongside but who have now shown that they might not be plastic, robotic Stepford wives, after all. She dares to wonder if perhaps they have the potential to become friends. Real friends, not the way she has pretended in the recent past.

Maybe, maybe, time will tell.

Vivacia covers her mouth with her hands as she contemplates the future. Could it really be that easy, having this new, exciting life poured into her lap like this?

Then, as she realises something is happening in the street outside, she feels a chill creeping over her.

Of course, it won't be that easy. It never is.

She darts up to the window, cupping her hands around her face and squinting into the bright day. There are people out there, many more than normal for this time of the morning. Much like yesterday, when Charles's body sprang from the well, they stand in clusters, morbid onlookers. But today, they are not shocked or horrified.

Today, they look like persecutors.

The police are there, not outside the fences, not around the well, but here, in front of Vivacia's home.

Door-to-door enquiries. The hope that they are just doing follow-up calls, because they would, wouldn't they? It's feasible.

But that's not what this is.

They are leading Rob from his home, from the place where he's lived for a year.

She wonders if this is what it looked like when she was led away, yesterday.

Why are they taking Rob?

Her breath catches in her throat.

Spurred into action, Vivacia races to the top of the stairs and peeks into the bedroom. Dallas is still in Rose's bed. Rose is sound asleep. The boy's eyes are the same as they were all last night. Tiny slits, dark irises glinting in the morning light.

'Stay here,' Vivacia whispers.

She closes the bedroom door fully this time, sprints down the stairs and yanks open the front door.

Portia is there, at the bottom of Vivacia's front garden. In a little cluster with Aster, Ruth and Chloe-Joy.

'What's going on?' Vivacia asks sharply as she hurries towards them.

'They're questioning Rob.' It's Ruth who speaks up, her normally friendly, sparkling eyes heavy with something that Vivacia can't discern.

'Why?' demands Vivacia.

Aster turns her cool gaze to her. 'Don't you think it's strange that your Charles went missing as soon as Rob turned up a year ago?' Her tone is as icy as her stare.

'What?' Vivacia utters a disbelieving laugh. 'That's... That's...'

'Possible.' Aster finishes for her.

'And Rob does like you.' This from Chloe-Joy. As she speaks, her eyes travel the length of Vivacia's body, up and down, a doubtful look upon her face, as if she can't understand why.

'They arrested him?' Vivacia asks.

'Yes,' replies Aster.

'No,' contradicts Portia, with a stern look at her friend. 'Just questioning him. They're speaking to everyone in Wolf's Pit.'

Vivacia doesn't want to hear any more. What questions are they asking of the residents? Will they be asking about Charles, about his personality, if he was well liked here?

How he could have ended up in that hole?

She shudders, cold in spite of the warm morning. She turns and heads back inside her house.

Will the police come here, to her home? She will be expected to let them in.

Her gaze darts upstairs. Is it possible the children will remain asleep, in bed, should the authorities come knocking?

She hates all this attention. She's always been the plain Jane, the beige in a community that is now full of rainbows. Overlooked, able to blend in.

Now, the spotlight is all on her.

She moves back into the lounge and dares to sneak a peek out of the window. The residents are dispersing now that the drama is over. The little groups breaking up, drifting back to their own homes.

To the left of the green, Vivacia sees Jackie Jenkins. She stands alone, arms hanging limply by her side.

Once upon a time, Jackie would have been the first person Vivacia turned to. Before her own mother, sometimes.

But years and tragedy have changed that, in a way that Vivacia can't explain, even to herself.

Vivacia pushes the curtain to one side to get a better view of Jackie. What is she doing? Nothing, which is odd. Just… standing, staring towards the main gate.

The irony of the scene doesn't escape Vivacia. Normally, it is Jackie on the other side of the glass, looking out.

The community is quiet now, everyone but Jackie has gone indoors.

But it's *not* quiet, she realises.

A steady beat is sounding a rhythm, like a drum, or the thrum of machinery.

Vivacia lets the curtain fall, anxiety in her chest as she desperately tries to identify this noise, and where it is coming from.

Upstairs!

The realisation is sudden and Vivacia is galvanised into action. She takes the stairs two at a time, thinking the worst – a seizure, an intruder—

She twists the old-fashioned doorknob and throws the door open. A flurry of motion, two tiny bodies scattering to the far wall. Rose's hands are clenched into fists, red marks on her pale knuckles.

The children couldn't get out.

She recalls the dirt under their nails, the fact that it looked like they'd dug themselves out of somewhere. Like they'd been shut in.

And now, Vivacia has as good as locked them in somewhere else.

She drops to her knees, hands clapped to her mouth. She hates herself. They will never trust her now.

'I'm so sorry,' she sobs. 'The door wasn't locked—' Abruptly, she cuts off her own words.

These children don't need excuses that make no sense to them. They need action. She needs to show them, not apologise or justify.

She wipes her face and surveys them. They have moved to the furthest side of the room, underneath the window, between the two single beds. They stare at her.

They are not crying. They have no expression on their faces at all.

'Look,' she says.

She pushes the door closed behind her until she hears it click into place. Slowly, still on her knees, she reaches up and grasps the doorknob in her hand. 'Watch,' she says.

She turns the knob, pulling at the same time, and glances over her shoulder at them as the door opens inwards.

'See?' she says. 'It's never locked. Never.' She pushes it closed again and stretches out her hand towards them. 'Come and try for yourself.'

It's no surprise when Rose moves first, Dallas trailing behind her.

'Good girl.' Vivacia takes Rose's hand and lifts it to the handle. 'Turn, towards me, that's right.' With her hand still on Rose's, they turn the doorknob together and watch as the door opens.

Vivacia pushes it closed again. 'Now you try.'

After a moment's hesitation, Rose does what she's told. Dallas peers over her shoulder. When the door swings open, Rose looks through the gap.

'Good.' Vivacia nods to herself and turns to Dallas. 'Do you want to try?'

He stares through her, past her, to the wall behind her.

Vivacia smiles sadly.

It's the first challenge of a day that will no doubt be filled with them.

They have a fear, these two, and for a brief second Vivacia imagines how they would react if she informed the police that she'd found them. If she brought the uniformed officers in here, let them crowd the children, looming over them with non-stop questions. The prodding and poking that would follow by doctors, social workers.

A little voice in her head tells Vivacia it doesn't work like this. More than that, she *knows* this. She's seen the trained professionals.

But, she tells herself, there is no better pro than a mother. And that's what she wants to be. That's what she is.

Rose and Dallas's mother.

Rose seems a bit fixated on the door now. She has closed it and opened it, stepped outside it and back into the bedroom again. With any other children, younger ones, Vivacia would think it's one of the games they play. But with Rose, Vivacia is pretty certain that she is testing her promise that she will never be locked in.

'Shall we have breakfast?' Vivacia asks.

She hauls herself up, suddenly realising she is starving. It's been a long morning already, a long, sleepless night, but Vivacia doesn't feel weary. Her body no longer aches. She is eager to start her day. She feels as though she could remain awake forever if it means spending her days with these two.

'What do you fancy?' she asks, conversationally, as she herds them down the stairs in front of her. 'I've got porridge, fruit, cereal...' She trails off, remembering the food orgy of yesterday and the subsequent vomiting.

She needs to be careful, mustn't allow them to stuff themselves silly, not until they're used to having three square meals a day.

In the bright light of the kitchen, she seats them at the table and scrutinises them. Is it her imagination, or does their skin look a little more... normal today?

She pulls out place mats and cutlery, squinting at their faces as close as she dares while laying it all out.

It does look better. They are pale now, but that awful green tinge to their flesh, though still there, is fading. Vivacia smiles.

She's winning. She's helping them. They're recovering. They've slept well, they're eating well, they are loved and they are safe. They have all the ingredients to grow up happy and healthy now they are home.

She takes an unopened box of cereal from the cupboard, one that proclaims to have iron-boosting goodness in it. Rob's words yesterday, about vitamin deficiencies, come to mind.

She pours full-fat milk on Rose and Dallas's cereal and sits at the breakfast bar while they eat slowly. All the thoughts spin on a loop in her mind. Then, a hammering at the door brings Vivacia back to the here and now.

She jerks in her seat, her eyes flying to the children, who have paused, spoons halfway to their mouths. Whoever is at the door is still knocking, a continuous bang that screams of urgency.

The police. Not here to enquire further about Charles, but come to get the children.

She is surprised that it isn't fear that she feels. It is fight.

'Wait here,' she demands, slipping off the stool and jogging to the door.

She takes a deep breath before opening it.

Noise and lights hit her. A fist aims for her face. Vivacia cringes backwards, closing her eyes, shielding herself with the half-open door. Only when the door is almost closed does she realise what's happening.

A stranger with a microphone. Behind her, a man with a camera.

'Mrs Lomax, can you tell us anything about the body of your husband that was discovered here yesterday?'

She's blindsided by the assault. Totally unprepared for the press to turn up at her door. It was inevitable, she supposes now. Her mouth opens and closes, a guppy fish coming to mind, long moments of hesitation before she can speak.

'My name isn't Lomax.' It's the first thing that comes to mind, and it sounds awful, even to her own ears, as soon as the words leave her mouth. Hardly what a grieving widow would say.

'Hey!' There's a shout from across the street and Vivacia looks over the journalist's shoulder.

Jackie, still out there, is now striding towards Vivacia.

As if sensing she's about to be kicked out of Wolf's Pit, the journalist turns back to Vivacia and fires off a series of questions, barely even waiting for a response, as if she knows that no reply will be forthcoming.

'...is it true they've arrested a man from this very gated community? Do you have any comments on that? Charles Lomax was a revered individual here, according to—'

'Enough, leave, please.' It's Clive, the private chef. He has overtaken Jackie, and is looking most un-chef like and more bodyguard as he holds up one hand to block the camera lens.

'Careful, mate,' says the cameraman gruffly. 'This is public property; filming is not against the law.'

Clive moves in closer. 'You're trespassing and you both know it.' He whips a phone out of his pocket and makes a show of dialling three digits before raising it to his ear. He switches his stare to Vivacia. 'You can go in, it's okay.'

She's so frozen with a strange combination of fear and anger that she can only nod at him. She lowers her face, reverses back into her hall and closes the front door softly.

Almost as an afterthought, she remembers Jackie, marching on over here. She can't open the door now, though, they're still out there.

She doesn't return to the kitchen. Instead, she leans her back against the door and breathes deeply. She should leave now, perhaps. Pack the children and herself into a taxi, and empty her bank account and just go.

The organised, sensible side of her retaliates. The police will no doubt want to speak to her again. And she needs to wait for Rob to return, to find out what they asked him.

Find out what he told them.

Find out what he knows.

She moves back to the kitchen and sees, to her surprise, that the children have moved to the patio doors.

She stands by the table, watching them looking outside, heads tilted upwards, looking at the sky.

A glance at the table tells her they've finished their cereal, bowls empty, spoons neatly inside them.

Even though Vivacia hasn't made a sound, Rose turns towards her.

'You finished your breakfast, well done you guys,' Vivacia says as she advances towards them. 'And what's this?'

She gestures to the paper that Rose has clutched in her hand.

Without pause, Rose hands it to Vivacia. Her heart does a little dance at this action, as she takes it and looks at the paper.

It's the same drawing that Rose was working on last night, she thinks. Nonsensical thick lines, just scribble, really.

'Beautiful,' says Vivacia. 'All those colours!'

She glances at Dallas, still standing by the door, still looking outside. It's a clear day today, no rain, and these two should really be outside. She moves past Rose, peering out of the glass to the garden and beyond.

It looks clear enough, and the bamboo panelling that Rob propped up against the fence certainly blocks out a view into her garden.

Vivacia opens the door a crack and listens intently. All is quiet. Nothing like yesterday, with the screams and moans and sirens.

Decisive, she moves fully to stand outside.

'Come on, you two,' she says. 'Fresh air, sunshine, it'll do you both the world of good.'

They follow obediently. A slight frown knits Vivacia's brow. Obediently... or eagerly?

Rose makes for the far fence, the one with the bamboo on it, and Vivacia watches as her tiny hands come to rest on it. Her fingers wrap themselves in the gaps and Vivacia draws a sharp breath as Rose tugs at the panel. It only gives an inch, though, and Vivacia sees upon closer inspection that Rob has cable-tied it to the railings behind.

'You can play here, sweetheart,' says Vivacia, putting a hand on Rose's shoulder and trying unsuccessfully to turn the girl back towards the garden.

Rose shrugs her off, and when Vivacia's hand comes towards her again, Rose turns to look up to her.

Just like earlier, when the journalist surprised her at the door, and yesterday, when Dallas held that knife, Vivacia finds herself dodging backwards.

It's the look on Rose's face. More than a scowl, more than a sulk. Her rosebud mouth is open in a silent hiss, small teeth bared like a dog.

Helplessly, Vivacia looks at Dallas. In turn, he is watching his sister as she faces the fence once more, pulling at it, ferocious in her intent.

But the panel isn't going anywhere. It's not moving at all, and suddenly lost, Vivacia moves back to sit upon the small, raised step outside the patio doors.

She's encountered children far more troubled than Rose. She's had foster kids who couldn't stand to be touched, screamers, criers, violent youths. Always, with the scant knowledge provided by social services, she was able to pinpoint the whys and hows. She understood and altered her own actions accordingly.

But with Rose and Dallas, she knows nothing of where they have come from. They are not feral, nor wild. They know to use cutlery, and how to get dressed, and how to use pens and drawing paper. They are familiar with phones, and the action of zooming in on an image. They are in awe of the television, though, eyes boggling at the cartoons she switched on yesterday, and seemed entranced by the various analogue clocks around the cottage. They're smart, Rose especially. Vivacia thinks back to the morning they arrived, how without speaking she was able to give Vivacia both of their names. But now, watching Rose continue to yank at the fence panel, Vivacia is at a loss.

A breeze whips up, interrupting her thoughts, and behind Vivacia, the curtain swoops inward. Vivacia glances inside, sees that the paper that Rose had has fallen to the floor. She reaches behind her and picks it up, smoothing it out to look at it more closely.

Thick, smudged lines near the top of the page, green criss-crossed pencil, six blobs in a shimmering brown with a red scrawl atop one of them.

Vivacia sighs, reaches back into the room and lays the paper on the seat of one of the chairs.

'Vivacia?'

The sound of her name has her jumping out of her skin. She pushes herself up, peering left, right, and when the small voice comes again, she realises it is someone outside her gate.

Not Rob. Not the police; the tone was watery-thin and hesitant.

She presses her hand to her mouth.

It is Ruth.

Vivacia stands up. 'Hold on, Ruth, I'll open the front door.'

Cursing to herself, she dodges back inside and pulls the patio door to. She opens the front door, slipping outside before Ruth can invite herself in.

It is a mistake. The journalist hasn't moved far. The cameraman is still there, down near the front now, as is Clive the chef.

'You shouldn't be out here, that's why I came round the back,' says Ruth as she comes up the steps. 'Come on, let's go inside, put the kettle—'

'No,' interrupts Vivacia. She attempts to soften her words with a smile. 'I'm fine, honestly. You don't need to worry.'

'But it must have been a terrible shock.' Ruth peers at Vivacia, narrowing her eyes. 'I know it was a shock for *me*.'

Belatedly, Vivacia recalls the scene. Ruth, staring as what remained of Charles slopped over the sides of Lady Well. The way she sunk to the wet, cold earth, her body and mind slipping into a faint at the spectacle.

Vivacia grips Ruth's arm. 'I'm so sorry,' she says. 'Are you okay now?'

With a spurt of impatience, Ruth pulls out of Vivacia's grip. '*I'm* fine. He wasn't *my* husband.' Ruth screws her eyes shut and takes a deep breath. 'I'm sorry, I didn't mean to be short. But… But Vivacia, how did this happen?'

'I… I don't know.' Vivacia shakes her head, repeats what she told the police. 'I thought he'd left me.'

Ruth takes Vivacia's hand, the one only a moment earlier she'd pulled away from. 'Poor, sweet girl,' she murmurs. 'Maybe what they're saying is true.'

Vivacia blinks. 'What are they saying?'

Ruth cocks her head and lets her eyes stray to the new builds.

'That the well was a hazard, that it was always open. That a child could have fallen in. That someone… inebriated… could have come to harm.' Ruth leans closer to Vivacia, her eyes darting about as if to check for onlookers, even though the only people in sight are the reporters, near the gate, and a few scattered rubberneckers. 'Did they tell you what they found inside the well?'

Vivacia blinks at her. 'No… what?'

'An empty vodka bottle.'

'Nobody has told me anything,' Vivacia ventures.

She recalls the day before, sitting in that interview room, her mind only on Rose and Dallas. *Had they told her that?* She has absolutely no idea.

'Look, do you want some company?' Ruth asks. 'A nice cup of tea.' She glances behind her, at the huddle of those who managed to get through the gate, and the onlookers and press that remain outside.

'No, I'm fine.' Vivacia manages a smile. 'Thank you, Ruth, for checking in.'

Ruth sets her mouth into a straight line and turns to leave. 'I'm always here, Vivacia. I've always been here for you.'

'I know that, Ruth, and I do appreciate it.'

Ruth stills, a faraway look on her face as she stares across the road that was once wildflower meadows – past Vivacia's house, past Jackie's, and the holiday home that Ruth owns, towards the back of the community that holds the relic of Lady Well.

'Ruth…' Vivacia moves a couple of steps towards the motionless woman. 'Are you okay?'

Ruth jerks her head towards Vivacia, startled as though she's only just remembered she is there.

'Hmm, yes, fine.' Ruth utters a dry little laugh. She reaches into her pocket, pulls out one of her foul cigarettes and clamps it between her lips. 'Just thinking, it's strange, isn't it?'

'What is?'

'The accident, if it happened like they all say, that he was falling down drunk.' Ruth raises her eyes and locks a stare onto Vivacia. 'But he didn't do that, did he, your Charles? He was never one for the booze, was he?'

The warmth that Vivacia felt only a second ago is pushed out by icy, glacial fingers twisting in her chest.

19

VIVACIA – BEFORE

The investor that Charles had taken to Vivacia's anniversary meal wasn't an investor after all. He was a developer. His name was Ivan, and he was interested in building plots on their land, and creating a specialist, fancy, gated community.

When he was home, Charles still acted as the go-between. He claimed to have no interest in either side, seeing as he himself had no land to sell – this always said with a sideways, accusing glance at Vivacia – and was acting purely in the everyone's best interests. He would decline on their behalf, or ensure they got the absolute, best possible price. Regardless of the outcome of the vote, their own homes would remain untouched, apart from the reduction in the size of the gardens.

Vivacia swung to and fro on her opinion. On the one hand, halving the land would be helpful. Nobody was getting any younger; nobody had ride-on lawnmowers to tend to the plots that had slowly grown into fields over the years. They were not unpleasant, though: wildflowers had sprouted, year after year, and privately Vivacia thought how lucky they were to have their own, personal meadows. But the money would be useful. The pay for fostering had dwindled somewhat over the years, and though Charles seemed to be hugely successful these days in his field – Vivacia still wasn't too sure what it was – she was aware that her own bank account was more diminished than it had ever been.

One day, Vivacia came home from shopping to find Kay and Stephanie at her kitchen table. Charles was there, brewing fresh coffee for the women. He brandished a bottle of rum. He nudged Kay with it, dancing around her, making her giggle until she let him add a splash to her drink.

Stephanie put her hand over her mug but smiled along with her refusal.

They remained all afternoon, Vivacia abandoning her chores as she realised this was the first time they had seemed like an actual family. Charles was at his charming best, laughing heartily with her mother and grandmother.

When dusk began to fall, they stood up to leave. Kay gripped the table, unsteady.

Charles rushed to her side. 'Oh no, you don't,' he said. His face was a caricature of a concerned man. 'You're staying to dinner. You've had way too much of that to leave on an empty stomach.' He tapped the bottle of rum, which Vivacia saw with alarm was almost empty.

Vivacia jumped to attention. 'I've got some lovely beef,' she said. 'Mum will help me, won't you, Mum?'

Charles and Kay retreated to the lounge, while Vivacia and Stephanie got to work in the kitchen.

'This is nice, Mum,' said Vivacia as they moved around the familiar kitchen, preparing a meal together in a way they hadn't done since before Charles.

'Mmm.' Stephanie was distracted as she peeled the carrots, her gaze fixed on the wall that separated the lounge from the kitchen, as if she could see through it. 'Just check on your gran, will you?'

Vivacia wiped her hands on a tea towel and went in search of her inebriated grandmother.

She was in the lounge; Charles was sitting on the old sofa beside her, chatting amiably.

Vivacia paused in the doorway, unseen, feeling something like hope as she watched the pair of them.

'...it's the future, Kay,' Charles was saying in a low voice. 'Think of the opportunities it would bring. A bigger community, the jobs that would come with it. And not just any community, but one with a certain status. A brand, if you will.'

Vivacia blinked as Charles put a stack of papers on Kay's lap. 'And all you need to do is sign. Life becomes better for everyone in Wolf's Pit.'

He slipped his hand into his shirt pocket and took out a pen.

Kay had a half-smile on her face, but it was the expression in her eyes that caused Vivacia the concern.

Confusion. Hesitancy. Two emotions that Kay rarely, if ever, possessed.

Then she saw it. Another bottle of rum on the table. A new one, not the empty one Vivacia had put in the recycling.

Kay reached for the pen. Vivacia hurried into the room.

'Dinner time!' she said brightly. She walked smartly over to Kay, gripped her by the arm and hauled her up. 'Come on, Gran. Time to soak up some of that rum.'

Furious. For the first time an anger simmered inside her. She looked at Charles as she led Kay past him, and he must have noticed the rage, because he averted his eyes and said nothing.

Later, after she and Stephanie had helped Kay home, she found Charles in the kitchen, heaping the dinner plates beside the sink.

'I'm on the payroll,' he said, even though she'd not asked him anything. 'Commission, okay? The more people I get to sign for the land sale, the more money I make. There's a bonus if I get everyone on board.'

She nodded. So Charles wasn't an impartial advisor after all. He was working for Ivan, the developer.

'You don't do that again,' she said, quietly, as she moved up to the sink and began washing up. 'If the residents want to sign, they will. You don't… You don't make them.'

'Your family are the only ones holding up the sale – them and that bald one down the road.' He spoke as quietly as her, and it was all he said as he left her to it and returned to the lounge.

Later, she read the notes that Charles had left on the kitchen table. He was right. Serafina Bastille and her own mother and grandmother were the only ones firmly against the development. Beside Jackie's name was a large question mark. Vivacia's name wasn't written in the notes at all.

The following day, she questioned him about her own absence from the notes.

He snorted, back to his normal, derisive self, his behaviour the day before seemingly forgotten. 'Does it matter?' he asked.

She didn't understand the context of his retort, so she remained quiet after that.

She wondered if Charles presumed her own decision one way or the other, or if in his eyes her opinion simply didn't count.

–

After more than three years of nothingness, of the drudgery of day-to-day life, three things happened.

Cally was officially reported as a missing person.

Kay and Stephanie decided to help Jackie by driving out in Steven's old Ford, searching.

Vivacia finally got her babies.

Charles was away. He had been for almost two weeks. He claimed to have been in London, as he always said he was, but when he returned, he smelled of the countryside and manual labour, of oil and old sweat. His suit had been replaced with sturdy boots and flannel shirts. Vivacia didn't question him. Things ran more smoothly when he was away. She never dared to admit the truth to herself: if she came in and saw that battered old red wallet on the table in the hall, her heart would sink.

She didn't mind the change in his physical persona, with the casual clothes and strange scent. It was better he had the aroma of the land, rather than another woman's perfume, or the mask of his own aftershave, like in previous years.

She was shocked at Jackie's decision to report her daughter missing. The rumour had been that Cally had moved abroad, was living it up in Ibiza or somewhere similar.

Belatedly, Vivacia recalled the last time she'd seen her friend. The neat hairdo, the pencil skirt and suit jacket. Thinking back now, Cally wasn't dressed for the laidback lifestyle that she'd so craved.

'Do you think Cally is in… danger?' asked Vivacia, as Kay and Stephanie came to the house to announce their intention to drive around looking for her.

Kay stared at Charles's shoes, all shined to reflective perfection, neat in a row in the hallway. 'There are different kinds of danger,' she murmured.

Drugs, Vivacia thought she meant. They all knew Cally was a wild child, a Peter Pan who refused to grow up.

'But Cally's got a new job, hasn't she?' Vivacia asked.

Kay scoffed. 'I highly doubt it. Anyway, Jackie is worried. It's not unusual for Cally to do a flit, but Jackie hasn't heard from her.' Kay narrowed her eyes as she stared at Vivacia. 'Have *you* heard from her?'

Vivacia shook her head. Had she been selfish? Spending all this time on her quest for children, so used to Cally going off over the years that she didn't realise the one time it was serious?

'Anyway, some people claim to have seen her, locally. We're here because we want to know if Charles will have a look over the old car, give it the once-over, make sure it's in good working order,' said Stephanie.

'Charles!' Vivacia jerked out a laugh. 'He doesn't know about cars; he's never even owned a car.'

She turned and fussed with the brand-new bassinets, waiting for the babies that would be laid inside them, so as not to witness the strange glance that her mother and grandmother exchanged.

'He works with them. That's where he's working, that car place in Dagenham,' replied Stephanie.

Vivacia reddened, kept her back turned so they wouldn't see her face.

Charles's words to her over the years.

You never listen to me. Is it any wonder I rarely share my successes with you anymore?

If it was true, did that mean he was off the board of developers? She frowned. The land sale hadn't been mentioned since that diabolical afternoon when he'd got Kay drunk to try and force her hand into signing the contract.

'He's not here, anyway,' she said in reply.

'He's back today, this morning, he told us,' Stephanie said. 'He wants to be here when the babies arrive.'

Vivacia's head felt fuzzy. Since when had Stephanie and Charles became best friends? Was Stephanie really oblivious to what had happened that afternoon while they had been cooking? Did Charles talk to Stephanie about Vivacia, about her lacklustre ways, her supposedly bad attitude towards him, her husband? Was Charles right about her paying more heed to him?

The worst thought of all: had he won them over, like he claimed he would?

She should be relieved, if that was the case, but there was something off. They had never taken to Charles, Kay and Stephanie. Vivacia was sure they'd viewed him with a slight suspicion. He had looked at them like they were inconsequential, too old, too trivial to be of any concern for him.

She tried to brighten herself internally. He was making an effort, for both the new arrivals, *and* with her mother and grandmother. Maybe he had given up on the development. Maybe he had got a real job in Dagenham.

Maybe Charles was right. Maybe Vivacia was the problem.

She *did* need to do more, for him, in every way that a wife should.

–

He returned at midday, just as the foster babies arrived. Not with Claire this time, but a new social worker, an older woman called Gillian, who gave Vivacia Aunt Lydia vibes with her thick brown coat, severely pulled-back hair and piercing eyes.

'I didn't think you'd be here,' she greeted Charles as he paid the taxi driver.

'I said I would!' he retorted, as he swept past her towards Gillian.

No, you didn't, she thought. Then, because she still felt a bit churlish after learning of Charles's sudden popularity, and her lack of knowledge around her own husband's comings and goings, she said it out loud. 'No, you didn't.'

He had reached Gillian by this stage, and he laughed as he leaned over the carrycots to examine the babies.

'She can be… preoccupied, forgetful, scatterbrained, but very good with the little ones, so you don't need to worry about these two!' he said to Gillian.

Gillian frowned, her forehead creasing into four deep lines.

'And I'm here, and these two wonderful ladies,' he said, sweeping out his arm to include Stephanie and Kay in his statement. 'We're all here to back up Vivacia. It's hard work, raising one baby, let alone two, but don't you worry, we've got her covered.'

It was a huge insult. Unless the foster kids were teenage girls or boys of an impressionable age, Charles had nothing to do with the children she brought into her home. Stephanie and Kay would always be on hand, and Stephanie often welcomed the children into her studio for arts and crafts. But Vivacia never asked them for help. She'd never asked anyone for help.

'Are you going to look at Gran's car?' she asked him.

Charles rolled his eyes, flashed a look at Gillian.

'We'll let them get settled in,' said Kay. 'Come on, Charles, you can make yourself useful at my place.'

Vivacia flashed her grandmother a wary look before ushering Gillian inside.

The babies were called Alex and Elizabeth. Four weeks old, fat, pink, with bright eyes and clear skin, and each sporting a cap of wispy, pale hair. When Vivacia settled them into their bassinets, they began to wail, high-pitched, a rising crescendo.

At the beginning of her journey, when any of the children had cried on drop-off, she'd felt like a failure. Panicked, embarrassed and uncertain of her own suitability. Now, things had changed. These days, Vivacia was methodical, working through the needs of the child, always hitting upon the solution eventually.

Hunger, fear, strange smells, sights, pain, the memory of trauma, thirst.

Today, whether it was because familiar Claire wasn't here, or maybe because Charles was, Vivacia didn't feel as confident as she usually did.

Gillian stood by the sink, eyes moving around the room before coming to settle on Vivacia.

Vivacia jerked herself forcefully back to the woman she knew she could be.

'Trial and elimination,' she said, chirpily, as she got the prepared bottles of formula out of the fridge and popped them in the microwave for a few seconds.

As the microwave pinged, Gillian's eyebrows shot up.

'Never had one of those myself,' she murmured, referring to the microwave as if it were a newfangled thing.

They didn't accept the bottles, both of them writhing, snatching their heads away, faces puce as they screamed in unison.

Vivacia patted their nappies through their clothing; both were clean and dry, and not at all heavy. She held them, one at a time, only to be met with squalls and tiny, flailing fists. She checked the temperature of the room on the thermostat. The babies were hot, worked up, and Vivacia said to Gillian that maybe she'd let them out of their clothes – a bit of air to the skin did wonders sometimes. She waited for Gillian's nod of assent, which wound up Vivacia even more. Had Claire been here, Vivacia would have announced her intention, not sought her approval.

She undid Alex's Babygro and peeled it off. Then, she stopped, frozen.

His tiny body was riddled with bruises, both fresh and ageing.

It wasn't the first time that a child had come to her with war-wounds. But those others, as heartbreaking as it was, were older. Their knuckles skinned and red where they'd fought back. They shouldn't have had to; they were still only children. Later, once the trust was there, Vivacia would clean the cuts and bruises borne out of their own defence. *Good for you*, she'd think.

But this one, Alex, four weeks old, not even able to hold his own head up.

She stared down at him. Her tears dripped onto his exposed stomach.

Gillian cleared her throat. 'You're sure you're up for this?' Her voice was rough, unkind almost, nothing like the passive-aggressive remarks Charles floated her way, but the intention was the same.

Vivacia wiped her eyes with the back of her hand and moved over to Elizabeth. She removed her Babygro, able to keep the shock from showing this time when she saw that her body was in the same condition as her brother's. She picked up the baby and laid her carefully into the bassinet, next to Alex.

The crying decreased, slowed, then stopped altogether.

Vivacia straightened and fixed Gillian with a cold smile. 'We'll be fine, thank you.'

'No raised voices,' she told Charles when he came in from checking over Kay's car. 'And please be very careful how you hold them, they've been… hurt.'

Charles kicked his boots off and lined them up neatly with his other shoes. He wandered into the lounge where the children were sleeping, still in one basket.

'Since when do I raise my voice?' he asked, lazily regarding her through hooded eyes. 'And why would I hold them?'

20

THE CHILDREN

'He was ever so handsome.' Mother darted a look at Dallas and her smile faded. 'He looked like *you*.' That last part didn't sound like a compliment.

Rose had thought they'd drained mother of both blood and life. As though they were vampires, pointed-tooth legends that Trinity liked to tell stories about.

Instead, somehow, Mother was revived. She wouldn't stop talking.

Her voice wasn't how Rose remembered it. Once upon a time, almost every word Mother spoke sounded like a laugh. Over time, it became dry, rusty, small, scratchy.

Now, Mother licked distractedly at her wrist. Her tongue came away from her skin burnished scarlet with her own blood.

'He was always smart,' said Mother. 'Lovely-looking.'

She was talking about Father, Rose knew. Mother had a strange look in her eyes when she referred to him. A small, secret smile played on her lips. She was being boastful, but then she remembered he was gone.

Rose had different memories about Father. Often, he scared her. Not because he was mean to her, since he hardly ever looked at her. It was more the way he was with other people. She couldn't explain it. He wasn't shouty or anything like that, but it was very obvious when he was displeased.

He used to quarrel with Mother a lot. But over time, Mother became quieter and softer, until she didn't answer him back at all.

Rose fiddled with the hole in the floor. All day long, and all last night and the day before that, for what seemed like *forever*, rain had smashed against the window. It heightened her thirst. All that water, yet nothing to drink.

'It's rotten,' said Mother, head hanging off the bed, peering down at the floor. Her voice dropped to less than a whisper, so Rose had to lean in to hear. 'It's... fragile.'

It was, realised Rose, as she pushed at the pulpy floor. Very fragile, even more so than any of them were, and that was saying something.

Mother pushed it, but she was so weak. She turned away onto her side, hunched over something that had caught her full attention in the couch cushions.

Dallas's feet did a better job at the old floor, and Rose made him stamp on it again and again. Later, when it got dark, she could put her hand through it and feel the cold earth below. They made the hole bigger. It was easy.

They were outside. It had rained so much. Indeed, it was still raining. Rose danced in it, spinning round and round, arms outstretched, not caring when she fell and landed upon the muddy ground.

A small shadow played near her. Dallas. Rose grinned. She'd thought she'd have to force him out, yank on his legs until his little body slipped out of the hole. But he was eager, wriggling down like a worm.

Now, she moved in a crouch to the underside of the caravan. The hole was bigger, she saw, even bigger than when she'd got out. It was indeed what Mother called *rotten*. A big gap now, more floor tiles scattered on the blackened soil.

Big enough for Mother!

Her heart did a funny little jig, a ripple that travelled from her belly to her ribs. Rose climbed back inside and ran to Mother.

'We can get out,' she said. Her voice was louder than she could remember it being. 'Come on, we can go now.'

Mother was still there, because Rose could hear her breathing. Long rattles, like sand inside a bottle.

Mother's hands came up to encircle Rose. Rose squirmed, because that sense of urgency was still there, and she didn't think they had time for cuddles. But Mother was insistent. Rose relented, folded herself against the funny-smelling, filthy form.

It had been a long time since cuddles had happened. The stench didn't go away, but it didn't matter so much and if she concentrated really hard, Rose could almost remember what Mother smelled like in that time before, when she used to laugh and dance and sing. Coconuts and tropical faraway lands.

'Mummy.' Rose dared to say the word that she never used.

Normally, it provoked A Reaction, but that was only from Father, and of course, he wasn't there, so she said it again.

'Mummy.'

Mother didn't answer, and it was only later, so much later that the sky was turning light outside, that Rose realised that Mother was sleeping again.

21

VIVACIA – NOW

Vivacia closes the door behind her and leans against it. Her heart thuds uncomfortably in her chest and there is a ringing in her ears.

She breathes deeply, the scent of Ruth's cheroot clinging to her. She feels a creaking in her breastbone. Despite the sunshine that has flooded the house, she shivers, suddenly cold.

Like the majority of those in Wolf's Pit, Ruth knows everything. That remark, about Charles and his sobriety. It was true, Charles wasn't a drinker, but where is Ruth going with her observations?

There isn't time to dwell. Before the older woman came knocking, Rose seemed to be on the verge of a meltdown. Vivacia knows all about those, remembers them from when there were children here before. Some of them wanted – no, needed – to be left alone. But Vivacia hasn't observed Rose long enough to know if that is what this situation calls for.

She pushes herself off the door, strides through the kitchen towards the garden.

She's almost at the doors when she hears it. A thin keening, like a trapped kitten. Something inside her cracks, an answering chasm of pain at the thought of her babies hurt.

She breaks into a run.

Dallas is there, in the middle of the garden. He's crying, his small chest jerking up and down, his cheeks wet. As he hears Vivacia, he turns to her, his fingers at his face, his eyes distraught.

'Dallas!' Vivacia falls to her knees and gathers him to her.

He wraps his thin arms around her and she buries her face in his neck as he sobs into her chest.

The moment should be lovely, should be special, because it is the first time he has looked at her, seen her, turned to her for comfort. But as she raises her head and sees the bamboo panel lying flat on the grass – and the gap in the damaged railings – the moment is awful.

She takes a hold of his shoulders and looks into his eyes. 'Dallas.' She tries to keep her voice even, though she wants to shriek. 'Where is your sister?'

Again, there is that lurching sensation of pride as he acknowledges her question. He points beyond the fence, past Lady Well, up the hill where he and Rose came down from the day before.

Vivacia stands, holding his hand in hers. Pulling him along behind her, she darts across to the fence, through the gap, and looks up the hill.

There is no sight of Rose. How long was she outside, with Ruth? Minutes, really, surely not long enough for the girl to have gone far.

The cable ties are on the ground and Vivacia scans the area for how they were removed. The secateurs, Kay's ones that she used almost every day when she was alive. Now they are blunted, brown with rust, but clearly still in working order.

She swears softly and moves on.

As she skirts a wide arc around the well, which still smells putrid, she glances towards the road. There is still a police car there, just one, but no officers in sight. She hopes – prays – that they are at the front gates, perhaps herding the journalists away, and she knows if that's the case she doesn't have long to find Rose.

'Come on,' she says, and scoops Dallas up into her arms.

She's not unfit, thanks to the classes that she attends along with her new neighbours, but she's far from athletic. The hill is steep, and she rarely ventures up it. There's nothing up there, apart from fields and sparse woodland, and the old rubbish tip that has been closed down and boarded up for more than a decade.

Sometimes, in the winter, kids come to this hill from the surrounding towns and villages, armed with their sleds. Vivacia has watched them over the years, indeed even joined it when she and Cally were kids. But snowfall is rarer now, and the hill never seemed this hard, back when she was ten.

Halfway up she puts Dallas down and grips his hand. 'Can you walk?' she asks him.

He doesn't reply but charges up ahead of her. Still holding his hand, it's *him* pulling *her* now.

'We'll find her,' she pants as she scrambles up the hill. 'We'll find Rose.'

But, oh God, what if she doesn't? This environment is wide-open space now; the girl could have turned off, gone west or east, into the woodland, circling round and getting lost, or charging on through and coming out onto the main dual carriageway.

The vision of her, of tiny Rose, stepping past the barriers onto four lanes of traffic.

Vivacia lets out a whimper.

Dallas stops walking.

'Huh.'

At the sound that Dallas makes – not a word, far from it, but more than she's ever heard emerge from him – she stops too.

'What?' she asks, urgently.

He looks across the sparse hill, to the right, and Vivacia follows his line of sight. Down there, there is a man. Vivacia sucks in a breath. It's Rob, she'd know that loping gait anywhere.

He has seen her too, and impatiently she waits while he raises a hand and gestures for her to stay there.

'Come on, come on,' she mutters, shuffling from foot to foot while he makes his way up the hill. When he arrives, he swipes a hand across his brow.

'It's hot,' he remarks. 'I'm not used to this after all that rain.'

There's so much she wants to ask him, about the police, about what they said, about what *he* said, but Rose trumps everything.

'Rose is missing,' she tells him, breathlessly. 'She took the panel off and got through the fence while I was talking to Ruth. We have to find her.' She narrows her eyes. 'Why are *you* out here?'

To his credit, he doesn't waste time with further questions, but he also doesn't answer hers. He gestures up the hill. 'She went this way?' is all he says, and then he is off.

They march on in silence for fifteen minutes. Vivacia hears the rattle in her own chest as the hill stretches on, no sign of it evening out anytime soon. She glances to her left. Dallas has resorted to crawling. His face, once sickly green, is now puce with effort.

'Wait!' she cries, and flops down beside the boy.

Rob stops, scrambling back to them, using the edge of his sturdy walking boot to slow his progress.

'Are you all right, mate?' Rob asks Dallas.

Dallas pants.

'Okay.' Rob goes on his knees and looks at the boy. 'Climb on.'

Dallas stares.

Vivacia throws a grateful look at Rob. 'Dallas, you're going to ride on him, like a horse, yeah?'

He doesn't look at her, instead shifting his gaze up the hill.

'I'm going to put you on him, you just hold on tight.' She lifts him, light as a feather, and places him on Rob's awaiting back. She leans close to his face and inhales his scent, his damp cheek hot against hers. 'You're safe,' she says.

They trudge on again. Vivacia sneaks looks at Rob, notes the way his mouth is set, how his hands grip Dallas's legs and hoist him up every so often.

She bites her lip. She wants to fire questions at him, wants to know everything that the police have said, what they know, what they think they know.

What they suspect.

And what he said to them.

But she hasn't the lung capacity to talk, and finding Rose is so much more important than anything else that is going on back in the community.

She's parched, her throat lined with a blistering heat. Dallas, though he is now conserving his energy, is still red-faced, his hair plastered to his forehead.

Anger bites at her. Not aimed at Rose, but at herself. She has no water, nothing to drink at all. She didn't think ahead.

Find Rose. That was all she'd thought.

No wonder she had never been blessed with children. No wonder Elizabeth and Alex had been removed from her care.

Because she wasn't good enough.

Because she was stupid.

'*Stupid.*' She spits the word.

'What?' Rob crab-walks over to her.

'I shouldn't have left them. I shouldn't have answered the door. I should have made sure they were inside the house. I shouldn't have left them in the garden.' She flinches away from his gaze, laden with concern. 'I'm so stupid.'

'Of course you're not!' Rob exclaims. 'I put the panel up, I thought it was secure. If anyone is to blame, it's me.'

Vivacia stares at him, breathing heavily.

Rob shrugs. 'That's what kids do. Crikey, V, do you think you're the first person that a child has wandered away from?'

She's not. She knows that. It happens daily. Everywhere.

It's how she got Rose and Dallas. They wandered away from someone.

'Don't,' she says.

'What?'

She swallows hard. 'Don't call me "V".'

He rolls his eyes. Throughout the entire exchange, Dallas lay splayed on Rob's back. Now, he pushes himself up and looks around.

'Mmm.' The sound, like the one he made when he spotted Rob, emerges as quiet as a tideless sea breaking upon a shore. 'Mmm.'

'What, darling?' Vivacia darts over to him, cupping his face in her hand. 'What do you see?'

She stands up straight and looks around. Far in the distance, she can just about see a tall wire fence. The old rubbish tip. Beyond it, the hill crests, spreading out into a patchwork of county-owned fields of nothing.

Not nothing. A chill comes over her as she remembers the quarry. Disused for decades, much like the rubbish dump. It has never been altered, though. Land developers haven't got to it yet. It remains as it did when Vivacia was a child.

A chalky canyon, fifty metres deep, with what she imagines will be a permanent pool with all this year's rain, deeper than the public swimming bath at the bottom.

Vivacia imagines Rose wandering through the fences that are as poorly constructed as the railings at the rear of her home. Over the edge she would go. No chance of survival.

Vivacia stuffs her fist in her mouth at the thought, as she looks wildly around.

To the left, a row of free-growing blackberry bushes stand in a cluster. They trail outwards, prickly, thorned arms drenched in the rain-soaked ground, no fruits upon them yet. The bright sunshine has caused the earth to steam. It rises upwards, creating a mist.

Vivacia is reminded of the strange light that broke through the clouds, an angel's halo, surrounding the children while they waited for her on Lady Well.

Dallas kicks out with his feet, startling Rob and Vivacia. Rob bends his knees. Dallas slithers to the ground. He takes off at a run.

Vivacia cries out.

They came to her like garden faeries, elves, mystical, mysterious children appearing like a miracle. She can see it now, what's going to happen. Rose has already gone. Dallas is away like a greyhound. Both of them, lost to the mist.

Her cry is shrill, threatening to erupt into a scream.

She won't come back from this, she knows, if she loses children again.

'Listen!' Rob is beside her now, his face too close to hers for comfort. He brings his hand up and grips her chin. '*Listen.*'

Her wail fades to nothing, dispersing into the steaming fog.

Two thoughts occur to her at once. The first is that Rob's hand is clenching her face, holding her in place, but somehow, it is okay. The second is the knowledge of why it is okay. Because she can hear a thin cry, somewhere in the mist.

And even though she hasn't heard it before, she knows it is Rose.

Rob's hand slips from her face to grab her hand. 'This way,' he says, grimly, yanking her onwards.

Dallas has found Rose first. Two shapes are there, close to the end of the row of blackberry bushes. He stands over her, one hand on her shoulder. Rose is curled into a comma. Roles reversed, Vivacia thinks, *him* protecting *her* now.

Indeed, when Vivacia approaches, he snaps his head towards her, lips bared in a silent hiss. Just for a second, though, then he stands back, the movement letting her in.

Vivacia sinks to her knees in the wet grass and pulls Rose to her. The girl is crying, huge, jagged sobs.

'Rose,' Vivacia murmurs into her hair. 'You mustn't run off; you could have got lost.' In amongst the relief is a slice of anger. She holds Rose at arm's length and looks into her eyes. 'You *did* get lost. Rose, what if I couldn't find you?'

The sobs subside slightly and Vivacia holds her close again. 'It's okay, we *did* find you, so it's okay. But you must never wander off again, do you understand?'

She doesn't expect a reply, but she hopes that on some level Rose understands the danger. She hopes she understands that she and Dallas are cared for now, and loved, and that they have a home with her. That they are a family.

'We should go, they need water.' Rob steps up to them, one hand on Dallas's shoulder. 'We can carry them, though. It'll be easier going down the hill.'

Vivacia nods and kisses Rose's damp cheek. 'Come on, baby,' she whispers. 'We'll go home.'

Rob is talking softly, and from the corner of her eye she sees him chuckling. She takes in the scene, trying to make sense of what she's seeing.

Dallas, pawing at Rob's back.

'He wants a ride,' laughs Rob, going down on all fours so Dallas can climb on.

Vivacia smiles too. She's not sure how it happened, this trust that Dallas has procured for Rob who is, essentially, a stranger.

Someone she knows nothing about.

Someone who, somehow, always seems to turn up exactly when she needs help.

It's not a comforting thought.

Rose sniffles and drags her sleeve across her face. Vivacia can see her throat is working, and she wonders if the girl is on the verge of crying again.

She waits patiently, ready to comfort, ready for whatever Rose requires from her.

Rose turns away, gazing up the hill, looking to the nothingness that's beyond the crest.

Rose draws in a deep breath and turns back to Vivacia.

The moment hangs, looming, like a threatening storm, or the mist that drifts lazily around their ankles.

Or the promise of a miracle.

'Mummy,' says Rose, her voice as clear as day.

22

VIVACIA – BEFORE

The summer stretched on and on, day after day of endless blue skies. Alex and Elizabeth thrived in Vivacia's care. Cally was still gone; Jackie had turned from worried to sullen, staying inside her house but always standing by the window, her head turned down the lane. Vivacia imagined the scene: Cally staggering along the road, hair in disarray, cigarette clamped between her lips, worse for wear but nothing that a good post-bender sleep wouldn't fix. Jackie would be angry, but underneath it, the maternal relief would be palpable.

Vivacia took to watching too, mirroring Jackie's stance at the front window, while the babies slept behind her. When she kept this strange sentry duty, she felt Jackie's eyes on her.

The developers came and went, even though there were still people who refused to sign, the meetings went on, the minutes emailed out. Vivacia ignored her inbox. She didn't care what they did with her front garden. All she cared about were the babies.

'I heard she's in Italy,' said Serafina Bastille one day, in a hushed whisper.

Serafina no longer wore her headscarf. Her hair had grown back. She kept it short. *My little pixie*, said Mr Bastille, while Serafina blushed and smiled.

Mr Bastille was up earlier and earlier every day. He had stopped spending all night on his porch, surrounded by empty whisky bottles and beer cans.

They'd mended, Vivacia realised. Serafina's cancer was gone for now. They had a second chance, and they were grateful. It was evident in Serafina's smile, and Mr Bastille's new kind and gentle personality.

'Who is in Italy?' asked Vivacia.

'Cally,' Serafina replied. 'That's what your Charles heard, anyway.'

If that was the case, why were Kay and Stephanie still heading out every day in Kay's old car? She watched them drive, knowing that it wasn't really a search for the girl who had moved away, but rather a small adventure to fill their days. *Thelma and Louise*, Kay had said, elbowing Stephanie in her side.

They giggled like schoolgirls while Vivacia watched on. Sometimes, Vivacia felt like the only responsible one in her family.

They asked her to come along on their drives, sweetening the deal with promises of pub lunches in the countryside. Vivacia declined – there was no way she was putting Alex and Elizabeth in that vintage old car with Kay behind the wheel.

There had been no more boozy afternoons at Vivacia's, not after the last one. Vivacia was summoned over to their home now, and Charles was never mentioned in these invitations.

Privately, Vivacia wondered if Stephanie was steering Kay clear of Charles.

She smiled ruefully. Maybe Stephanie wasn't as irresponsible as she thought.

'Are you selling up your land?' Serafina changed the subject with a shrug.

Vivacia, lost in Elizabeth who had just started smiling, looked up at the older woman. 'I don't know.' She offered a shrug of her own. 'I don't think I mind, either way.'

Serafina's face broke into a smile. 'You've got more important things to think about.' She took baby Alex's hand and grinned even wider as his fingers wrapped around hers. 'They've been here a while now.'

Vivacia felt a thrill. It bubbled up inside her, gold flakes shivering through her body. She leaned closer to Serafina. 'I want to find out about adopting them.'

'Oh!' With her free hand, Serafina pulled Vivacia in for a hug. 'Wonderful. They'd never find a better mother than you.'

It was validation, a confirmation that Vivacia didn't even realise she'd been seeking. She thought that she was doing great, that the babies were happy. No longer did they wail all night, no longer did their bodies bear the brunt of heavy, unloving, cruel hands. Gillian seemed pleased with their progress on her visits, and Vivacia was, for the first time, in love.

'I think if they were going to be returned to their birth parents they'd have gone by now,' she confided in Serafina. 'I think… I really believe that I'm good for them. I don't want to lose them.'

It was the cardinal sin of fostering, growing too attached. Always when she waved off her wards there was sadness, sometimes deep and dark, sometimes tinged with relief. This time, with Alex and Elizabeth, she couldn't even envision them not being here.

Charles had been gone for a month this time, a fact that Vivacia hadn't even realised until he returned that night. He slammed into the house, flung his red wallet on the table and didn't even kick off his shoes as he normally did. Instead, he strode through to the lounge, glaring at the Moses basket that was in his favourite chair.

'Fuck,' he said.

The banging of the door and his particularly vicious curse woke Elizabeth with a jump. She began to cry in earnest.

'Fuck!' shouted Charles again.

'Don't!' cried Vivacia, rushing in and scooping Elizabeth up.

He didn't normally swear. He was usually eloquent in his insults and remarks.

He turned to her, turned on her. His finger was up, extended, in her face. Vivacia darted left and right, her hand cradling Elizabeth's head. Charles followed her, a strange dance around the living room.

'Adoption.' He hissed the word at her. 'What were you thinking?'

He'd spoken to Serafina, then. She wasn't surprised. She acknowledged that some part of her had wanted the woman to divulge their conversation to Charles. Plant a seed. She'd been hopeful, though, that Serafina might relay it in a way that meant it was the older woman's observation, rather than Vivacia's idea.

'All week when I'm at work, I'm surrounded by noise and crying babies and shit,' he fumed. 'I come here for respite, for peace. And here you are, thinking you can mess with me.'

His words made no sense. As far as she knew, he had moved on from the Dagenham car plant, was back to wearing his silver suit and polished shoes, back to sales meetings in the city. Why would there be noise, crying babies and shit?

'Where do you go?' Her voice trembled, but she looked him in the eye.

She'd never asked him, not once. Despite what he thought, she listened when he deemed her fit to be a conversational partner, but she was never the one with the questions.

'Right.' His lips pressed together, his eyes narrowed, a vein throbbed in his temple. He nodded, as though to himself, and said it again, 'Right. I see.'

She didn't know what he saw, but she knew what she felt. Impending doom, danger, a sense of being hemmed in, trapped for whatever was building inside him.

She dodged out of the room, still holding Elizabeth. In the hallway she skipped smartly towards the front door and snatched it open.

She glanced down and saw Elizabeth's eyes – wide, round pools – *him* reflected in them. He circled around her in a pinched arc, nudging her with his hip until Vivacia and the baby in her arms were backed against the wall. His face loomed close. She felt the heat running the entire length of him. It turned to ice against her own body.

They'd been here before; he'd pinned her against this very wall, in this very spot, and just like then, she felt his excitement again at this sudden turn of events. She'd diffused the threat last time by becoming submissive in her stance. He had wilted, drifted away, no longer interested. She should do that now, she realised. It would be so easy to lower her head, round her shoulders, become mouse-like. He would tire of playing with her, then.

It was more important than ever that she return to meekness. Alex and Elizabeth needed safety, security, warmth, care, love, protection. The baby would not know what she was seeing when Charles tore away her clothes and her heart and her sanity, but Vivacia knew that the girl's very marrow would be sullied by even being in close proximity to such an attack.

But the image only served to heighten Vivacia's temper. She juggled Elizabeth as she brought her knee up, up, up. Not just once, but as many times as it took to catch him finally in the right place, and make him stumble back, curses falling freely from his furious lips.

Vivacia darted away. He gripped her hair. She did not scream. Elizabeth was on the verge of tears already. She kept moving determinedly onwards, Charles still holding her hair. She saw a bag of wine bottles just inside the door, on the mat, gifted to Charles by customers who had fallen for his charm.

Vivacia kicked the bag, heard the crack, watched the liquid seep out, spreading like blood. His grip slackened. Vivacia leaned down, still holding Elizabeth, rising again with wine-stained fingers and a shard of bottle.

'No!' she screamed, or at least hoped she did, and she held the broken glass out like a sword as she backed out of the door.

The door swung closed, but Vivacia knew he was still there, standing behind it, enjoying the fight, loving the thrill of her fear. Alex was inside. She should go to Kay's house. Kay would sit with Elizabeth while Vivacia and Stephanie returned to collect Alex.

Then she remembered the new, odd, almost-friendship her mother had with Charles. But Stephanie would stand beside her daughter, surely?

Wouldn't she?

The door opened again. There he was, bathed in the glow of the late-summer afternoon sun that trickled through the house. From inside, Alex's thin wails could be heard. Charles cocked his head at her, an expression on his face that Vivacia couldn't fathom.

'Are you going to see to him?' he called across the driveway.

His hand wandered to the front of his trousers, lingering on his zip. A miniscule movement, but all Vivacia saw was the attack that would happen when she returned to the house to rescue her second baby.

She tilted her head back and screamed. Pent up over years, the sound she made frightened both Elizabeth *and* herself.

'Fuck!' Charles swore once more, and his footsteps clattered down the steps towards her.

Intimidating her inside the house was fine, but God forbid the neighbours witness it, she realised.

Other feet pounded the pavement, a circle of bodies surrounded her.

Thank God, she thought. She recognised the arms of Serafina, alongside Ruth's face, familiar since she was a girl. Even Ivan, the developer, always loitering in the village now, and Blind Iris's grown-up children had come running.

Vivacia remained in place, cloistered in comfort, shielded by the bodies of her neighbours.

Then, it all changed.

'So sorry, I'm really sorry.' Charles's voice, loud amongst the murmured concern. 'It's hard, two babies, sometimes it just gets too much for her.'

Wait, what? No! Vivacia turned her head, seeking her mother and grandmother, someone to attest to why she was out here, barefoot, clutching poor Elizabeth. It was because of him. It was always because of *him*.

'No!' She found her voice and looked to Serafina, the friendliest face in a suddenly hostile crowd.

'The baby's bleeding,' said Ruth, bluntly.

A collective intake of breath. Vivacia stared down at the red patch on Elizabeth's head. It was wine, she realised, the red that stained both her flesh and the baby's.

'It's wine,' Vivacia protested, realising too late that the fact there was alcohol on her baby was almost as bad as if it had been the child's blood.

Charles was there then, easing the broken piece of bottle out of her fingers and putting a guiding arm around her shoulders. The glass slid free from her grip. She felt a strange sensation. Looking down, she saw that Charles had dragged the shard across her palm. There was no pain. Just numbness.

'It's okay, folks,' Charles said. 'We're sorry to have disturbed your evening.'

'I'll come in with you.' Serafina spoke, finally, stretching herself up taller than her five-foot self and maintaining eye contact with Charles.

Vivacia smiled through tears, a silent thank you.

She gets it, she realised. *She knows.*

Blind Iris's children swept Ruth away. Ivan, the developer, clapped Charles on his shoulder, averted his eyes and bade him farewell.

If Serafina was with her, nothing else could happen. Vivacia succumbed to be led towards her home, the older woman's hand on her arm, gripping, squeezing, comfort without words.

At the door, Charles took Elizabeth and reached out to lead Vivacia inside.

Serafina's hand dropped from her arm. A muted mutter, a shadow falling over them. Vivacia looked up to see Mr Bastille, Serafina's husband, beside them.

'Don't get involved,' Mr Bastille told his wife. He looked at Charles. 'Sorry, mate. We'll see you later. Goodnight.'

Serafina was gone.

Vivacia followed her husband into the house.

The door closed gently behind them.

23

VIVACIA – NOW

'Oh!' At Rose's first word – *mummy* – Vivacia brings her hands to her face, her smile wide and joyous. 'Yes, darling.'

She opens her arms. Rose steps into them, her small body heavy now with the fatigue that's evident on her face.

Over Rose's shoulder, Vivacia surreptitiously glances at Rob. He has moved away, started the return to Wolf's Pit, Dallas on his back. He is out of hearing range, she sees with relief.

The journey down is so much easier than going up. It is still a long way, but now that she has both children again, Vivacia feels like she's walking on air.

She bubbles inside at the breakthrough with Rose. The elation dims a little upon the approach to the rear of Wolf's Pit but, as they make the final descent, Vivacia sees that the police car has now gone from the lane.

She ducks back through the fence, waiting inside her garden as Rob follows.

Gently, he lowers Dallas to the ground. The boy ignores his sister, moving towards the house. Rose, eyes downcast, follows him. Rob busies himself with picking up the panel and propping it back up against the fence.

'I'll secure it better,' he says, scrutinising it. 'There's a drill in Ruth's shed; I'll screw it in place.'

Vivacia scoops up the hacked-up cable ties before he can inspect them.

She shoves them in her pocket and relives that glorious moment on the hill.

Vivacia lifts her face to the sun, enjoying the warmth after so much rain.

Real life crowds in her mind again and she clears her throat. Might as well get the other thing over with.

'What did the police say?'

'Huh.' He turns from the fence to face her. 'The usual: they asked when I came here, if I knew Charles, if I saw him.' He utters a stale little laugh. 'If I *liked* him.'

Vivacia shades her eyes from the sun. 'What did you tell them?'

He shrugs. 'That I never saw him, never even knew he existed when I got here.'

She nods.

He wanders over, coming to sit beside her on the step. 'I didn't tell them that if I had met him, I don't think I'd have liked him much at all.'

Her heart begins a slow thunder.

'Thanks for your help today.' She gives him that much.

He nods his head, offers her a smile. 'Any time,' he says.

–

Later, they eat together. A concession on her part. An almost-family.

Anybody looking in would assume they were just that.

As she eats, Vivacia can't quite believe it. The day before yesterday, she had nobody. Just surface friends, like Portia, or old-timers who feel a sense of responsibility for her, like Ruth. But she had nobody *real*. Hasn't had for years and years.

Now, today, she has a table full. Two children, who are dependent on her. And a man, Rob, who... She tilts her head as she regards him.

Who what?

Who... cares?

Who... turns up wherever she seems to go?

She's shaken from her reverie by the ringing of her phone.

It's Detective Andrews. He has nothing relevant to say to her, no further questions – just yet – he says, and is that a warning? But right now, he's 'checking in', making sure she is okay, that she has support. Letting her know that the family liaison is still an option.

Vivacia moves away from the table and surveys the three people seated there.

'Yes, Detective,' she says, 'I have support.'

She can feel Rob's eyes on her. She turns to face him, covering the phone with her hand. 'I'm going to take this upstairs,' she says, with a meaningful glance towards the children.

He gives her a thumbs up.

She slips into the hall, closing the door behind her, and takes the phone upstairs. In Rose and Dallas's bedroom, she pulls the door to and walks over to the window.

DI Andrews talks a little more, his words dipping in and out as he talks of process and procedure, of positive identification. It's not the phone service that makes his voice dim, even though it is often bad out here. Tonight, the line is as clear as a bell, but she barely hears him as he drones on.

She barely *listens*.

'If we need to speak to you, you'll be around, yes?' he finishes, smoothly.

'Yes,' she says, obediently.

There is a pause, a silence as the one-sided conversation winds down. She could interject here, she thinks. She could tell him about Rose and Dallas, and report them as found.

She *should* tell him.

Night is falling now, Lady Well and her police tape and secrets are vanishing in the twilight.

She takes a deep breath.

'Detective…' she says, 'thank you so much for your call.'

Later, with Rob despatched, Vivacia puts the children to bed. Their eyes close as soon as they hit the pillows, and Vivacia knows they will sleep well tonight.

Rose has said no more words since that single one spoken up on the hill. Vivacia tries to bring back that joy that coursed through her when she called her mummy. It was a break-through; for Rose, for finding her voice. For Vivacia, a salve to soothe all the past hurts away.

She replays it now, in her head. She sees Rose, her throat working to push out the single word. She sees her own elation, her arms open wide, Rose stepping into them. The perfect mother–daughter fit.

But the truth has pushed through the barrier of delight. Rose, saying that word, not looking at Vivacia as she speaks it, but looking off into the distance, seeking her real mummy, the one from whom she has somehow been separated, leaving Rose untethered, swirling in the mist of the hill.

It is painful. Vivacia has experienced a lifetime's worth of hurt, but this new knowledge is raw and savage as it bites at her.

Too difficult to agonise over.

It is as though the village she's lived in all her life is closing in on her. She shivers. Her thoughts go to leaving. Upping sticks and vanishing in the night.

But at the very least, with the lie she has told Rob, she's bought herself some time. Time with Rose and Dallas. Time to think and plan for a future.

Time to work out how to get out of this mess without losing her children.

24

VIVACIA – BEFORE

Gillian, the Aunt Lydia-esque social worker, arrived at dawn the day after the incident and took the babies away.

Vivacia knew there was no arguing to be done, though she tried anyway.

'It can be tough, I know that.' Gillian shuffled papers and juggled the babies. 'Even *we* need respite, at times.'

'But I don't!' protested Vivacia. 'Not from them, never from the children.'

Charles stood in the doorway, arms folded, a sympathetic look on his face. 'So sorry it didn't work out,' he murmured to Gillian as she passed him on the way out. He grabbed Alex's hand. 'I'll miss you, little buddy.'

The desire to scream rose ferociously in Vivacia, before flickering and dying out.

Still in the kitchen, she closed the door, unable to watch them leave.

Charles left her alone for the rest of the day.

She sat at the table, wondering who had called Gillian. It could be anyone, she realised, any one of the neighbours.

A terrible thought: that it was Charles himself who made the call.

She clenched and unclenched her hands. Her palm stung now from the shard she'd held towards Charles. Pain had finally arrived.

She saw last night's debacle from the neighbours' eyes. Vivacia, screaming, mad, having what appeared to be a breakdown. Waving a broken bottle, smelling like alcohol from the spilled wine, while holding a baby. They would have seen Charles as he wanted to be seen. Apologetic, confused, embarrassed, concerned.

Kay and Stephanie came over after hearing the news on the Wolf's Pit grapevine.

Sequestered in the kitchen, she waited for them to bustle in. They would surround her with love, their special protective force. She would tell them everything, she decided.

The forming of the words would be difficult, though. What was there to tell? That she was weak, that her husband knew it and regarded her accordingly?

When the front door closed, she sat up straight in anticipation.

'They're going to look for that misfit again,' said Charles. 'I told them you were resting.'

Vivacia slumped in her seat. He had sent them away.

They were looking for Cally.

But what about me? She wanted to bleat the words, pitifully, whine in a way she'd never done.

Vivacia turned away from him. What she'd do to have Cally by her side right now. She would have taken charge last night. She would have gathered the babies, got a hold of Vivacia and marched them to Jackie's house. She would have thrown vitriol and swear words in Charles's direction, and towards any of the other villagers who sided with him.

Charles was still talking. Muttering something about looking at Kay's car again before they set off. He said that he was leaving straight after, he had a business trip that he couldn't put off, and that maybe when he returned, Vivacia might think about pulling herself together.

'Madness is a stigma that lingers,' were his parting words.

The house returned to a bone-numbing quiet.

The village was peaceful once more.

Then, just before darkness fell, Vivacia's world shattered again.

-

She drank from the bottles of wine that Charles had left by the door. He had cleaned up the mess she'd caused the day before, and the unbroken bottles were still there. She plucked one at random, not caring if it were red or white, just seeking oblivion.

He had only cleaned around the bag, she noticed, and the alcohol from the smashed one clung to the plastic, already staining the wood floor. She sat on the bottom stair and drank straight from the bottle.

She was a third of the way through it, on the way to becoming comfortably numb, when, through the glass portion of the door, a fireball explosion lit up the early-evening sky.

Senses flattened, she remained seated, blinking.

Bonfire, she thought dully. But then screams ripped through the night.

The bottle fell from her hands, wine spilling out to pool on the floor once again.

The air pierced her sharply as she staggered down the steps and moved cautiously down towards the road.

A car accident, she realised. One of the golfers perhaps, always speeding down here.

The screams, though, that still pealed out across the land. A driver trapped, perhaps?

Charles, hit, she thought. And something sparked inside her, causing her to break into a run.

The temperature of the night was intense, like it had been all summer. Tonight, it was a different sort of heat. It was from the fire, she realised.

The car was in the middle of the lane, facing the fields that served as their gardens. The explosion had stripped the vehicle of its colour, but Vivacia recognised the shape immediately.

Nobody else drove an old car like that anymore.

She sobered in an instant, not feeling the heat until it became a wall that impeded her.

'Mum,' she said, 'Gran.' Her words were drowned out by the sparks that flew and the ongoing screams.

Hands were on her, an arm enveloping her from behind, tugging her away.

'Come on.' It was Jackie. Her face grim and twisted, her eyes red and watery. 'You don't need to see.'

Vivacia imagined it then, and for years after, the burned-out shells of the two women she loved most in the world.

Jackie manhandled her up the bank, only allowing Vivacia to sink to the ground when they were at a safe distance.

'Oh, Jesus,' muttered Jackie, looking further down the lane. To Vivacia, she said, 'Stay here.'

Vivacia, kneeling, stared after her. In the road, ten feet from the burning vehicle, lay a figure. Not burned, this one. Dressed smartly as always, short hair almost white against the blackened tarmac. Body contorted and broken, life and spirit gone.

The screams that had summoned Vivacia from her house were still ongoing. They belonged to Mr Bastille, she saw now, and finally his voice went, though his mouth still yawped in a wounded, silent cry.

He bent over his wife, scooping Serafina up as though she weighed nothing. She lay childlike in his arms, her twisted limbs dangling towards the fire-scorched ground.

25

THE CHILDREN

Dallas came up through the floor. He didn't have the strength to pull himself up into the caravan, so he sagged where he was, dull eyes staring at Rose. He had a piece of flint in his hand, the sharp edge causing spasms of concern to Rose.

She eyed him sternly, didn't allow her voice to tremble like it wanted to. 'Mother needs to sleep.'

She crawled onto the couch alongside her. The sense of urgency had faded a little because they could get out now, and she'd already opened her mouth to that rain and had drunk and drunk and drunk.

She sat beside Mother, so her knees nestled against her spine. Like the earlier cuddle, she relished it. Normally, it was Dallas in this position. But he was still half-in, half-out of the hole. Childishly, Rose smiled. It was her turn for snuggles now.

And sometimes it was better for him to be a little further away.

The couch was littered with stuff. As she sat, Rose rifled through it. Nothing interesting: drinking bottles, cups, a plate, a packet which once held seeds. All empty. Everything in this caravan was empty.

Rose squinted and clambered further up Mother's body, towards her curled hand.

Gently, then, when it became clear Mother was sleeping soundly, Rose opened her mother's fingers.

Paper! Rose let out a gasp as she pounced on it. She remembered this stuff, but she hadn't seen it for a long, long time.

Rose picked it up – three pieces in all – and smoothed them out on the dirty sheet.

Two had letters written on them. She sounded them out, but they were boring and senseless.

The other one, though, was exciting. A treasure map, like she had seen in the kids' books, back when they were allowed books.

It wasn't hastily scrawled. It had been worked on for a long time, going by the different types of pens that had been used. Rose lifted it to her face and sniffed hard. Crayon, red and green and blue, and a thick black pencil which Rose suspected to be Mother's eyeliner.

She hadn't seen that for a long while, either.

A memory distracted her. Many years ago, Mother standing in front of the mirror (when they still were allowed mirrors), lips all askew as she drew big black lines around her eyes. A little tube of dark paint with a tiny brush (a wand, said Mother) that made her eyelashes long and spiky.

It was back in the days when life had been fun. Before Father decided they were changing the course of their lives, and rather than seek to have everything, it was better to have nothing.

The wand with the paint had gone, onto the bonfire, probably, and Rose had thought the eyeliner had suffered the same fate. Apparently not, because here it was on the treasure map.

Rose looked over at Dallas. Still half-in, half-out of the caravan. He had wedged his hand down, was cradling his stomach. He was hungry. She knew that. She was starving too. Her own hunger made her sad and empty. Dallas got angry, edgy, eyes darting here and there, small fingers landing upon anything that he could throw or jab.

Not at Rose. Never at her. But there was only one other person here, and Rose knew the boy needed to be fed before that strange emotion of his exploded in full force.

Water had been paramount; now her thirst was sated, but that only served to highlight the other emptiness.

She tried to remember their last dinner and couldn't. There had been bread and biscuits, both hard like stones. That wasn't today, nor yesterday, nor even the day before that, or even last week or month maybe. There had been a tin, with fruit inside it, left open a while and the juices had gone. That also was not in her recent memory. There had been red stars in Rose's vision, which she thought came along when she realised she was really, *really* hungry.

But that was so long ago that she'd kind of forgotten what it was like to live without the stars and blotches and blurs in her eyes.

She looked back to the map that lay on the bed next to her mother's inert form and squinted.

The caravan was there, near the top of the page. The fences were below it, just past the little drawing of the bonfire.

Rose looked at her mother. She wondered when she had drawn this, because the bonfire had not happened for a long time, at least fifteen moon phases ago. They had been locked in this caravan for about twelve moons, Rose reckoned.

It was a primal sense that had Rose picking up the map and the other pieces of boring paper.

Crouching next to Dallas, she pushed at his shoulder until his body slid back to land, once more, upon the sodden grass beneath the caravan.

Carefully, she put the papers in her pockets and lowered herself down the hole to land in a crouch beside her brother.

The sharp flint rolled to land beside him. Rose kicked it away, out of reach. Sometimes, sharp objects were best when they were lost.

There was no food left here. No more caravans that she could investigate. All of those were gone, along with the cars and the trailers that had once filled this little site. They had to follow the map, get out of the place they once called their garden, and travel wider, further. Somewhere out there was food, and other things even better than water. Juice and exciting drinks, the like of which they'd never been allowed before and wouldn't even know about had it not been for the other travelling people who used to come inside the fences.

Rose's head was full of plans now, and she knew what she had to do, kind of, but it was a little bit scary, going out to the beyond.

She threw a glance at her brother. He was standing now, at least, but he swayed in place, and his eyelids were drooping lower and lower like he needed to sleep.

Rose stood so her head and shoulders were back inside the van.

'Mummy, we're going to get some food,' she said quietly.

And then, because it smelled really bad in there, and her mother didn't answer, Rose ducked back into the fresh air and made her way down the scorched, blackened, wet meadow, towards the fence.

26

VIVACIA – NOW

Vivacia doesn't see Rob the next day, or the day after that, or for almost the whole week that follows.

She wonders if he has actually left Wolf's Pit.

The police call her, on the phone and in person. She declines their offer of an FLO, keeps them at arm's length on the doorstep. Continuously, she reassures them that she is okay. 'Coping' is the word she uses.

In truth, the discovery of her husband's dead, watery body is not the first thing on her mind.

Confident that her garden is utterly secluded, even more so now that Rob has vanished, she takes advantage of the sunshine and lets the children play outside.

At night, they sit in the living room. Rose and Dallas's eyes glued to children's TV channels. Vivacia watching them.

She orders groceries in for the first time in her life. Standing at the front window, ready to yank open the door, take delivery of her food and get back inside as quickly as possible.

As well as the police, she fields calls and visits from Ruth, Portia, Aster, even Clive the chef.

She smiles at them, gives them assurances she's doing okay, answers their questions that are cloaked as concern, but which she suspects are really a need for gossip about Charles.

She wonders about Rob and his vanishing act. After all that concern, all those times he popped up beside her, it seems strange that he didn't say goodbye.

She could ask Ruth if he's coming back.

But she's never before enquired about anyone in Wolf's Pit. It would look strange if she started now.

On the sixth day of Rob's absence, the police knock on her door again. Not Andrews, but DI Ola Demoski. Vivacia slips outside onto the porch, heart beating like a drum in her chest.

She waits for Ola to tell her that she knows the secret Vivacia is keeping inside her house.

But that's not the reason for her visit. They are closing the case, she tells Vivacia.

Vivacia feels elated that the DI is not here for Rose and Dallas. Her mind is blank, though.

Which case?

It's been deemed an accidental death, Ola continues.

Vivacia jerks in a breath. The case of her husband's corpse.

Apparently, the ill-fitting lid and the vodka bottle found inside the well helped in their assessment and subsequent conclusion.

Chloe-Joy is passing by on her morning run. Shamelessly, the younger woman jogs up to them, her bright eyes curious.

Inspector Ola stops talking, waits patiently for Chloe-Joy to move away.

She doesn't.

'It's okay,' says Vivacia, signalling at the policewoman to continue.

Ola gives Chloe-Joy a long look before turning to face Vivacia. 'That's all, really. If you wanted to make plans for a memorial, a burial, you're free to do—'

'She could sue, you know,' Chloe-Joy interrupts. 'The council, the county. That lid was a shambles, a hazard. Her lawyer will be on to the authorities, right, Vivacia?'

Vivacia excuses herself and slips back inside the house, leaving the two women to it.

She thinks of the last funerals she went to: those of her mother, her grandmother and Serafina Bastille.

She has avoided the church since. Now she will have to go again.

One more funeral. One last time.

She doesn't want to harbour thoughts of death, even though the decay of Charles is embedded in her brain forever.

She takes her mind off visions of him and turns to the children. She feeds them, bathes them, tries unsuccessfully to get Rose to speak some more. After dinner, they sit each side of her on the sofa. Not so stiff and statue-like anymore, but resting against her.

The softening of them makes Vivacia's heart soar.

Rose clutches her drawing at all times, the colourful page of blots and lines with no discernible shapes on it, just scribble. It's getting worn now, ripped in places, but still Rose insists on having it with her.

She looks at it a lot, and she lets Vivacia marvel over it.

When Vivacia has it in her hands, she can feel Rose's eyes boring into her. Vivacia offers Rose more paper, the crayons as yet untouched. But Rose simply takes back her page, holds it close to her chest. Her eyes pierce Vivacia's, a strange mix of pleading and fury.

Often, Vivacia remembers that first night, when she asked Rose if the little girl could show her the route she took when she ended up in Wolf's Pit.

Rose had held her hand, as if to lead Vivacia.

It had been night-time, dark, the weather outside gnarly.

I didn't mean tonight. Vivacia's words, Rose's little face, the cloud of resignation Vivacia was sure she saw there.

The sun has been shining for days now; the relentless downpour has ceased. But Vivacia hasn't asked Rose again.

She knows how wrong this is. It is just as wrong as not reporting their appearance to the police. She tries to ignore it.

The children look better, physically, anyway. Their skin has a rosy hue now, and if she were to take them out, they would attract no stares apart from admiring looks for being such a cute matching pair.

But she can't take them out. Not in public, anyway.

The journalists and the police have gone, but nobody in Wolf's Pit knows they are here. And all of them would know they are not supposed to be here.

It is at the forefront of her mind, all the time.

And she can find no way to get out of the lie that she's told without losing these precious two.

Early the next morning, when the sun isn't too hot, Vivacia takes them out into the garden.

Dallas moves around, stopping to look at flowers, at stones, at the toys of the children who came before. Rose stands by the new fence panel. She stares at it as though it is a window, looking to something beyond that only she can see.

Something niggles at Vivacia.

Then, before she can fully concentrate on what is needling her, Rob is there, at the back gate. It is always locked now, and he is calling her name.

She's troubled by the way her heart sinks, though she can't put her finger on *why*.

And so, it is with a scowl upon her face that she sees Rob again for the first time in a week.

She refuses to ask him where he's been, lest he thinks she cares.

He greets her, looks past her to the children and throws them a wave.

Dallas wanders over, his eyes narrowed, looking Rob up and down. Rose allows Rob a somewhat withering glance, then goes back to studying the new fence panel.

'Sorry I haven't been around,' Rob says to Vivacia as he comes into the garden.

She bites her lip to stop herself replying.

'How's their mother?' he asks, as he sits himself down on the raised section of the patio.

Her 'cousin'.

Vivacia shrugs and suddenly feels cold as ice.

'The same,' she manages to reply.

And, because she doesn't want further questions about the children or their fictional mother, she changes the topic.

'Where have you been?' she asks, despite herself.

He gives her a lopsided smile. 'Home,' he replies. 'Had to go to a funeral.'

'Oh.' Vivacia frowns. 'I'm sorry.'

'An old friend,' he says, even though she hasn't asked. 'We served together.'

She looks up at him. 'Served?'

'A couple of tours, overseas.'

'I thought you were a medic.'

'I was,' he says mildly. 'In the army.'

'Oh.' She's at a loss for what to say. She wonders what he's seen.

'They called it shell shock in the first war. Then battle fatigue. Now it's PTSD.' He shrugs and looks down at his feet.

'You… You have PTSD?' She thinks of the body, of Charles in all his watery glory. Rob was there, right up at the well. 'I'm so sorry.'

'Not me. My friend.' He looks at her sideways on. 'The funeral I went to.'

Reading between the lines, she understands it was suicide. It seems wrong to ask that, and she doesn't know what else to say, so she repeats her last sentence. 'I'm so sorry.'

'It was a nice service. Flag on the coffin, and all that.'

'You didn't want to stay with your family?'

He laughs. Bitter, brittle. The way she herself laughs.

'No. We're not close.'

It strikes her then, the backstory she's made up for him without ever enquiring. She knows he comes from Essex, the next county along. He was travelling, she knew that much. She'd imagined he was coddled and loved, that he had people like she once had, like Kay and Stephanie, and even though he wanted to head out into the world, he didn't want to leave them too far behind. So close was he to his blood kin, he'd only managed to cross one border.

Not true, she sees now.

She thinks of Charles, of the way he was. Coming here seemingly from nothing, leaving nobody behind, and she's chilled even more at this newfound similarity between the two men.

She narrows her eyes. 'Is that why you stay here?' she asks. 'For the community?' She resists putting quotation marks around the word, but her tone gives away her scorn.

'Kind of. I like it. A sense of belonging, everyone in it together.' He shrugs once more. 'It's nice.'

It's farcical, is what it is. Wolf's Pit holds no sense of belonging. Not for the old, not for the new. Nobody talks to each other and when they do, they squabble and argue.

She tells him this now, sitting down on the patio step, one eye on Dallas, who is walking in circles, stopping every now and then to pick dandelions.

'You don't think that's what makes a community, or a family?' he asks, mildly.

She turns back to Rose, who is still standing at the fence, still looking at the panel.

Dallas turns in slow, lazy circles, arms outstretched. Vivacia smiles as she watches him.

She regards his sister again.

Still at the fence. Staring and staring and staring.

Vivacia's smile slips from her face.

The unknown, unseen thing that has been needling her bursts inside her head like a firework. It won't be ignored or pushed away any longer.

'Oh…' she breathes.

'What?' Rob asks.

She moves past him to stand next to Rose at the fence. Beyond it, unseen, is the well, and above that, the hill that

181

Rose went up when she ran away. Vivacia remembers how determined she was, how distressed Dallas had been.

How, once Vivacia had found her after her aborted attempt to run away, she'd cried out the word 'mummy'.

How delighted Vivacia had been that Rose saw her for what and who she was.

How she had ignored the little girl's struggle to release herself from Vivacia's grip. How, when Rose had said that magic word, she hadn't been looking at Vivacia.

Her face had been turned away, up the hill, to some unknown place Rose had desperately been trying to get to.

Something else comes to Vivacia's mind and she passes a hand over her forehead. This knowledge isn't as sudden, as raw, as it seems. She knew, or at the very least suspected.

She didn't want to let it in.

What has changed?

Rose has.

The girl is desperate. Tied with a maternal cord that is affixed to her brother, here, in Wolf's Pit, and stretches all the way to somewhere else.

Some place where her parents are.

And Vivacia knows how to find them.

Without speaking to Rob, she turns and walks swiftly back into the cottage.

The house, once spotless, now shows clear signs of children living in it. Vivacia loves it for that very reason, but now, the mess that has built up hinders her.

She starts with the table, rifles through the various papers on it, the toys discarded, the half biscuits, sticky straws, badges and stickers.

'Vivacia, what is it?' Rob comes in, Dallas at his heels.

Vivacia looks up. 'Dallas, get your sister.'

Obediently, Dallas trots off, returning with a drooping Rose at his side.

Vivacia pounces on her. 'Rose, my darling, where is the paper you were drawing on?'

Rose glances helplessly at the reams of sketchbooks that are now on the floor.

'Not those. The…' Vivacia looks furtively at Rob before turning her attention back to Rose. 'The map. Where is it?'

In one fluid movement, Rose pulls it from her pocket.

Vivacia deflates a little. Now, there is no going back.

She picks up her mobile from where it is charging and shoves it in her pocket. To Rob, she says, 'I'm sorry, we have to go out. I'll catch you later, okay?'

He is confused as she sidles past him, ushering the children ahead of her, stopping at the fridge to grab a bottle of water, remembering the *last* trek they took.

He follows her, reaches out a hand, catches at her wrist.

Her breath hitches in her throat and she raises her eyes to meet his.

Two, three seconds pass and he lets go of her arm.

'I promised them I'd take them out,' she says, aiming for breezy, while knowing that her eyes are wild and the panic is coming off her in waves. 'We'll see you later.'

She edges past him again, a child in each hand, now flicking him a smile that is her grin of old: bared teeth, and a clear message. Out of my way.

She realises her error as soon as they leave by the front door. That anyone could see them. That anybody could ask questions.

Too late now. She urges them on faster, her breath coming in short little bursts, not relaxing until they have made it to the land where there is minimal chance of being overlooked.

She looks at Rose's paper as they walk. The kids are ahead, as if they know where they are going. Angrily, Vivacia balls her hands into fists. They probably don't need the bloody map.

The walk is long, but the children are not flagging like they did before. This time, it is Vivacia who hurries to keep up with them. Every few steps, she darts a glance back over her shoulder. There is no sign of Rob.

Good, she thinks.

Because if she discovers what she thinks she will, her lie will be blown wide open.

Eventually, they pass the cluster of blackberry bushes where she found Rose last time. Then, this land was shrouded in mist. Today, it is hot, sticky, and they have not passed another soul on their walk.

'Kids, drink, please!' Vivacia calls out.

Reluctantly, they come to her, opening their mouths obediently for the water she gives them. They are sloppy, spilling it, in too much of a hurry to stop for long.

They are off again. Dallas as animated as Rose now, their little legs pumping as they push the final peak until the land opens out in front of them. Patchwork green fields in every direction, marred only by the A-road that slices through the landscape, a mile to their left. Before that lies the quarry, the land leading to it chalky white, the path overgrown, a forgotten landmark.

She takes the paper out again and studies it from the bottom up.

Four squares in a row. On the left, at an angle, one more, and another one opposite at the other end. She knows now that the blobs denote Mr Bastille's house, Blind Iris's place, Vivacia's cottage, Rob's rental, Jackie's home, and below it, Ruth's place, which once belonged to Stephanie.

Above them, a circle, denoting Lady Well.

Higher up the page is a green scrawl. Up further still, black scribbles.

Vivacia looks up and left, to the bushes that spring up and trail outwards with their lethal, snake-like tendrils.

Though Rose has carried this paper since she arrived, she did not draw on it. This was done by an adult hand. Someone older than Rose and Dallas. For the most part it isn't in crayon or pencil, either. It wasn't in Rose's pocket when Vivacia undressed them that first time, not like the note which had *that name* on it, which she's successfully pushed far from her mind.

Vivacia lifts the paper to her nose and sniffs, as though the artist will be revealed by scent alone. But it is old now. It has been a long time since anyone other than Rose, or Vivacia, held this crudely drawn map.

It isn't to scale. The page runs out. A scratchy, ink-free biro has made deep indentations at the top.

The instructions are over.

'Rose, darling.' Vivacia breaks into a run to catch up with the girl, who is still thundering on.

She catches Rose's hand, hopes that her love will still the little girl who is, Vivacia sees now, on the verge of panic.

'Rose.' Vivacia drops to her knees in the dry grass. 'I'm here, I'm with you. Show me where to go.'

They remain there, and Vivacia feels it as Rose calms. Dismay remains in the girl's eyes, though, and it bounces off Vivacia.

She stands up.

'Show me.'

They walk on, methodical now, rather than frenzied. No more words spoken, saving breath for the onward march.

Finally, the landscape is broken by the appearance of the old rubbish tip. The fences surrounding it remind her of those erected around Wolf's Pit, but unlike her village, there is no life here.

She wonders if she is wrong. If they will skirt the small site, continue on over the other side, but to her surprise, Rose drops her hand and makes a beeline for the fence.

The sun is at its highest, cutting off her vision. To Vivacia, it seems as though Rose passes right through the metal, Dallas along with her.

Stupid, panicked thoughts of alternative universes crowd her mind – a blind fear that they've crossed over to another place, somewhere she can't follow. Just like that time when she thought they'd vanished into the mist. Much like how they appeared on Lady Well in the first place.

She is breathing fast. She can follow them, she sees with relief, as she peels back the hanging fence and crawls through the gap.

It's a small plot. Overgrown grass that turns into a concrete centre full of tall weeds. An engine block, abandoned, and the stench of oil. Grass black from fires; pages upon pages of books, torn and charred, collect in a pile in the far southern corner, blown there by the wind. The name that was in Rose's pocket was written on a page from a book. Vivacia shivers and turns away from the pile of discarded paper.

A solitary shack stands forlorn. A caravan, old-fashioned, the sort that a car would tow. Yellowed with age, rust adorning the metal trims, the windows battered by rain and sun, dust and filth.

Vivacia feels her face crumpling with sadness. Rose and Dallas were living *here*?

In amongst the awfulness, hope creates a heat in her. If they live here, they will be removed from their caregivers, surely?

There is hope, yet, that she won't have to say goodbye to them like she did Alex and Elizabeth, all those years ago.

The kids are at the caravan already, cementing her suspicion that this is where they call home.

What now? Hammer on the door, demand to be let in, call the police in case it turns ugly?

Anybody could be in there. Drugged to the eyeballs, armed with a knife or worse.

She finds her stereotypical way of thinking distasteful, but… *come on*. There is only one reason why somebody would choose to live here. There is only one reason why the children would have come to her so terribly malnourished and uncared for.

She walks towards the van, scanning the ground in front of her for evidence of needles and paraphernalia.

There is nothing. Apart from the strange pages collected in one corner, there is very little here at all.

The silence, from both inside and out, is chilling.

Vivacia turns to gather the children close to her, to shelter them from the vibe of this place. Dallas is within reach. Clinging to him, she turns in a full circle. Rose is gone.

'Where'd she go?' Her voice is high with distress.

Dallas twists his body and pulls away from her. Vivacia snatches up his hand. 'Where did Rose go, Dallas?'

He yanks his fingers free from hers, drops into a crouch and shuffles underneath the caravan.

The day they came to her, when she bathed them, washed their fingers, inspected the broken nails, the grazed tips.

Like they've dug themselves out of somewhere.

A cry escapes her. She falls to the ground, feels the caravan scraping her spine as she crawls underneath it in pursuit of Dallas.

He's there, squatting in a crouch, thumb in mouth – something he's never done since he's been with her – gazing upwards. The bottom half of Rose, disappearing up into the bowels of the old caravan.

She lurches after her, mindless of the filth on the ground beneath her, pushing her body through yet another oil patch. It doesn't smell, this one, no fumes of fuel like the one near the fence where they came in.

She closes her eyes. The oil patch probably *does* have an aroma, but it's overpowered by the stench coming from the hole in the floor of the caravan.

Her stomach churns. A mixture of vomit, filth, stale air, shit. *Death.*

She knows then that she was right. Rose and Dallas's parents *are* inside. Dead, rotting. She has a sense of what she will see: lifeless forms with belts binding their arms, needles hanging from collapsed veins which no longer carry life's blood.

Hot, fetid air cascades over her. She gags, angles her head to one side and spits out the vileness. She is underneath the hole in the floor where the children made their escape. She lowers her chin to her chest and takes one, long, deep breath, before busting upwards.

The first thing she sees is Rose. She mimics her brother below her, in a crouch, thumb in mouth, staring with a vacant expression in her eyes across the room towards a filthy old couch.

Vivacia stands in front of the child, desperate to shield her, and looks at the figure on the worn and tattered sofa.

The air surrounds her, stifling, covering her so she can't breathe. No needles, no belts, no drugs.

Vivacia sees how wrong she was.

Much like the old, damp, rotten floor beneath her, the bottom falls out of Vivacia's world.

27

VIVACIA – BEFORE

In the final days of what had been a blistering summer, Vivacia attended all three funerals: Kay, Stephanie and Serafina.

Charles stood by her side, dutiful. His hand hovered at the small of her back. He didn't touch her. He gave no words of comfort.

'It was a wonderful service,' Ruth said as they filed out of the church after Kay's cremation. She enveloped Vivacia. 'You poor thing.'

Jackie was there, too.

'Have you heard from Cally?' Vivacia asked.

'No,' said Jackie. 'Living it up, somewhere, I suppose.' But she didn't sound sure.

The short conversation was exhausting for Vivacia. She wilted noticeably. Jackie's hand made its way under her arm, propping her up.

'You… You can come to me, if you need to,' said Jackie.

Her meaning was horribly clear. Vivacia had lost both of her mother figures. Jackie's daughter had left.

It was almost offensive. As if Vivacia could ever replace Cally. As if Jackie could even begin to fill the Kay-and-Stephanie-shaped hole.

She shook her head, not trusting herself to speak.

Jackie moved away.

'She was better, you know. *Healed.*' Another voice boomed in Vivacia's ear.

It made her jump. She turned to see Mr Bastille, looming over her.

She withered inside at the alcohol fumes that emanated from him.

So were you, she thought, *for such a brief time.*

'Mowing her down.' His face twisted, red and purple. 'Like she was a *dog*.'

She thought about it all the time. Kay, in the driver's seat, losing control on that long, deadly steep hill. Pumping the brakes but somehow hitting the accelerator instead. Stephanie screaming in the seat beside her, grabbing the wheel. Serafina, pottering along the lane as she did every evening.

'She knows,' said Charles to Mr Bastille. 'Vivacia is so terribly sorry.'

He led her away, steering her by her elbow to a waiting taxi.

'What did you mean when you told him I was sorry?' she asked, breaking the silence of the journey.

Charles looked out of the window and didn't answer her.

'Charles?' she prompted.

He sighed. 'They're saying you shouldn't have let her drive. You shouldn't have let them out in that old car.'

Vivacia felt her mouth fall open. 'Who says that?' she demanded.

'Kay was losing her marbles. Your mother was always… absent-minded.' He fixed her with a look, overly stern. 'You were preoccupied,' he said. 'Both of those babies, it was too much for you, really.'

She remembered the times when Kay and Stephanie had implored her to come along with them on their drives. The way she'd scoffed inside at the thought of getting in that decrepit old car, of allowing the children inside it.

She'd thought all that but had never cautioned them against it.

Mr Bastille was right. Charles was right. It was all Vivacia's fault.

The pit that Vivacia slipped into was dark and dank. Like a cell, she imagined, or a circle of hell. It was her penance, though. She took it, willingly.

–

Bed. There had been a lot of bed. Charles had ushered her up there after the funerals.

'You are going to take such a long time to heal,' he said as he tucked her in under the sheets, still fully clothed. 'You'll rest here, you'll find your peace here.'

It had sounded nice. A dark room, a quiet room. Rest.

She nodded, crossed her hands over her chest like an obedient girl.

Later, hours or days – it might have been weeks, she couldn't tell – the room was stifling. She craved air. She wanted to go to Kay's house and put her face in her grandmother's and mother's things. She wanted to inhale them, drink in their scent, touch the things they had touched.

'Not a chance,' said Charles, intercepting her on the landing. 'Best you're not seen out there, not for a while.'

But… But aren't people worried? she wondered. Ruth, Blind Iris, Jackie, all those people who had known her for thirty years.

Then she remembered Mr Bastille, his accusatory tone when he'd spoken to her.

She recalled Charles's words.

They blamed her. She'd been so wrapped up in her own little world that she'd let Kay, an eighty-year-old woman, go off driving in a car that was almost as old as Vivacia was.

Vivacia returned to her darkened bedroom and lay down in the stale sheets.

Charles fed her. He brought her soup, tea, fruit. He brought her stews and casseroles. Sometimes she wondered when he had learned to cook. Oftentimes she didn't care.

Finally, Vivacia ventured downstairs. At first, she couldn't put her finger on what was wrong. The house was so... cold. The bright sunshine and the heat were absent. She peered out of the window in the hallway and staggered back to land heavily on the bottom stair when she saw the coating of frost outside. It was winter. She had been in her room for more than three months.

Lots of cars were there, parked neatly. Good cars, she saw. Decent, rich men's cars. It looked like the golfers had made a wrong turn and parked up on her verge.

A murmur of voices, she could hear now, coming from the dining room. Belting her dressing gown, she ran a hand through her hair and opened the door. It was no longer the dining room that Vivacia remembered.

In the doorway, she frowned. Where were the long, hand-made, table and cushioned chairs that had been *in situ* since Vivacia was a child? Where was Kay's sideboard, stacked with tiny figurines that were little horrors in miniature, jostling for place alongside Stephanie's earlier glazed works, which were also gone? A mahogany desk stood in the centre of the room, a large swivel chair behind it. There was a sofa in dark red leather along the wall where a bookcase had been. In front of it was a long, low coffee table, also mahogany, filled with crystal ashtrays, which housed the butts of cigars, and several brandy bottles.

She gaped at the men on the new sofa.

Charles, on the chair behind the huge desk, tilted his head.

'You're up!' he exclaimed. 'How do you feel, darling?'

He came around the desk towards her, arms up and outstretched. Vivacia flinched involuntarily.

'What... What is this room?' she whispered to him.

He tensed. She felt it through his arms that encircled her.

'Come on, back to bed,' he soothed into her ear.

He chatted as he tucked the sheets in around her. Her arms pinned by her sides, like she was in a little prison of old, faded, bobbled cotton.

'The fences are going up, groundwork starting tomorrow. It'll be noisy for a while, but the end result will be worth it,' he said. 'Now, what would you like? A drink, a sleepy tea, perhaps?'

The phrase jolted her. Her grandmother called it that, *sleepy tea*. Camomile, to be taken after dusk, before bedtime. But it wasn't dusk, or bedtime.

Was it?

She turned her head towards the heavy drapes. Charles's words niggled at her like fruit flies.

'What groundwork?' she asked, bemused.

'The development!' Charles exclaimed. 'The gated community!'

It was happening, then. The reality hit her, hard. Without Kay, Stephanie and Serafina there would have been no opposition.

'Did… Did I have my say?'

He smoothed down the sheet, trapping her further. 'Yes, dear. You signed the paperwork.'

She opened her mouth to ask more questions, but he covered it with his own. He tasted of aged brandy and cigars.

'Hush, now,' he said. 'Rest.'

–

Another whole season passed before Vivacia emerged again from her cocooned prison. She sat in the kitchen of her home in the early spring and perused the land. She heard people coming and going, voices that were at once familiar and unknown. Ruth's voice, sharper than she'd ever heard it, before dissolving into pleading tones.

'…just need to see, to check…'

But nobody apart from Charles came to her.

Later, she would acknowledge it was likely a dream. Wishful thinking. Then she remembered Ruth's sharp tone, almost angry, and figured that she, Vivacia, was still the enemy.

Now, in April, the fields were gone. All those cornflowers and poppies flattened to become a sandy landscape. Tyre tracks all over the place, men everywhere, surveying their work on the new development. A sea of yellow vests and hats where there had once been daffodils and crocus flowers.

Charles was often not around. When he was, he was on site, as he called it. Overseeing the new builds, chumming up with the foremen. Vivacia wondered if he got his bonus money for the land sale.

When the skeletons of the new homes were up, potential buyers came to view them. Suited men with their shirtsleeves rolled up, big watches on display. Their wives wore oversized shades and tight dresses, their handbags on show, the same way the husbands' wristwatches were. They reeked of money, and they frowned as much as their filled, frozen faces would allow when they passed Vivacia on her front step.

Some mornings, Vivacia walked the perimeter. Charles didn't encourage her to remain inside any longer, because he was rarely at home to insist upon it.

They had erected new iron railings at the back of her place. She was hemmed in, she thought; even though she'd finally wrestled her way out of Charles's bed-cum-prison, she was still fenced in.

They had left Lady Well alone, though, she noted. The new boundaries skimmed past it, but the old hole had been given a new hat.

Nothing fancy, because after all, this portion at the rear of the compound was for the old-timers, not the brand new, shiny newcomers. They could keep it cheap and basic back here.

She bent to examine it. Nothing more than a drain cover. Already brown and dirty-looking.

She straightened up and looked back over the building site. Cattle class to the back, those who turn left when walking onto a plane up at the front.

—

By the last days of spring, Wolf's Pit looked totally different. The cluster of new builds were finished. The fields were gone forever.

The village was now a community, filled with new blood. They had parties which started with boxes from Fortnum & Mason being delivered early in the morning, and white-dressed staff sweeping and cleaning the exteriors of the homes. By midnight they'd descend into a debauchery that she knew Cally would have loved to witness. Squeezing into hot tubs aglow with fairy lights, glasses clinking, champagne flutes shattering.

On one such night, Vivacia watched those at number eight from the upstairs window. A familiar figure cut through her eyeline.

Charles, on the new people's patio. That old suit was shiny with overuse, his best shoes were scuffed and faded. He clutched a whisky glass. He never drank from it. He was all alone, on the fringes of the group, desperately seeking a way in.

Vivacia uttered a dry laugh to herself as they closed ranks against him. Just like the original villagers had done to her.

He left, carefully placing the glass on a waiting server's tray.

She expected to hear his key in the front door, but instead he moved in a different direction, outside of the community, walking on, on, on, until he'd vanished altogether.

Hours later, just before dawn broke over the community, she looked out of the back window and saw him again. On Lady Well this time, the lid off to one side, shiny suit jacket abandoned on the grass beside it. Charles lay half-on, half-off the well lip, peering down the hole.

Vivacia went downstairs, out of the patio door, and made her way to the iron railings.

'What are you doing?' she asked him.

In the still of the morning, she heard his shirt rustle as he shrugged.

Vivacia slipped through the dented railing and made her way over to him. He shaded his eyes as she approached, even though there was not yet any sunshine, and looked past her.

'Who damaged that?' he snapped.

She turned to look at the iron pole that had been shifted to one side.

'One of the builders when they put it up,' she replied. 'He hit it with the digger.'

He'd been full of apologies, the driver, but only when he realised Vivacia was there, perched on the well, watching him.

'It doesn't matter,' she'd said to him. 'Not back here, where nobody ever goes.'

Happy that no extra costs were to be incurred, the builder had gone merrily on his way, probably never to think of it again.

She told Charles this, now. 'If it had been at the front, where *they* live, there would have been uproar,' she said. Her tone was amused in a way she hadn't heard herself speak in a long time. Maybe never.

Charles beat his hands on the side of Lady Well. 'That's the problem,' he hissed. 'You are so weak. You are so boring.' He raised his eyes to the heavens and sighed heavily. 'Why do I stay? You are the reason why they don't accept me.' He swept his hand out in a wide arc. 'Because of *you*, because of the way you *are*.'

'Because I don't pretend to be something I'm not,' she said.

He let off a torrent of vitriol then, all the more impactful because the words were spoken in his normal, neutral tone.

Stupid. Mental. Crazy. Ugly. Worthless.

He stopped when he saw no blows had landed and flopped back to lie on the ground, spent from exertion.

'I had this vision,' he started, 'of a grand society, of filling our community with funds and status.' He rolled over to peer

196

down the well. 'I think I got it all wrong. I think perhaps it's better to have a place where nobody owns anything, nobody can lay a claim to anything.'

'Imagine all the people, living in a world of peace...' she said, ironically.

He blinked at her, annoyed again, and flapped his hands to dismiss her.

Later, he was still there, no longer looking down the well, but staring towards where he'd walked before, to a place of nothingness.

More contractors came, this time to concentrate on Lady Well. They stood around with their clipboards, and samples of pipes and tubing. They came after dusk or before it got fully light.

Before the neighbours can ask what's going on, Vivacia realised.

Once again, she found she didn't care enough to enquire. Her questions would be brushed aside, she knew from experience.

Perhaps because she didn't ask, Charles told her. 'Fresh, spring water,' he said. 'Free running water. Just imagine the possibilities!'

She couldn't imagine. They had water, fresh in the taps. Why they needed another source was beyond her.

'We can lay water pipes,' Charles continued, enthused. 'Expand this land even more, create a place that's special.' His eyes were shiny and faraway. 'I can do that. I can make that place.'

She should care, she knew. Even if it wasn't about Charles's exploits, she should care about something. She resumed her walks around the newly gated community. Bravely, she offered quiet greetings to the newer residents, sought out the older ones, the original ones, but they mostly stayed within their own homes and gardens now.

She spent a lot of time hovering at Jackie's gate, remembering the times she'd wander through, let herself in and up to Cally's room.

Somehow, since Cally had left for good, without even so much as a goodbye, and Stephanie and Kay and Serafina had died, everything had changed. This place wasn't her own anymore, and all the people she'd loved were no longer here.

Stephanie's house had been sold to Ruth, of all people. Vivacia remembered that, recalled signing the papers that Charles had thrust at her. It had been in those dark days, when she was confined to her bedroom.

Odd, she thought now, that she remembered signing that paperwork, but the agreement to the gated community was still missing from her recollections.

She wandered over to Stephanie's old house, wondering vaguely what Ruth was planning to do now she had two homes. She was only one person, after all.

Ruth intercepted her at the gate and seemed pleased to see her. She folded Vivacia into her arms. Vivacia breathed in the familiar smell of Ruth's hand-rolled cigarettes and found she didn't want to let go.

'Holiday rental,' Ruth said, in hushed tones, as though it was a scandalous secret. 'They're the in-thing, you know?'

Vivacia didn't know. She glanced at the McMansions, and wondered if Ruth had somehow penetrated their protected, closeted walls.

'You're renting out Mum's home?' Vivacia asked in surprise.

Ruth shook her head, her big earrings giving off little musical notes. 'No way, darling. I love this place; I'm living here myself. All that light, the beautiful studio.' She put a hand on Vivacia's arm. 'You're okay with it, aren't you?'

Vivacia was, she found. She couldn't live there herself. All those warm memories would become like a furnace, burning her from the outside in. She'd hate to see strangers there too. The Widow Ruth having occupancy was fine. A happy medium.

'You need to come outside more,' said Ruth, her voice suddenly strict and assertive. 'The whole neighbourhood is a mess. Bastille drowning in his drinking habit, Jackie hiding in there, you sequestered in your place.'

Vivacia stared at her. *Where were you when I needed you?* she wanted to ask.

But, ever mindful of respecting one's elders, she said nothing.

She also left the obvious unsaid: the accident that had taken three of the most prominent residents had stunted the lives of those who remained.

'No news about Cally?' asked Vivacia.

'Nothing. I heard she's abroad, found a swanky rich bloke and she's holed up there.'

'Abroad?' Vivacia frowned. 'Where?'

'Germany!' Ruth exclaimed now. 'Good nightlife, apparently. That's what your Charles heard, anyway. Jackie got a postcard, so she's no longer on the missing persons list.'

Something twitched in Vivacia's mind. The fog, all-encompassing these days, and the already strenuous conversation she'd had with Ruth brought a shutter down on the half-thought that tried to emerge.

Exhausted, suddenly, Vivacia bade Ruth goodbye and went home.

Later, in bed, on her own because Charles no longer shared her room, she turned her face to her pillow and wept until sleep caught at her.

She dreamed of those loved ones, all gone.

When she woke, she thought of those still here: Ruth and Jackie.

And Charles.

–

'Do you think it would be all right to call on Jackie?'

Vivacia had snagged Ruth, early the following morning, once more outside the gate of what had once been Stephanie's home.

Ruth's mouth turned downwards. 'To be honest, darling, she's kind of a loner these days.'

Anger bloomed in Vivacia's chest.

'I was a loner. I really needed someone after... after they'd gone. I was alone for months, but I didn't want to be.'

Ruth gaped at her. 'We all came. You wouldn't see us; you turned us away.'

It was Vivacia's turn to be shocked. 'Did I?' she asked, her voice an equally hushed whisper. *Or did Charles?*

Ruth patted her hand. 'You ate the meals we prepared, though. And you are your mother's and grandmother's girl. I knew you'd come back eventually.'

Vivacia remembered the meals. Recalled wondering vaguely when Charles had learned to cook.

She should have known.

Her temper spiked again, and she grabbed on to the emotion, grateful for it after so long of feeling nothing but an empty ache.

'Jackie can only tell me to go away,' she said. 'You stay here, all of you, in your ivory towers, ignoring everyone whose life doesn't currently smell like roses.'

Ruth, open-mouthed, watched her go.

Jackie did let her in. Or rather, when she answered the door, she didn't tell Vivacia to go away.

Instead, she looked her up and down, and retreated to the lounge and her window seat, leaving the door open.

Vivacia took it as an invitation to enter.

'Have you not heard anything from Cally?' she asked as she slipped her shoes off and followed Jackie into the front room.

'Apparently, she's in Germany now,' said Jackie.

Her voice was hoarse and deep, as though she was a forty-a-day smoker.

Or like she was no longer used to talking to anyone.

'Who told you that she's in Germany?' Vivacia asked, cautiously.

'Ruth,' said Jackie.

'And where did she hear that?' Vivacia felt awkward, questioning the other woman, but there was a need prickling at her that made her press on.

'Iris's kids,' said Jackie. She turned back to stare at Vivacia. 'Did you want something?'

'I wanted to make sure you are okay,' said Vivacia, stung.

Jackie barked a laugh, but it was laced with scorn.

'Have you heard from Cally, though?' Vivacia pressed her.

Jackie gestured to the mantle, a postcard upon it. Barcelona. A nightscape scene. Glittering fountains, bright lights.

Vivacia plucked it off the shelf and turned it over.

Cally x

That was all it said, the handwriting surprisingly neat and tidy.

Vivacia let herself out of the house then, pausing at the midway point between Jackie's home and hers. Her head was pounding, an ache that ran down her neck into her shoulders.

She clutched at the wall closest to her, bent over and suddenly exhausted, until a gentle hand came to rest on her shoulder.

She jerked upright, expecting Ruth, and found herself staring into a pair of warm, bright, brown eyes.

One of the new ones.

Vivacia cleared her throat and moved out of reach of the woman's hand.

'Hey. Are you okay? You looked like you were about to keel over.'

Vivacia studied the woman in front of her. She was so… glossy. So perfect-looking that Vivacia was lost for words.

'You want to come in for a coffee?' the woman asked. Then, with a sudden wink that jolted Vivacia, she added, 'Or something stronger.'

Vivacia shook her head. 'I'm fine, thank you,' she managed.

A sudden hammering had them both looking to Ruth's house. Ruth was there, one fist on the pane of glass, the other hand struggling with the catch. Finally, she opened the window and leaned out.

'Hi, girls. Vivacia, are you all right?'

'I'm fine,' she snapped, her tone harder than she meant.

'Come in, I've got something I want to show you.' Ruth beckoned.

'Jesus,' Vivacia muttered.

The woman, the stranger, still there, let out a laugh that sounded like delicate piano music.

'I'll let you get on. I'm Portia, by the way, I live at number three. Drop by if you like. Anytime, the coffee machine is always on.' With a hand raised in a friendly wave, she started back on her way. 'See you, Ruth,' she called over her shoulder.

Vivacia turned as Ruth emerged from her house. 'Do you *know* her?'

'Of course, darling, that's Portia.' Ruth trotted down the path and encircled Vivacia's shoulders, leading her firmly towards Stephanie's old house. 'Come in, I want to show you something I found.'

She'd not been in the house since Ruth had bought it. As she was pushed inside, she faltered, as though she was walking on quicksand.

It was like stepping into a dream. Everything was familiar; the number of steps it took to reach the kitchen hadn't changed. But it wasn't Stephanie's place anymore. It smelled like Ruth: of coffee, freshly baked biscuits, vanilla candles.

The 'something' that Ruth had to show her was a folder that had belonged to Stephanie. An album, really, of portraits. Watercolour paintings, charcoal drawings, acrylics and oils and coloured pencils.

'I thought you might like them.' Ruth patted Vivacia's hand. 'There's some of you in there.'

Vivacia opened it at a page towards the end. Encased in the plastic was a graphite drawing, astonishingly realistic, of two babies.

Alex and Elizabeth, instantly recognisable.

Vivacia drew in a sharp breath. She was glad for the plastic covering, as two tears dripped onto the page. A tear for each, she thought. A river, an *ocean* for those babies.

28

VIVACIA – NOW

That moment. The instant she recognises the body on the couch, the sight has the potential to send her into a direct descent of madness. Insanity.

After the initial shock, however, the mist dissipates, the world becomes clear. Her mind, teetering on the brink of potential mania for a long time, is suddenly whole.

The children, Rose, and Dallas, whom she's loved irrevocably since the moment she set eyes on them, are not a gift sent from a higher power. The link she has with them is because she has a connection to them. Her best friend's babies.

She sobs hard as she sinks to her knees beside Cally's body. She doesn't see the sunken face, the grey skin, the wide open, staring, glassiness of her eyes.

She sees her how she was. Spirited, fiery, joyous, scrappy, wild.

She slips a hand underneath Cally's neck, cold as marble, and draws her in to hold her oldest friend close.

She understands that now the police must be called. There is no more room for the lie. This is – *was* – Cally. She shouldn't touch her, but she leans forward and kisses her lips anyway. They are cold and hard and bloodless.

She glances out of the filthy window. The children have retreated there. They stand together. Not touching, staring at the caravan that holds their mother's body.

Still weeping, Vivacia yanks on the door handle. It doesn't budge.

Locked in. They were all locked in.

Cally is still locked in.

She slips out through the hole in the floor, staggering around to the door. Underneath the steps, partially hidden in the weeds that surround the van, she finds a piece of metal. Jagged and rusted, it looks like it was once part of an exhaust.

Sweat combining with the tears on her face, she shoves the pipe into the miniscule gap between the door and frame, and wrenches at it.

It gives a little, and she pushes, ignoring the flakes of rust that break off, and the pain in her arms and shoulders.

Finally, the frame, old and worn, buckles. The hinges fall at a crazy angle. The door springs open.

She stares again at the interior. The fierce daylight only serves to heighten the terrible scene.

To be enclosed in this place, smaller than the bedroom that Rose and Dallas share back at her house.

With the body of their mother lying inches away.

The tears are endless as she walks back inside, circling the few feet of the perimeter. The cupboards, devoid of anything. There is a pile of cans in the corner. Wrappers and packets too, all empty. Licked clean. She twists the tap over the sink. Nothing comes out. The windows don't budge an inch.

Off the main room is a tiny bedroom.

Vivacia walks into it.

It is mostly as bare as the rest of the caravan. A towel, draped on the bed, a single shoe, on the floor.

She sees it on the bedside table.

The fear is visceral. Her throat clicks. She swallows desperately, repeatedly. Her body stings as though a hundred bees have landed on her. Her stomach roils.

The tears have gone now, to be replaced by a deep, dark heat within her.

All the things she felt before, all those years ago when she would return home and see his red wallet on the hallway table. The same red wallet that she is seeing now.

On reflex, from muscle memory, she braces herself.

She darts to the wardrobe and flings it open. It is not empty in here. Flannel shirts, half a dozen of them, alongside a shiny, worn, silver-grey suit.

The clothes still hold his scent. It assaults her nostrils. The way he was, slathered in that cheap aftershave, and the way he became, the earthy smell, a mixture of oil and sweat.

His final words to her, that night on Lady Well, when he attempted to explain what he wanted, his gains, his goals.

I think I got it all wrong. I think perhaps it's better to have a place where nobody owns anything, nobody can lay a claim to anything.

He had tried to weasel his way into the gated community, but they had seen him for what he was. They closed ranks against him.

He had started again, changed his approach. Instead of trying to come in at the top in a place that was already established, he'd attempted to form his own community.

A cult-like place.

And Cally had been taken in by him. Won over by his ideas and his charm.

Vivacia spins away from the clothes, past the dresser where his wallet lies, a beacon in the gloom, flashing red in her peripheral vision. Danger.

All the blanks are filled in. The control that he exerted over Cally, the same coercion he'd tried on Vivacia. With Vivacia it was mental, because that was where she was weak. But Cally wasn't. Cally was emotionally strong, so he'd had to use physical force.

A locked door.

A depleted stock of food and water.

How many times had he locked her in here, softening her persona, making her pliable, ensuring that she had to rely on his return?

And he would have returned. He did, time and time again. Until that last time, when he ended up in the well. He couldn't come back then, couldn't walk up that hill to unlock the door.

A sharp pain worms a hole into Vivacia's temple.

She doesn't realise she is crawling until she feels the rough, dirty flooring beneath her palms. She hurls herself back out of the door, into the air, which is fresh and clean but does nothing to cleanse her.

It runs in a terrible sequence through Vivacia's head.

Charles lured Cally, who was always up for an adventure, to this barren place.

Somehow, for some reason, probably because she was wilful, it went sour.

Charles locked Cally and the children inside when he went back down to Wolf's Pit.

Charles never came back.

Cally could never get out.

Through fresh tears, she sees Rose and Dallas, peering curiously at her. She turns away.

She can't look at them. Can't stand to see the trust they have in her.

Then she hears her own name, and the devastation inside her turns to fear.

Rob.

He has followed her, his trusty backpack ever-present, his eyes squinting in the sunshine as he darts his gaze to the children, before looking back to her.

'V?' He crouches down, frowning now, his eyes concentrated on her face.

She sees it: the moment when his attention is caught by the open door behind her.

She hears it: his exclamation as he moves past her to peer into the caravan.

'It's Cally. Cally is their mum.' Her words are broken by her own gasps for air.

'Cally!' His volume rises even as the confusion drowns his features. 'Jackie's girl? But... But she's not...' He trails off, looks at the children.

She's not your cousin.

The words he was about to say.

She scrubs at her eyes and sees the moment the confusion clears for him.

The fact that he now knows her lie.

His face drops. 'Oh, Vivacia.' He is practically dripping with disappointment.

The fear and the sudden horror inside her twist into something else.

Fury.

'I didn't know!' she shouts. 'I didn't know she was here!'

He shakes his head sadly and passes a hand over his eyes.

'Vivacia.' He says her name again, once, and suddenly, he is no longer Rob.

She's back where she was during all those years, being the disappointment, the fool, the wife who could never live up to her husband's expectations.

Anger sears her insides, red hot.

'They've not been placed with you. You're not their foster carer.' He stares at her. 'You did steal them.'

'No!'

She looks at the children. Rose, eyes averted.

Rose thinks they are fighting. And she doesn't like it.

Vivacia bites her lip. How many fights did Rose witness between Charles and Cally? Because Cally gave as good as she got.

Dallas catches her eye. He has a tiny smile on his face, one that doesn't reach his eyes.

Vivacia can hear her own breathing. Shallow and quick. Dallas clenches his fists over and over, a look on his face as though, bizarrely, he finds this latest drama… thrilling.

She sees it then, just how damaging their formative years have been.

As if further proof was needed that she must step in, love them, protect them.

Save them.

Rob is still there, inside the caravan now, gagging and swearing. He practically falls out of the door, glaring at her while he digs his phone out of his pocket.

'I'm calling the police,' he announces. He shoots her a look, heavy with disgust. 'I'm calling the social, too.'

Vivacia plants her hands on the ground before her.

'Wait!' she cries.

His fingers hover over the phone, mid-dial.

She is sobbing again now, staggering to a standing position. This can't be it. This can't be the end. The children's mum is gone, as is their father. These kids really do need a mother now. And there is nobody better than Vivacia to fill the shoes of her best friend.

She can't fail now. Not at the last hurdle.

But he is serious. He flashes her one more glance, his lip curled, and looks back to his phone.

'Please don't take them away from me!' she cries.

'You can't do this, Vivacia,' he says, not even looking at her now. 'There are laws for a reason. I mean, God, if you'd not lied, a search could have been launched. They might have found… *that* in time. Still breathing. Still *living*.'

Vivacia cries even harder.

Is that true?

If it is, she wants to die.

She thinks about sinking down to lie upon the scorched, dry earth and ending it all here, yards away from Cally's inert form.

A hiss, sudden and sharp, at the same time as a cry rings out. Not hers. Not Rob's, either.

She swings her head to the right. Sees Rose standing, arms outstretched. Dallas, giving them one glance over his shoulder as he runs away into the undergrowth.

Vivacia's tears stop. Panic moves from her loss to Dallas's safety.

She knows what's on the other side of the wood into which he has disappeared.

'DALLAS!' Her shout is no longer laden with tears. It is primal, instinctual, maternal.

She starts towards the trees, pausing at Rose's side.

'Do not move,' she tells the little girl. 'Stay here, wait for me.'

Two seconds was her delay, and already Rob is charging past her, following Dallas through the canopy of trees.

'Shit!' Vivacia takes off at a run after them.

She takes the overgrown path that leads west, beating at the tall grass with her hands. Blackberry tendrils snatch her arms, blood beading up on her skin. She pays no heed, doesn't even feel it.

She hasn't been down this path in twenty years. So far it is unchanged, forgotten, just like the rubbish tip. But the old dump is not a hazard. Unlike what they are all headed for.

'STOP!' she roars, and it takes all the breath she has left after her sprint. 'Please, stop!'

She can see it, as the land suddenly opens up. The soil, still sodden, not yet dried underneath the trees, changing. Paler, stonier, then a chalky white earth.

The edge of the quarry.

And Dallas and Rob are heading straight for it.

It is fenced off, but the wire boundary is weather-beaten and useless. Sagging in places, completely down in others. She runs between the barrier posts, Rob ahead, the sound of his backpack thudding against his spine loud in her ears. She sprints in a zigzag, desperately trying to see around him, searching for Dallas's small form.

She can see no sign of the boy.

She screams. A crow bursts from a low tree branch, startled by the ferocity of her cry.

There! She sees Dallas. He has stopped running, is facing them. Relief drenches her that he is no longer running, but a chill clambers up her throat as she sees he isn't standing still.

He is walking backwards.

Towards the quarry, mere feet from the edge that would send him to his certain death.

She covers her mouth with her hands. Something tells her not to scream, not to startle him.

She freezes. A whisper emerges from her.

'Dallas…'

Not even a whisper. A moan.

Rob, just in front of her, has no such instincts.

'STOP RIGHT THERE!' he shouts, so loud that Vivacia flinches.

Rob takes off again, aiming at Dallas, and now Vivacia does scream.

She keeps her eyes focused on Dallas, still stepping backwards. Holds her breath when Rob is nearly upon the child.

Then, three things happen at once.

Dallas smiles, showing all his little white teeth.

He steps to the side, quick as a whip.

Rob, arms outstretched, catches at nothing but thin air. He plants his heels in the ground, puffs of white chalk floating up around his boots. His backpack shunts into his spine.

The weight takes him over the edge.

The sound of rocks knocking against each other, a small landslide of loose stones. A single cry. A thump, a small splash.

Then, nothing but silence.

–

On her front, because she dares not stay on her feet and peer over, she inches towards the edge.

He is forty feet or more down.

So far that if she didn't witness him going over the edge, she wouldn't know he was down there. She can see a patch of light-coloured material. His shirt, perhaps, and the shape of a bulky item which must be his backpack. She can't see him clearly, but she imagines that his body is crooked, legs and arms askew at unnatural angles. An unwelcome memory: Serafina lying in the road.

Rob is gone.

A shadow falls over her and she turns to her right. Dallas, in a crouch beside her. He has his thumb in his mouth, and his eyes are huge and watery.

'Dallas…' she whispers.

He glances at her, lower lip trembling now.

Her heart stings with love for him. She scoots backwards, opens her arms, the flame inside her hot as he tumbles into them.

'It's okay,' she says. 'It was an accident.'

His body jerks and she stiffens at the motion.

Is he… laughing?

No. He is crying. In the space of an hour he has witnessed two terrible deaths.

His tiny hand makes its way into hers and he pulls on her.

She releases her grip on his body, holds his fingers tightly in hers as they move away from the edge of the quarry.

–

The walk back takes them fifteen minutes. Constant tears roll down Vivacia's face. She wipes them hastily with one hand, the other one gripping Dallas's tightly.

Her chest jerks with sobs she tries to hide.

She doesn't know if she is shedding tears of grief, or relief. The whole day has been the worst of her life, or at least on a par with the night when her mother and grandmother died.

She searches inside for the positives.

Dallas and Rose are safe.

The only positive that matters.

'It's okay,' she whispers. 'Everything is going to be okay now.'

She isn't sure if her words are for herself or Dallas.

Rose is where she left her, by the fence, head down. She looks up at the sound of their approach, eyes narrowing when only the two of them appear.

'There was a terrible accident,' Vivacia says. 'But your brother is safe. He's unharmed, see?'

Rose stares at Dallas.

Vivacia watches her carefully. Something like anger flashes in the little girl's eyes. It changes almost immediately to look like resignation, or perhaps disappointment.

Vivacia pulls them both into a hug.

'I'm not going anywhere,' she whispers. 'I'll be here for both of you forever.'

She herds the children outside the rubbish tip, to the highest point of the land where she can just about see where the road ends, half a mile away.

From there, she pulls her phone out of her pocket, and calls the police.

It is a nightmare scenario. It takes her so long to tell DI Ola Demoski what has happened here today. Long pauses, periods of sobs that wrack Vivacia's body. One awful moment when she stops, averts her head, sure she's going to throw up on the oily, patchy ground.

The DI calls for reinforcements, directs some to the caravan, some to the quarry.

Vivacia watches, quieter now, in shock at the turn of events this day has taken.

Two dead, in entirely different circumstances.

Two children, officially parentless.

–

Vivacia takes a deep breath.

'They came down the hill, I saw them at the back of mine. I waited a while, in case they'd just wandered away from their parents, but the little girl… Rose, she was crying, pointing up the hill.' Vivacia breaks off, rubs a hand over her forehead. She

is suddenly sweating. 'Neither of them said anything, just…
They just led me up here.' She pauses, shakes her head. 'Rob
must have been out walking. He appeared out of nowhere.'

They have been moved to the station, Rose and Dallas in
the room next door.

A medic had come to the scene, checking them, proclaiming
them in relatively good health, if a little underweight.

Vivacia felt a thrill at that, at their improvement compared
to a week ago, when she *really* first found them.

She tells the DI as much as she can without implicating
herself. That the dead woman is Cally, that the wallet and
clothes in the caravan belonged to Charles. That after seeing
his mother, Dallas ran, Rob taking off after him. The terrible
accident that followed.

The DI leans back in her chair, observing Vivacia with an
intensity that makes her nervous.

'Charles locked her in… locked *them* in. And never went
back.'

Vivacia feels tears on her face. She nods, searches for appropriate words.

'I'd… I'd like to look after them. In the interim,' she says.
She wonders if it is an inappropriate comment, too soon, too
sudden, but if she doesn't say it now, they will be arranging care
for Rose and Dallas.

Ola Demoski flips through her notes. 'Jackie is their grandmother.' It isn't a question.

'Can she deal with two young children?' Vivacia leans
forward, already knowing the answer.

Jackie couldn't deal with one child, and that was when she
was twenty years younger.

'I'm equipped for children; I've taken in emergency fosters
before.' The blood drains from Vivacia's face as a thought strikes
her.

What if they come home with her, see the beds already made
up, the house full of toys and clothes that Rose and Dallas have
been playing with and wearing for a week?

214

Ola frowns, makes some notes on a pad in front of her. Vivacia tries unsuccessfully to read them.

She thinks of something else, of the incident four years ago when her last charges were removed. Is that on file? The black-list she's always imagined she is on, though she never checked, never tried to foster again after that heartbreak.

Ola excuses herself. Vivacia watches her through the window, tapping away on a computer, making calls, cradling the phone on her shoulder as she makes more notes.

The wait is eternal, but finally Ola hangs up the phone and makes her way back to the office.

Vivacia waits, hands clenched, not even breathing.

'Are you sure you're up to this?' Ola flings herself in her chair, that concerned look still on her face. 'You've had some pretty big traumas yourself this last week.'

Vivacia exhales. A big woosh of air, worry and panic escaping with it.

She smiles, bittersweet. She gazes at the wall, as though she can see her two babies in the next room.

'I'm sure,' she says to Ola, with a firm nod. 'I've never been more certain.'

–

They come for their checks, those in authority, but it is two hours after Vivacia is taken home. She has cleared up, and shows them the room, the beds, the clothes. All ready and waiting.

The children are now at the hospital for a more thorough looking-over, possibly to stay in overnight, after being assessed by both a doctor and a child psychologist.

They won't talk.

They won't talk.

They won't *tell*.

They know everything, Rose and Dallas. They know they've been with Vivacia for a week. They know Rob arrived at the caravan today, full of threats and disgust at her lie. Rose knows that Rob went into the woods with Dallas and didn't come back out again.

The risk of them being in the hands of professionals is huge. Rose and Dallas will decide all their fates.

If the children should speak, should tell, Vivacia will take her punishment.

If she were to be found out today, she promises herself and God she would tell the police everything.

The truth about when she found the children.

And the other secret she has been keeping.

–

She gets the call at nine o'clock. The children are okay, physically. There is no medical reason for their lack of speech, the gravelly-voiced physician tells her. It may simply take time. He talks on as Vivacia holds her phone to her ear, her hand gripping the edge of her table until her knuckles cramp painfully.

'...drop them off in about one hour,' she hears him say.

She gasps, unlocks her fingers and covers her mouth.

'Thank you,' she stammers. 'I'll be here, and I've ensured they have everything they need all ready.'

She falls back into her chair and puts her hands to her face.

She is close.

She is within touching distance of having everything she has ever desired.

But she also knows that there is one person she must see, must speak frankly with, must be truthful with. Because when it comes down to it, it is not God, or even the children, who will decide Vivacia's fate after all.

A pair of headlights cut through the dark night. Vivacia stiffens, and goes to peer out of the window. It's a police car, rolling slowly around the looped road, cruising to a stop outside Jackie's house.

She waits, her heart in her throat, hating the sudden silence in the house.

216

Even though Rose and Dallas don't talk, their absence is excruciating.

Outside, a fox screams.

Vivacia pulls back the curtain again. The police car is still there, its occupants inside Jackie's now.

Vivacia replays that scream in her mind. A fox or... Jackie?

She shivers, her body wracked with a chill. She drops the curtain and wraps herself in the blanket that Kay crocheted.

She leans forward and opens the drawer set into the coffee table. From inside, she plucks the piece of paper that Rose had in her pocket when she arrived in Wolf's Pit. She folds it into her palm.

Outside, a car door closes. Vivacia resists the urge to look out of the window again.

She lays the paper out flat. The name written upon it screams in Vivacia's head.

Jackie Jenkins

If she'd taken the trek up the hill the day she found that paper, if she'd scrutinised what transpired to be a map earlier, could Cally have been saved, like Rob claimed?

Horror simmers inside, burning her chest.

She throws the blanket off her shoulders.

—

Ola is the one who opens Jackie's front door.

She looks weary, and sad, too.

'I was making her a cup of tea,' says Ola.

Memories pummel into Vivacia. Years of hidden, needless childhood recollections. Jackie, hunched over her kitchen table as a ten-year-old Cally screamed upstairs, a tantrum over something and nothing. Jackie, gulping the steaming black liquid, her eyes filled with helplessness.

Later, when Cally was older, Jackie would sit on the steps at the front of the house, cloaked in darkness, one hand wrapped around the mug, the other reaching out for Cally's shoulder when she returned home hours after her curfew.

How tired Jackie must have been, for all those years.

Vivacia keeps the door open as she slips inside. 'She prefers coffee,' she says to Ola. 'I'll stay with her. You can go if you like.'

Ola glances at her watch. 'The children are on their way?'

Vivacia nods. 'I've got everything ready for them to stay,' she replies. 'Jackie can stay too, if she wants.' Vivacia drops her voice to a whisper. 'She's pretty independent, though.'

Ola raises her eyebrows. 'Seems you all are, round here.' She smiles, gentle, kind, an expression Vivacia knows she doesn't deserve. 'She'll want to see the children, obviously. Once the shock has worn off,' says Ola, conversationally.

She will probably be offered guardianship of them, reckons Vivacia. She wonders how Jackie will do in that role. Poor, worn-down Jackie.

Vivacia goes through to the kitchen and flicks the kettle on. No fancy machine here – not like Portia's sparkling, steaming, silver one. Just good old-fashioned coffee granules in a jar.

She passes Ola on the way out. The officer grips Vivacia's arm and offers her a hushed thank you.

'You're amazing, after the shock you had. If either of you need anything…'

Vivacia nods but is unable to force a smile.

'I'm getting a family liaison officer to call this evening. She'll stop in soon.'

She watches the door close softly behind Ola, takes a deep breath, and walks into the lounge.

Jackie is on the sofa. Her post by the window has been abandoned. She looks up when Vivacia comes in.

'Oh, Vivacia.' Jackie's words are laden with weariness. Her face drags with sadness. Her eyes, however, are bone dry.

'I'm so sorry,' whispers Vivacia.

She thinks of her mother and grandmother, of how if they were here, they would envelop Jackie in their arms. With what she is about to tell the woman, it doesn't seem right for Vivacia to do that.

Another memory slips in. Jackie, marching over to Vivacia's house, a year ago, demanding to know Charles's whereabouts.

It was the first time Vivacia had said the words. *He's left me.*

Now, after this latest, awful discovery, Jackie's near interrogation holds new meaning.

'Did… Did you know they were together?' she asks.

Jackie's mouth twists but she says nothing.

'If… If I'd known…' Vivacia trails off.

Jackie makes a noise that is supposed to be a laugh but sounds nothing like one. 'If you'd known, what? What would you have done?'

Vivacia takes a deep breath and stares at Jackie.

'If I'd known they were together, I wouldn't have killed Charles.'

29

VIVACIA – BEFORE

The days grew clearer, little by little. At the beginning of another summer, Vivacia realised how much time she had lost in her grief. The knowledge that entire seasons – indeed, three whole years – could pass her by without her realising was frightening.

Ruth wasn't maudlin or depressed. It was like her little holiday-home business and living in Vivacia's mother's old home had sparked a new lease of life for her.

'You're glad the land sale went ahead, aren't you?' Vivacia said one morning as they strolled the woodland beyond the confines.

'Yes,' answered Ruth, truthfully. 'I'm busy, and I'm happy.'

What must that feel like, wondered Vivacia.

'I feel awful, sometimes,' confessed Ruth. 'If it wasn't for what happened, that terrible, awful thing, it wouldn't have gone ahead, the land sale.' Ruth stops, leans over as if winded and peers sideways at Vivacia. 'I'd give it all up, to have them back. You know that, don't you?'

The conclusive vote. The irony of it, that with the three opposition parties gone, their opinions were null and void.

Ruth had straightened up then, moved away, her small feet leaving tiny tracks in the undergrowth.

A coughing fit struck Vivacia. She thumped her chest once, twice, three times, but the blockage wouldn't clear.

'Are you okay, dear?' Ruth had returned, eyes full of concern. Vivacia waved her away.

'Better go back,' she choked.

It was absurd, that sudden knowledge that had struck her just then. So terrible that she tried hard not to let it become a fully-fledged thought.

But it wouldn't leave her. It hovered around the edges of her mind, needling her, pushing to find a way in.

The three opposing members in the village. Gone. The land sale, free to proceed.

She wondered if the police had examined the car. If something untoward had been found, she'd have known about it.

Surely?

She caught up to Ruth and asked her. Ruth's face was a picture of pain.

'There was… nothing to examine,' Ruth said, her voice a tiny whisper. 'There was… It was… too damaged.'

A shell. That's what Ruth meant. The old Ford had ended up nothing more than a burned-out skeleton. Just like its occupants.

'It was very quick,' said Ruth. 'You know they wouldn't have felt a thing, don't you?'

Vivacia nodded but knew it was a lie. Those screams that hadn't only been Mr Bastille's spoke of a different truth.

'Why were they even going out in the car?' she asked now. 'Serafina said Cally was abroad; you did, too. Jackie received a postcard. Why, then, were they driving round here, looking for her?'

'Charles thought he'd seen her.' Ruth looked sharply at Vivacia. 'Dear, don't you know all this?'

Vivacia felt increasingly colder the more she persisted in finding out the timelines of that strange day.

Maybe stop here, she thought. *Leave it be. What's done is done.*
But she couldn't.

'It's a blur,' she said to Ruth. 'I know I've been told before, but…' She dropped her eyes. 'I don't remember much from that time.'

221

Ruth patted her arm tenderly. 'Charles thought he saw Cally down the lane. He went to Kay's, told her and your mother. He didn't want to go straight to Jackie and get her hopes up.' Ruth looked skywards, eyes shining. 'I can imagine those two, up for an adventure, looking for a happy ending for Jackie.'

That day, the babies had been removed from her care. Vivacia had been in a deep pit of depression. Charles had been there, telling her to pull herself together. She remembered something of his words… that he was going to give Kay's car a once-over before heading off on his business trip.

Vivacia shivered violently. Charles was gone again right now. These days, he was away more than he was home. Vivacia wondered if this feeling, this sudden desire to know, would pass by the time he returned.

–

She attended the Pilates session with Portia and Portia's equally fake, plastic-looking friends.

Vivacia waved a cheery goodbye as she left and hurried along the sun-warmed path to her own home.

She paused in her own front garden and tilted her face up to the sky. It was dark, the sun long sunk, but the night carried the heat of the day.

To her left, the sunflowers drooped, untouched by rain or a watering can for too long.

She felt a crack in her chest, remembering the days when Kay would tend to the blooms, religiously, without fail, every morning and evening.

Another pain followed, not as sharp, but there all the same. The thoughts she'd had about Portia and her mates. They weren't so bad, not really. They'd welcomed Vivacia into their homes, into their funny little activities, and all she did was laugh at them behind their backs.

It had been a ploy, really, a stupid thing, to hang around with them. She'd started because she was lonely. She only had Ruth; the community as she knew it was fractured badly, beyond repair, and kicking back with the new lot – join in their exercises, and sample and swap recipes that Vivacia would never eat or cook – had passed a fair few hours in days that would have stretched into isolation.

Charles had returned, off and on, sometimes here, some-times who-knew-where, and she liked the way his face creased and crumpled when she told him airily that she was off with her new friends for the afternoon.

She'd joined in with Portia's gang simply so she would forget that newfound half-knowledge that burned a hole in her soul. It was ridiculous, really, thinking that Charles might have had something to do with Kay and Stephanie's car accident. It was Vivacia who was at fault, for not keeping an eye on the two older women. But that knowledge hurt just as bad, so Vivacia sought a distraction with the new, rich lot in their shiny homes and mindless activities.

These days, she found herself enjoying the simplicity of Portia's conversation, the banality of just sitting in amongst the women, nodding along at the right moments, imparting a sentence here and there.

'Vivacia!' She heard her name, hollered from across the street, and saw Portia sprinting over to her.

'You forgot your yoga mat!' Portia exclaimed.

Vivacia smacked the side of her head. 'Silly me!'

Portia giggled, her blonde ponytail bouncing up and down, and looked past Vivacia towards her house.

'Charles away again?' she asked, her tone laden with sympathy.

'Yes, hopefully back to spend the weekend here,' Vivacia replied, the lie tripping too easily off her tongue.

Portia gave a wide grin. 'We're having a barbeque Sunday. If he goes back to the city early, come and join us.' She darted forward, grasped Vivacia's hands in her own and squeezed. 'Thank you so much for coming tonight, see you soon, lovely.'

There was so much to unpack there, thought Vivacia as she scooped up her yoga mat and let herself into the house. Come to the barbeque, but only if you're on your own. In other words, Charles is not welcome here.

Vivacia barked a laugh as she made her way upstairs, not bothering to put any lights on. She moved to the back bedroom, the one she slept in these days, still smiling over the exchange with Portia.

How she'd love for Charles to know the little conversation that just took place in their front garden.

She'd never tell him, of course, because even though she no longer feared his words or his fists, he could still be very difficult.

Or... could he?

It struck her that she had no idea, because she so rarely saw him.

These days, she breathed easier, knowing he was gone far more often than he was here.

One day, she hoped fervently that he would be gone forever.

As she pulled off her sports tee and slipped an old jumper on, she imagined sharing the reality of life with Charles with her new neighbours.

She knew exactly what Portia would say. *Why don't you leave him?*

She thought about it, often. How she came from a line of independent, straight-talking women, but had garnered nothing of their strength in her own DNA.

Had it been the other way around, they wouldn't have hesitated to ask questions about *that night*. They would have pushed and pushed and pushed at Charles until they had every piece of information.

They would know if he was lying, too.

The new ones were like Cally in that way.

In the window she caught sight of her own reflection.

It stared back at her, small and sad.

Vivacia marched to the window to yank the curtains closed.

She paused, staring across the field beyond the fence.

By the bright moonlight, she glimpsed a figure making its way unsteadily along the track. She recognised the height, even though the person was stooped almost double. She knew that silhouette, didn't know that red cotton jumper which must be new but looked ancient.

Vaguely, she realised her heart was beating a ferocious rhythm. She glanced around the room on instinct, to check all was clean and tidy, before remembering she didn't do that anymore.

Muscle memory was hard to shake.

She turned back to the window, a hiss of breath steaming the pane at the realisation that the figure had vanished. She blinked, saw her own reflection again. No longer small and sad. Rather, a set jaw, a hint of determination.

She scanned the landscape.

There he was!

He sat atop Lady Well. She couldn't tell his expression, not in the dark, not from this distance, but in his stance, he seemed... morose.

There was no thought, no planning, just acting upon an instinct that ordered her to confront him.

Vivacia hurtled down the stairs, through the patio door, and across the grass towards the damaged fence.

One time, her body grazed the sides of the gap. These days, she slipped through easily. She had lost weight, too much of it, in those dark years since Kay and Stephanie's accident. Although, the pounds had been steadily falling off her since her wedding.

'What are you doing here?' She was pleased with her voice, authoritative, as though he were an intruder or a trespasser.

Which he was, really, she told herself.

He didn't belong here. Not in her house, not in this gated community, not in her life or her bed, or her grandmother's house.

It took an age for him to respond. *He must be drunk*, she realised, as she moved closer to him. Steaming, falling-down intoxicated.

'Wife.' The single, slurred word was enough to chase away any potential concern.

'Did you do something to Kay's car?' The words were out before she could overthink them. Before she could change her mind.

Charles giggled.

Despite the hot night, Vivacia felt ice on her skin.

He was not just drunk. There was something else as well. Something he must have taken, to emit a sound like that in response to the question she asked. It was absurd, because Charles didn't drink or take drugs. He abhorred people who did. He always needed to be in control.

His fingers curled over his lips in a childish motion. He pulled his knees to his chest and lowered his head.

'I just wanted to be a part of it.' His voice was so low that Vivacia, in spite of herself, moved to sit next to him on top of Lady Well.

'What do you mean?'

He looked at her sideways, his dark eyes flashing with… something that looked an awful lot like hate.

'You all had each other, you all knew each other. Such a clique! I didn't fit, not the way it was. I had so much to offer but you…' He scowled, suddenly more like the Charles she married. 'All set in your ways, weren't you? All closed off. Living in the past. Couldn't see the future, could you? Couldn't see my potential, could you?'

He jabbed at his own chest, so violently that he lost his balance and swayed, almost in slow motion, to land on his side, looking away from her. He drew his knees up again, foetal-like now.

An overgrown baby, matching his childlike words. The exhaustion that followed a tantrum.

Vivacia stared at his spine and felt everything at once. Regret for not insisting he leave her home, sadness that she had been so insecure and married a man like this. Anger, for all these years she'd longed for a child.

She could cut him loose now. Easily. He was lost here. Even though he'd got his desire of this grand sense of place, he wasn't in it. Would never be in it.

The strength was there within her to do it, as well. Kay on one shoulder, Stephanie on the other, reminding her of something she'd forgotten for so long. Who she is. Where she comes from. *Who* she comes from.

Do not come back here. The words would be easy to say. Because he was right. He didn't belong here, but she did, she always had. She'd begun to adapt too. Like Ruth, she had become somebody in the new community. People, Portia and her pals, seemed to like her. She had already started a new life without Charles, but the threads of the old one held taut during his sporadic visits.

She could snip those threads.

Instead, she asked his back, 'What did you do to Kay's car?'

He struggled a little to get upright but gave up and simply turned his face towards her. A beetle on its back.

He said, tone laden with weariness, 'Does it matter?'

Cold fingers tapping down her spine. 'Yes,' replied Vivacia. She licked her lips, suddenly dry.

'A sacrifice for a new start.' He coughed and lay his head back to rest upon the centuries-old bricks of Lady Well. 'You have to see that, surely you understand that there is always an offering, to make such a big change.'

His words were almost religious. An offering. A sacrifice.

She'd known it. That day when he'd muttered something about looking over Kay's old car. He'd done it before, when they'd asked him. Was that where he got the idea from, to tamper with the brakes? To see off two of the people who wouldn't agree to the land sale?

There was no way he could have foreseen Serafina walking down that road. She, the other opposing party, had simply been a bonus. Three for the price of two.

All along, so deep inside that it could be ignored. She'd waited years – had to, because she hadn't been strong enough until now. She'd had to heal herself before confronting him.

The thoughts – the *knowledge* – were like a footnote, a postscript, just idling along one side of her mind. The other half was hot, a brutish heat piercing at her insides until it was all she could feel.

He watched her, almost wary now, his pupils huge in the moonlight.

Vivacia's hand moved of its own accord, a swinging fist that landed on his cheek.

The blow glanced off him. Indeed, Charles seemed not to even notice.

The heat simmered before boiling over.

Vivacia planted her hands into the earth, scrabbling around to push herself to standing. A wedge of the bricks that made Lady Well a little piece of folklore history crumpled. Vivacia didn't know what it was when she swung it. A long arc, the muscles in her shoulder hardly feeling it. Her tendons felt light as air, as she smashed the brick into the side of his head.

It wasn't a huge chunk of concrete. It was nothing more than a roof tile, half the size of one, actually. Not that heavy, not something that could cause irreparable damage.

It shouldn't have been enough to kill him, she would muse later.

But kill him it did.

30

VIVACIA – NOW

The moment Vivacia speaks the truth, she hears a rushing noise in her ears. The world tilts, Jackie's swirly, brown rug undulating on the floor. Vivacia blinks rapidly. This is it.

This is bigger than Charles, bigger than Rob's tragic accident. Bigger than both of their deaths combined.

This is about Cally, now.

'What?' Jackie's voice is too loud, glass shards in Vivacia's ear.

Vivacia jumps. Jackie has moved, is in front of her now – her arms outstretched, her nails, bitten to the quick, her hands like claws.

Vivacia leans forward and closes her eyes. She will take whatever Jackie wants to bestow on her. Punches, slaps, those raggedy nails dragging down the fair skin on Vivacia's face.

She'll take it all.

Gladly.

Instead, Jackie's hand holds Vivacia's shoulder in a vice-like grip. She shakes her, just once.

'What?' she says. 'What did you say?'

Vivacia opens her eyes. 'I killed Charles.'

She's said it twice now. She wonders if it gets a little easier to speak the words the more she says them. Maybe by the time she is in court, after repeating it to various police officers, her voice will be as clear as a bell.

Jackie staggers back until she reaches the fireplace. Her hand comes up again, not to strike, but to grab the shelf above.

'Tell me,' Jackie says. 'Tell me what you did.'

–

Vivacia's face is wet when she finishes her story. She pats at her cheeks, stares down through blurred eyes at Jackie's hideous rug.

Time passes.

Jackie doesn't move nor speak.

Eventually, Vivacia stands.

'Jackie…' she ventures.

Jackie raises her hand, a 'stop' gesture, but she doesn't look at Vivacia.

Fear grips Vivacia. She had expected shock, and once that had passed, she'd anticipated a thunderous response.

This nothing is awful.

Vivacia stands up and dares to approach her.

Jackie's hand comes up again. Not a threatening gesture, but Vivacia flinches all the same.

'Go,' says Jackie. Her voice is hoarse. 'Just… go.'

'What are you going to do?' Vivacia isn't asking if Jackie is going to call the police. She doesn't care about that. Hell, she expects it. No, there is something else here. The emptiness in Jackie is concerning.

'I don't want to leave you on your own,' says Vivacia, bravely. 'Not tonight.'

'Go.' Jackie turns away. Her hands are now clenched, knuckles white.

One more night, then. One more night with her babies. It's more than Vivacia could have hoped for. Though she'd dreamed of forever.

She backs away from Jackie, all the way to the door. 'I'll see you tomorrow,' she says. 'Whatever you need to do, whoever you need to call, I'll be ready. I'll be waiting.'

She slips outside and closes the door quietly behind her. Gulping huge breaths of the hot night's air, Vivacia races home.

She waits for the children to arrive. They will be exhausted, will want to go straight to bed.

She will tuck them in, all the time praying it won't be her last night doing so. She will sit with them until they fall asleep, watching as Dallas drifts off, cat's eyes peering at her in the darkness.

She wonders what Dallas has seen in his short life to make him sleep with his eyes half-open.

She shudders.

Charles and Cally. An extraordinary force between the two of them. Charles, sly and clever, charming and ambitious. Cally, a tornado, always ruffling feathers, prone to fighting, never shying away from sharing her thoughts and feelings.

She would have been a challenge at first, for Charles. He would have seen Cally as someone to tame, like taking in a feral cat.

Vivacia stares out of the window and up the hill.

They can't have lived there, mere miles away, all these years.

She thinks back to the very last time she saw Cally. That day on the road, Cally dolled up in a pencil skirt and jacket, clutching her suitcase. Looking so *un-Cally* that Vivacia had laughed. She remembers that interaction as though it were yesterday.

'*Do you have a job interview?*' Vivacia had asked.

'*Something like that.*' Cally had pulled Vivacia in for a hug and told her, '*You deserve to be happy. You're wonderful. You need to move on.*'

Cally had not been expecting to go a few miles up the hill to live in a caravan in an abandoned tip, not dressed like that. And perhaps they didn't, not straight away. Maybe there was another place, lies that ran on until the money ran out. A promise of riches, of city living, of far-flung places of paradise.

Yet, Cally had died in squalor, starved of food, water and sunlight in a caravan where the doors and windows didn't even open.

A pain grips Vivacia, sharp like glass, across her stomach. She bends double, tears silently falling down her cheeks.

She moves to the front of the house, watching out the window, just like Jackie used to.

Used to.

To the left, Ruth's holiday rental is in darkness. She thinks of Rob for a moment. His accident was horrific. But she can't deny that the threat that he turned out to be softens the blow of his death.

The car rolls up an hour later than they'd said.

Vivacia has spent the time pacing, chewing at her fingernails, wondering, worrying that one of them has spoken up, or Jackie has made the call. And instead of them coming home, a police car will arrive in their place.

For her.

But the car that arrives is sleek and black, and holds just a woman, and Rose and Dallas.

They've been sleeping, she can see, as she yanks open the front door and hurries down the path. Rose's face has a crease in her cheek; Dallas is yawning widely.

She scoops them up, sagging with relief as Rose's little arms reach around her and squeeze tightly. She tries her best to put on a professional front, as the social worker talks a hundred words a minute, nodding and agreeing in all the right places.

When the woman – Tara, Vivacia thinks her name was – leaves, Vivacia herds the children upstairs.

She offers them a drink, a snack, because nobody told her if they'd eaten, but Rose answers for both of them by pulling back her duvet and slipping into the bed.

'I'm here, all night, you just come and get me, okay?' she says as she kisses both of them.

She will shower, she decides. She will shower and then she will stay up, keep a watch on them. That way, she will be fresh for when the police turn up on her doorstep. And she won't miss a single moment of her last night with her babies.

After she's done in the bathroom, she drifts around her house, alternating between checking in on Rose and Dallas, and peering out into the dark night.

She ties her hair back in a messy bun, pulls on her trainers and a plain red T-shirt.

She's ready.

It's not even sunrise, but she's ready for them to take her away.

The world is monochromatic, the early morning grey. Soon, the indigo of the sky will burst into another day.

Vivacia pauses on the landing and looks out of the small window. Summer has truly arrived now. Not that she'll see it.

She drifts down the stairs, anticipation a cold, hard lump in her midsection.

The curtains are open. The community is quiet. The sky has turned from grey to yellow. It will be a lovely sunrise. It will be the last she sees for a very long time.

She forces herself to look over at Jackie's house. It is quiet, like nothing stirs inside.

What did Jackie do last night? Did she sleep? Did she move away from her constant position at the window? Did she look at the space where she has sat and stood and paced for years, knowing she'll never need to resume that position again? Did the family liaison officer that Ola promised turn up? If she did, Jackie would have sent her away.

Did Jackie break then, on her own on the first night without her daughter in the world? Did the tears finally fall from those steely grey, stern eyes? Did her home seem suddenly huge and empty, a stark realisation that there is nobody left for her?

A shiver wracks Vivacia's body; the stone that sits in her stomach grows, spreading until her arms and legs are tingling.

What if Jackie... hurt herself last night?

She's out the door in an instant. Charging down the front, speed-walking as though she's Portia or Chloe-Joy. But her steps falter as she nears Jackie's house. What is she going to find? Is this it? Is she destined to continue stumbling upon corpses, like Charles, like Cally, like Rob? A strange half-thought: is that her punishment?

The sound of an approaching car brings her to a complete stop. It rounds the corner, an unmarked car, but the driver is unmistakable. Detective Inspector Ola Demoski. Beside her, a younger officer, the same one who came that first day with all his bravado, and then was sick when he saw Charles emerging from the well.

They don't look in her direction, but head straight to Jackie's house.

She feels eyes on her, looks to the left and sees Ruth, standing outside her rental, her face twisted with sadness, cigarette almost burned down to the butt, forgotten in her hand.

They walk towards each other, meeting in the road near Ola's police car.

'I... I was going to see how Jackie is,' says Vivacia.

'You've got the children,' says Ruth.

Vivacia covers an ironic smile. One thing about Wolf's Pit will never change. News travels fast within this gated community.

'Yes,' she replies, simply.

There, at the edge of the road, Ruth beside her, Vivacia waits. Either for the private ambulance that will come for Jackie, or for Ola to come over to arrest her.

–

Ola emerges from Jackie's house after ten minutes. This time, she sees Vivacia. The other officer, the young one who vomited upon seeing the spectre that Lady Well flushed out, stands by the car. He gazes over their heads, past Vivacia's home, towards the well. He is pale, his expression unfathomable.

Ola throws a glare his way as she heads towards Vivacia.

Vivacia trembles, grips her arms to stop the tremors.

'I thought you were going to stay with her.' Ola's voice is sharp, accusing in its tone.

Vivacia draws a breath. 'Is she… Is…'

Ruth leans forward and says the words that Vivacia can't seem to. 'Is Jackie okay?'

Ola gives her a withering look.

'I mean, she's… coping?'

Ola sighs, as though this question is ridiculous. The exasperated exhalation pulls Vivacia back to the present.

Jackie is alive.

'She wanted me to go, last night. I stayed with her for a while and was heading over again now,' Vivacia says.

'Me too,' pipes up Ruth.

'Fine,' says Ola.

Vivacia hesitates. 'It's… okay to go over there?'

'Yes.' Ola frowns, throws them a small wave and turns to go back to the car.

The young officer snaps to attention at her approach, yanking open the passenger door and slumping into the seat. Now he averts his gaze, turning his head so he doesn't have to look at Wolf's Pit any longer.

Vivacia takes a step off the pavement towards Jackie's.

Ola's car does a neat three-point turn and trundles off the way it came.

'I'll come with you,' Ruth says.

Vivacia shakes her head. The children are inside, sleeping still. She doesn't want them to wake up alone. But she doesn't want to send Ruth to Jackie's in her place.

'Would you…' She stops, swallows and takes a deep breath. 'The children are asleep. I want to see Jackie, but I don't want them to wake up and find nobody in the house.'

Ruth pulls Vivacia to her and hugs her hard. 'It would be my honour, darling girl.'

Jackie's door is ajar, and the silence inside hangs heavy like fog. Vivacia pauses in the doorway, remembering the times when she would walk right on in without invitation.

A movement catches her eye: Jackie, in the lounge, her steps measured as she paces through towards the front door.

She stops sharply as she sees Vivacia.

Vivacia stalls too, unsure what to do or say.

'I'm going to tell the police what happened, you know,' says Jackie, steely eyes flashing.

'Yes,' Vivacia says. Her voice only wobbles a fraction, barely noticeable. Vaguely, she wonders why Jackie didn't tell Ola the truth when she was here only minutes ago.

She looks down at Jackie's feet, at the trainers she wears.

'I'm going up there first,' says Jackie in response to Vivacia's unasked question. 'I need to see.'

Panic rears, before Vivacia comes to her senses. Cally won't be there; they would have taken her away, zipped up in a black bag. Like Charles, but more solid.

Vivacia is unsure how to respond. Does Jackie want her to go too? She gives her the once-over. She looks fragile, thin, just the anger holding her together.

'I'll take you,' says Vivacia.

It will be hard, awful, horrible. Another punishment. Vivacia is glad to go back up that hill. She deserves to be there again.

'Where are they?' Vivacia's heart leaps as she realises Jackie is talking about the children.

Her own grandchildren, she reminds herself.

'Ruth is with them,' she replies.

Jackie says nothing further.

They skirt around the side, the same route that Vivacia took when she tracked the children. Jackie walks slightly ahead, purpose in her long strides.

They are quiet for a while, until Lady Well comes into view.

Vivacia doesn't want Jackie to look at it, or dwell on it, this unintended monument that was the catalyst for Cally's demise.

She focuses on the one thing that Jackie has so far steered clear of.

'Do you... Do you want to see the children?'

She sneaks a sideways glance at the older woman. Jackie stares ahead, up the hill, her eyes resolutely fixed in the distance.

'No,' she says.

Vivacia is stung on Rose and Dallas's behalf.

'They... They're not like *him*,' Vivacia says. 'They're all Cally.'

But how correct is that? she wonders to herself. It's true of Rose, she thinks. The stubborn nature, the beauty, the leadership. For Dallas, she isn't sure yet of who he really is. Yesterday's accident comes to mind. That small smile on his face as he stepped smartly to one side. Rob, skidding over the quarry's edge.

She shivers, unbidden.

It was an accident. Dallas is too young to know the consequences of his actions. He was simply being... a child.

He's not Charles, neither of them are.

They *can't* be.

'Children...' Jackie practically spits the word. 'She had children, by *him*.'

'They loved her, though.' Vivacia doesn't look at Jackie, can't stand the embittered look.

'And her, as a mother.' Jackie's voice is a sigh on the breeze.

'If you see them, I'm sure—'

'No.' The word shakes with finality. Just in case it's not clear, Jackie marches over to her until they are shoulder to shoulder. 'No, okay?'

Jackie turns, walks on once more, up the hill towards the place where her daughter died.

Vivacia, as always, follows.

There's police tape around the old refuse site, woven in and out of the railings, piercing the barbed wire, flapping in the gap in the fence, the place where Dallas and Rose made their escape.

This morning, Vivacia looks at the site with fresh eyes. When she came here, yesterday, she was solely concentrating on the children as they surged forward. She'd felt their emotions coming off them in waves: fear, urgency, despair. Their feelings matched her own, a sense of dread incoming.

There is none of that today. She's already seen the worst of it. Now, she can stand back, pause on the periphery, and take in the place where the two people who had once been such a big part of her life spent their last months or years.

Charles died around a year ago. Cally and the children were locked in here all that time. She recalls the empty food packaging in the caravan. They had food, a good enough bounty to last that long. When did it start to run out? When did the water stop working? How long did it take for Cally to starve to death? What had it felt like to live in one tiny room for a whole year?

She looks around the land from the outside, turning to take in the surrounding landscape.

It's a wilderness here. These fields that lead up from the hill don't belong to any local farmers or landowners. The land here is uncared for, and untended; nettles and weeds and wildflowers stand tall, competing in height with the grass.

Through the shrubbery, she can barely see into the old dump. If anyone were to walk past here, which nobody does, they would avert their gaze from the eyesore. Nothing to see here. Abandoned land.

Did Cally shout, regardless of the isolation? Did she scream for someone to help her, help her children? Did her dread grow, with each day that passed and there was still no sign of her children's father?

Vivacia glances at Jackie. The older woman has her arms wrapped around herself as she gazes forward.

'You don't need to go any further,' says Vivacia.

Jackie drops her arms, lifts her chin as though Vivacia's words are a challenge. She strides to the fence, pushes the wire roughly aside and ducks through.

Vivacia follows.

'What were they doing here?' Jackie looks at everything: the oil patches on the dried grass, evidence that once there were other vehicles here. The charred remains of bonfires once set. The windblown pages of books burned.

Vivacia hesitates for just one moment before telling Jackie her theory. Of how Charles came seeking something. Acceptance, a place where he could be as recognisable as Mr Bastille, or Ruth, or Blind Iris, or even Jackie herself. They all had their roles in the community and they were all sitting on a virtual goldmine with all that wasted land.

'He played the part of the foreman back home, of the organiser, the mediator,' says Vivacia. 'But then, even after he'd pulled it all together, he was still on the outside.' Vivacia barks a laugh, humourless and dry. 'Did you see that? Did you notice?' She feels her lip curling in a sneer.

Jackie's eyes are on her, small and hard. Vivacia rearranges her face, sombre and serious.

'He said that to me, one night.' Vivacia pauses, swallows again and again.

'What?' Jackie asks. 'What did he say?'

'He said, he'd had this vision, of filling the community with funds and status. But he'd got it wrong, and maybe it was better to live in a place where nobody owns anything.'

As one, they turn back to the land in front of them: a single caravan, broken down, sad and lonely amongst the scorched and charred grass.

'A cult.' Jackie spits the words.

Vivacia nods unhappily.

'Do you think there were others here?'

'Probably. Until they realised what Charles was really like. I imagine they left then.' The theory grows and strengthens, suddenly so clear to Vivacia.

'Once they started to leave, he felt like it was all slipping away from him again. Just like Wolf's Pit.' He would have seen what was coming, that Cally and her children would up and leave too.

He saw the risk, stopped it from happening.

The door to the caravan is ajar. Jackie hooks it open. The smell hits them both like a wall. Somehow, it seems worse than it was yesterday. Or maybe, the day before, the sight of Cally lying dead dulled all her other senses.

Jackie crumples, one hand still on the door, her knees in the dry, scratchy earth. Her head hangs low, her rounded back heaves.

31

THE CHILDREN

It was an adventure, Rose told herself as she chivvied Dallas along. It was something exciting and new, and it was going to be Good Fun.

Mother used to like Good Fun. Back when Father wasn't angry or burning things. When there were other people with them or when they were in that place before. The bonfire would be going but it was for nice things like marshmallows and keeping warm, not for putting books on. There was music, and everyone laughed and there were other children to play with. The adults danced and all of them apart from Father drank stuff that didn't smell nice but seemed to make them happy.

That was Good Fun, said Mother, back when she was allowed to be called Mummy.

This adventure was a little different. So far, Rose had to admit it wasn't Good Fun. It was raining again, and earlier that had been brilliant because she'd been so thirsty, and it was drink coming from the sky. But now it was cold and not enjoyable at all, and she was so hungry that she was sure there were little teeth in her stomach, and they were eating her insides, and it was just so wet out here.

They took a wrong turn, Rose not even realising they'd veered off the path until the white-bordered quarry's edge came into view.

They sat there a while anyway, staring over the huge crater in the ground.

Dallas scuffed with his shoe, sending showers of stones tumbling down into the centre.

Rose took his arm and pulled him back. 'Stop it,' she told him. 'If you fall down there, you won't come up again.'

He looked back into the cavernous hole, his eyes wide with wonder.

'Back this way.' Rose dropped his arm, fought her way back through the narrow path.

She didn't check if he was following.

She wondered if he would, or if they would go their separate ways now.

She tried to imagine life without her twin. Marvelled at the freedom it suggested, not having to keep an eye on him all the time. Not having to think ahead of possible dangers, wondering if he had picked up an item that was something seemingly innocent but with the potential to cause harm.

She heard his footsteps behind her, the sound of his breathing as he fought to catch up.

Rose sighed, waited for him to reach her.

They moved down a hill, carefully because the grass was slippery, and even though they moved with caution, Dallas slid over a couple of times. He glared at her each time and bared his tiny little teeth.

It was a huge hill, Rose saw now, just going down and down and down, and looking like there might not be an end to it.

There will be, she told herself. *There has to be.*

—

So much of the journey was missing. She didn't realise until later. Big gaps in her memory. She remembered swatches, like a snatched dream that faded in and out. Wet grass, more rain, a deep hunger. Dallas falling, time and time again. Dallas swaying until she made him sit down. Dallas hissing while silent tears tracked a clean path down his muddy face.

She cleaned him as best she could, doing the spit and polish with her sleeve like Mother did once upon a time. The mud went, but his face looked grass-stained now, no matter how much Rose scrubbed at him.

She looked at her own hand, saw the same shade of green.

Something wrong, she realised, only thinking in clipped sentences now, unable to form full trains of thought.

The sun vanished entirely, and for a while there was a period of nothing but blackness. Dallas snarled some more and Rose made him sit again. No point walking in darkness.

She dug in her pockets, pulling out Mother's paper. The map was there, another one too, but the third was missing. The long, boring letter was gone.

Rose cried a little. She had so little to own that to lose something was disappointing.

Later, when Rose's tears had dried, a stripe appeared in the sky, the smallest glimpse of a crescent, only to vanish almost instantly as the clouds moved in again.

The remainder of that night on the hill was a mystery. Rose didn't think she slept. Dallas was quiet. The next thing she remembered was a hazy sunrise, sweeping red and purple.

A shepherd's warning.

More rain.

She dragged Dallas up again, made him march on.

The landscape changed a little. The never-ending hill stopped being quite so steep, though they continued to stumble time and time again.

She recalled looking at the map, wet now, the eyeliner bits causing rivers of black on the page like tears. The one remaining scrap of paper she tried to protect by leaving in her pocket.

Later, maybe the next day, maybe more days had passed, the ground levelled a lot more. There was undergrowth now, and bushes with fruit on. She recognised the gooseberries. They were green and veiny, hard and sour. She plucked them and stuffed them in her mouth in abundance.

She pulled Dallas to sit atop a circular, brick-ringed thing and put some in his hand. He stared down at them, his face blank.

After the fruit, her eyes saw things a little bit better. She could see houses. Proper, brick-built ones, like the one she remembered from years and years ago.

These ones were even fancier, she thought now. Not the ones at the back, directly in front of her. Those were small. But beyond those, there were new houses. Red bricks, and rich people lived in them; she could see the fancy balconies that were affixed to the back.

She left Dallas where he was and scooted to the right, following the line of the black iron fence.

The fence made her shiver. There was a fence where they'd lived up the hill. It had kept them imprisoned just as much as the door that wouldn't unlock.

But there had been a tear in that fence.

Rose peered closer, trailing her hand along the wet bars.

There. A gap.

An escape.

Satisfied, Rose left the fence and travelled further along it until it turned a corner.

She walked past the last small house, and she was on the other side, directly opposite rich man's land.

The gardens were beautifully kept. *Manicured*, the word was, like how Mother's nails used to be. In one of them was a swimming pool!

Rose stifled a gasp as a woman emerged from the rear of one of these homes. She had some children with her – three children, two boys and a girl.

Rose stared in envy at the girl. Her coat, a proper rain jacket, and a hat and most of all the wellington boots she wore, red and shiny.

Rose glanced down at her soaking wet clothes that were dirty, old and torn, and felt a bolt of longing in her chest.

One of the boys spoke, his voice a loud yell, and Rose, after hearing nothing but silence and tears for so long, blanched.

The woman, the mother, shushed him as she pulled a ringing phone out of her pocket and began speaking to someone at the other end.

The woman paused, turned her head back towards her house and yelled out, 'Richard! Are you coming or not? Hurry up!'

Rose darted her gaze to the house, expecting to see another child. But it was a man who came out, grinning, hopping from foot to foot as he pulled on his own wellies.

The woman's husband. And yet, she dared to speak to him like that! And even more thrilling for Rose, the man didn't seem to mind. His face didn't go all twisty like Father's did when Mother had disrespected him. This man seemed to think his wife's words were amusing!

Rose's mouth hung open at the sight of this new world.

She ducked away, walked back to where Dallas sat, awaiting her return.

'This is the place,' she whispered to him. 'But we've got to be careful.'

Stranger danger. Words not from Mother, nor Father. Who was it who explained it to her?

Heather. A woman called Heather. Rose was pleased at her ability to remember, because Heather had been a long, long time ago, when Rose was really small.

Heather had come to live alongside them. She grew plants in her trailer that smelled funny. She hooked up electricity to keep her plants warm, and she was Mother's friend back when Mother was Mummy.

'There are people who don't like the way we live, Rose,' Heather had explained. 'They might come here and take you away, and if they do, you don't tell them a goddamn thing.'

'Heather!' Rose's mother had sounded shocked. 'Don't frighten her!'

Later, Mother admitted Heather had a point. 'You don't talk to anyone that you don't know,' she warned.

Rose remembered it now, and she pulled Dallas's arm to make him look at her. 'No talking,' she said. 'When they come, you don't talk.' She looked him up and down, and added, 'And you don't do anything... bad.'

His eyes were faraway, as if he wasn't really listening. Rose figured it didn't matter. Dallas didn't talk, not even to her anymore. Not out loud, anyway.

She saw a man first, one with a large bag on his back. He huffed and puffed his way out of the trees, coughing as he stumbled past them.

Rose remained still. She pinched Dallas's hand so he wouldn't move. The man didn't see them.

Not long later a woman appeared. She glanced once at the man, now halfway up the hill, and then looked straight to them.

Like she was expecting them.

As if she had been *waiting* for them.

Rose almost said something, remembering her own rule just in time. She clamped her mouth shut as the woman approached.

She stood in front of them, held out her hands like Mother used to do.

The woman waited until they were both holding her hands and told them that they were going home.

32

VIVACIA – BEFORE

She expected fear and remorse in equal measure, as she remained in a crouch over his dead body.

Fear won out, pulsing through her in red waves, pushing and growing until there was no room left for remorse, anguish, guilt or regret.

She was glad, but she was scared.

It was getting late, not much chance of anyone stumbling upon her. Vivacia knew the routines of her neighbours as well as she knew her own. At the crack of dawn, that chef sometimes came down here, foraging for berries to put in the freshly made porridge, prepared with oats that would even now be soaking overnight. Ruth sometimes joined him, rambling along, doing her best to insert herself into the newcomers' lives. Portia might be out for an early jog. The husbands would leave early to get a round in before heading off to their Very Important Jobs.

She had six hours. Five, to be on the safe side.

She could leave him here, she figured, reeking of alcohol. The conclusion might be made that he fell and hit his head while intoxicated.

Vivacia crawled as close to him as she dared and inhaled.

But he didn't reek of alcohol. He smelled as he always did these days, when she saw him, of earth and soil, slightly musty, a little bit unwashed.

Vivacia sat back and observed him.

What had become of him? When – and why – did he transition from that smart gentleman who never had a hair out of place and smelled of too much cologne?

Before the accident that took her family's lives.

She heard a sharp gasp, realising as the fury rose again that it had come from her.

It wasn't an accident, was it? He'd said as much. He'd admitted what he'd done.

She hissed, clenching her fists to stop herself pummelling his dead body. Instead, she turned and hit out at the grass, at the wedged-in bricks of Lady Well, at the very earth itself.

The lid of the well shimmied and shook, letting out a clatter that resonated across the quiet land, echoing as it came to a slow stop, slightly askew.

As silence descended once more, and nobody came to investigate the racket, Vivacia knew exactly what she was going to do.

The lid was relatively light. *Flimsy, cheap*, she remembered thinking when the contractors came to fit it. No expense spared inside the gates, but here, round the back, cosmetic appearance didn't really matter.

It was around the size of a truck tyre, made from an inexpensive alloy.

Vivacia peered into the open well. It was deep, dank, black, and smelled rather foul.

He was hard to move. Inch by inch he shifted, her hands underneath his arms, her progress measured by the tracks that the heels of his boots made.

As she tugged him the last few feet, she thought of *that night*. Of Charles going to Stephanie's house, of what he might have told them to lure them out in the car. He thought he'd seen Cally in the lane. That she looked wary, undecided whether to come home to Jackie or not. That he was unsure about approaching her, because let's face it, Cally never really took to Charles. He didn't want to knock on Jackie's door either, and the reasons were twofold. Jackie might be angry with Cally, might startle her into flight again. Also, Charles might be mistaken, and he'd hate to shoot down Jackie's hope in such a manner. Maybe Cally needed a friendly face or two, people she'd known her whole life, to coax her the rest of the way to Wolf's Pit.

Vivacia imagined Kay, her excitement at being a possible hero, and Stephanie, not thinking twice about what her daughter's husband was telling her, thinking only of the girl she'd considered one of her own when growing up.

Kay hadn't even stopped to put her shoes on. Vivacia knew that because she'd counted them in the hallway, later, after. Her wellington boots, her walking boots, her summer shoes and her sandals. All there, which meant she'd gone out in her slippers, so desperate to aid her neighbour in her search for her missing daughter.

Never before had Vivacia allowed her musings to go any further than her mother and grandmother leaving their house. Her mind would shut down, before she even envisaged the door closing behind them.

Now, however, as she felt her muscles screaming in her shoulders, she let herself go there. She needed the strength that it would lend her.

Kay, driving in her slippers, so used to these roads that she knew as well as the lines on the palm of her hands. The descent down the steep hill, normally driven in a flash, the belated thought that they needed to slow, to look out for the missing girl. The pump of the brakes, once, twice, then the subsequent horror that she couldn't stop the car.

What was she thinking at that moment? Was she already thinking ahead, planning on keeping control until the road levelled out, enabling her to roll to a stop on the incline?

The thought would have been dashed, though, as the slight figure of dear Serafina appeared in the road.

Maybe just a single moment for the thought to cross Kay's mind. *What have I done?*

249

Then came the fire and the flames.

Vivacia let out a half-grunt, half-shriek, and pulled Charles's body once more with all her might.

So hard she pulled, that his upper body overshot the well opening, his hips, legs and feet dangling over the top.

Vivacia sobbed, released her grip from his arms and watched as he slid down, down, down.

She dry-heaved, bent over, hands on her knees, hawking and spitting into Lady Well.

Then, she straightened up with effort, pulled the flimsy lid over without looking inside and staggered dizzily back home.

—

Charles, and her murder of him, was not her first thought upon waking. As normal, as it had been for three years, when she opened her eyes, it was Stephanie on her mind, and Kay, followed swiftly by thoughts of Alex and Elizabeth, how they would be now, where they would be and who they were with.

But that morning – the morning after – thoughts of Charles followed swiftly on the heels of those he had taken from her.

She examined herself carefully as she lay in the bed at the back of the house. Still no angst, no remorse, no guilt.

Regret was there, in a small dose, that she hadn't acted sooner. Hadn't done this a long time ago.

She decided she would go to Portia's barbeque. She would prepare something, a side dish, maybe a dessert too. A pie, and she would source the fruits from the thick, lush bushes that lined the outer fences. They wouldn't be ripe yet, not this early, but she could counteract that.

She'd learned from her grandmother, after all.

It would mean walking past him. Past the well. But of course, she knew that. She *needed* to do that, she acknowledged as she pulled on a pair of jeans and a shirt.

From the kitchen, she grabbed a basket, one of Kay's old ones. As an afterthought, she rifled in the old cabinet, pushing aside things until she found what she was seeking. Stepping outside, she made her way down the garden to the gap in the fence.

She headed to the bushes to the left, pleased to see the green fruits in abundance. She picked handfuls until her basket was full.

With no more time to stall, she made her way to Lady Well.

She placed the basket on the ground by her feet and took a furtive look around. Nobody here yet; the joggers and dog walkers had either been and gone or had yet to pass by.

A thin trickle of sweat rolled a path down her shoulder blades as she pushed the lid to the side.

One second, just a single half-glance was enough to see a length of red material, the flesh of a hand, the flash of a wristwatch.

From beneath the fruits in her basket, she brought out the three-quarter-full bottle of vodka. She poured it into Lady Well until it was almost empty. She tossed the bottle in after, watched the dregs as they soaked into that red cotton jumper.

Vivacia pulled the lid to cover the well. Only when he was once more concealed did she let what she had done sink in.

Not a dream.

Not a glitch of her mind, which he always said was stupid, nor a fantasy.

It was real.

She grabbed her basket and fled.

—

In front of her house, she sat on the stoop, the gooseberries now forgotten by her side. She would have to sit out here, she thought, in the coming days or weeks, maybe even years. The rear of her home – that lovely landscape that was still untouched by machinery and bricks and mortar – was sullied now.

Vivacia smiled and tilted her face up to the sunshine. It was a small price to pay.

'Have you seen him?' The voice was so stern, so ragged, that Vivacia didn't recognise it.

She jerked upright, shaded her eyes and found herself looking at Jackie Jenkins.

'Jackie.' Vivacia pushed herself up to standing.

She hadn't seen the woman for ages.

She remembered the day of the funeral, three years past now, the hand Jackie had extended, the unsaid words: we're both alone, I need a daughter, you need a mother. One single day she'd paid a visit to Jackie, and it hadn't gone very well.

Now, three years after Kay and Stephanie's death, Vivacia was slowly coming back to life. Jackie, seven years after Cally had left for the final time, was still sullen and bitter.

'Are you okay, Jackie?' Vivacia asked.

'Where is he?' Jackie avoided Vivacia's question and stared down at her. 'Charles, where is he?'

Vivacia was aware of a dull, thudding beat in her chest. 'I–I don't know. He doesn't come home very often.'

The sun dipped behind a rogue cloud and Vivacia barely managed to stop herself gasping.

Jackie's face! Since Vivacia could remember, it was on the slightly harder side – always had been, having to deal with her errant daughter – but these days... Jackie looked a hundred years old.

'He was here, last night, I saw him.' Jackie narrowed her eyes.

'I didn't see him. He didn't come home.' The lie came easy and fast, as natural as breathing.

Jackie glared past Vivacia, sweeping the hallway behind her, as though Charles was in there, hiding.

'Shit.' The hard look fell from Jackie's features. In that moment she was crestfallen, her face filled with despair.

Vivacia blinked at her, not knowing what to say. Why was Jackie looking for Charles? She never bothered with him, not even when he appeared to win around Kay and Stephanie.

'Do... Do you want a cup of coffee?' Vivacia reached out a hand, her fingers grazing the soft fabric of Jackie's top.

Jackie moved away, out of reach. The granite face returned.

'He's not come home?'

Vivacia shook her head. 'I haven't seen him for a long while now.' There was a sudden idea, a spark inside her. She raised her eyes to Jackie. 'I think he's left me.'

Jackie's mouth worked, all the lines and wrinkles shifting. She put the back of her hand to her forehead and stared at Vivacia for what seemed an awfully long time.

'Good,' Jackie said, eventually.

Vivacia swallowed.

Then, Jackie was gone, striding away from Vivacia's house, heading not towards her own, but towards the pedestrian gate, left open as always.

Vivacia sat back down on the step and tried to get her breathing under control.

—

Later, the well drew her in again. This time, she observed it from the back window of the bedroom.

The lid had been left off in the past. By kids messing around, by ramblers who were interested in the folklore of Lady Well, by large foraging animals perhaps? Who knew?

Vivacia didn't, and before now, she'd never given it a second thought. She hadn't cared if the lid was on or off.

Some residents did. That Aster Gould who lived in plot two. It was almost the furthest new build from the well, but Aster was a workout freak, and a helicopter mum. She led her little tribe of mini-me children on a stomping walk three times a week, out of the gates, down the lane, up past Ruth's new home, which was once Stephanie's, past the back of Jackie's and Ruth's old bungalow, through the woodland and past Lady Well.

If the lid was off, they all knew about it. A couple of times, Aster had actually gone through the trouble of printing little leaflets and posting them through all the doors, asking for them all to be vigilant and, *if the lid is off, put it on*. She'd called a meeting, once, Vivacia recalled, wanting the well to be permanently covered, filled with concrete, welded shut.

The older ones had piled in then, Ruth, Iris, even Mr Bastille. Lady Well was an historical site. The new, rich people might not have any respect for it, but the original residents did.

Vivacia didn't go to that meeting, but she heard about it from both Iris and Portia.

Vivacia shivered despite the heat of the room.

She could weigh it down, maybe. Take those old bricks that looked like roof tiles – like the one she killed Charles with – and stack them on top of the lid. Children might be less inclined to move it, then. Foxes and the like would find it difficult and would leave it be.

She turned from the window, drifted down the stairs, through the kitchen, and headed over to the fence.

How many times will she have to do this? she wondered. Will this damn well and the horrible secret inside bring her here every day, every night?

No, she told herself. She just needed to make sure it was secured, that the bloody lid wasn't going to be popping off every five minutes.

Alongside the fence at the back of Vivacia's house, trailing ivy grew, long tentacles intertwining with the blackberry bushes. She pulled the ivy, draping it over the well, and picked up a few of the bricks to lay atop the lid.

She looked at the one she held. Was this the one that had delivered the final, fatal blow?

She hefted it in her hand and frowned. Like that night, it seemed far too light to inflict much damage.

'Hello, there!' The voice, one unknown to Vivacia, startled her.

Carefully, she set the brick on the lid of the well and observed him.

A stranger. Tall, wearing a huge backpack and good rambling shoes.

She flicked a look at him, what she hoped passed for a smile between people passing each other on a walk. Brushing her hands on her knees, she turned back towards home.

'Do you live here?'

She stopped, regarded him carefully. 'Why?' she asked.

If he noticed her brusque tone, he didn't show it. 'I just moved in,' he said. 'I'm Rob. Rob Caver. I think we're neighbours.' He gestured towards Ruth's house. 'Neighbours might be pushing it. You're pretty isolated back here, aren't you?'

His words could have been perceived as a threat. This man, the fact that he knew she was alone, at the back, where nobody came and nobody saw. She scrutinised his face. Was that a genuine smile? Or a leer?

Her gaze drifted to Lady Well. If only he knew. *She* was the threat now, not him, this stranger who had come to stay.

'Hi, I'm Vivacia,' she said. She started to walk, was almost past him, when he spoke again.

'Can I call you V?'

She blinked. 'My name is Vivacia.' She regarded him a little closer. His face was either friendly and open, or entitled and expectant. She had been alone for so long that she could no longer tell any intentions.

She cleared her throat. 'There's really no need to call me anything.'

He said something else as she walked away.

This time, she didn't turn around.

33

VIVACIA – NOW

Vivacia rushes to Jackie, puts a hand on the older woman's spine. When Jackie doesn't move, Vivacia slides her hands under her arms and pulls her to standing.

'Come on,' she says. 'I'm taking you home.'

Jackie, to Vivacia's horror, doesn't protest.

Vivacia berates herself silently as she guides Jackie back down the hill. What was she thinking, letting Cally's mother go up there?

What is wrong with her?

Why is she so... so *stupid*?

She shakes her head violently to dispel Charles's words. So deeply imbedded are they, so often he's been proved right.

She is stupid. Soon, the police will come for her, and what then for the children? Jackie isn't interested in them. Jackie dislikes them deeply, purely for who their father is.

They will be put in the system, spinning round and round to be released once they are eighteen.

Vivacia whimpers and stuffs a hand to her mouth.

Jackie, smothered by her own grief, doesn't notice.

As they begin the descent of the last part of the hill, and Wolf's Pit comes into view, Vivacia drops back. She studies Jackie through narrowed eyes, surveying the stooped shape, the shoulders that hang heavy.

Onto the road they move, and as Jackie is about to veer off onto her own pathway, Vivacia reaches out a hand. She touches Jackie's wrist lightly.

'Come to mine,' she says. 'Nobody is there,' she lies. 'Ruth will have taken the children out.'

Jackie's hesitation is barely noticeable, but Vivacia pounces on it. She curls her fingers around Jackie's hand, applies pressure.

In the hallway where Jackie has been a thousand times before, Vivacia feels the old cottage settle around her. It's dead quiet, no sign of Ruth or the children. Anxiety pinches at her. Where are they? Where has she taken them? Have they spilled everything to her, the kindly, friendly stranger who was there when they woke up?

She runs upstairs, darting into their room, seeing the empty beds.

Then, a single noise, a laugh, coming from outside. She opens the window and peers into the garden.

There they are. Ruth has a skipping rope, is using it nimbly, expertly, as though she's a child herself, and not a woman in her seventies.

Dallas and Rose stare at her. Like Vivacia, they can't seem to believe their eyes.

She closes the window quietly, moves downstairs, past Jackie, who is still standing in the hall, and moves into the kitchen to flick the kettle on.

She reaches for the coffee granules, scoops in three spoonfuls, good and strong, and busies herself with mugs and milk.

She feels Jackie's presence in the kitchen, rather than hearing her. She turns around, sees Jackie looking at the table in the centre of the room.

It's a family table now, Vivacia realises, with everything it holds. Sticky patches from days-old breakfast juice. There's a lone crayon, snapped in two, a discarded hairband from a collection that Vivacia had found and tried, unsuccessfully, to use in Rose's hair.

Jackie slumps into a chair, stares at the wall in front of her.

Vivacia thinks of that other piece of paper, the one with Jackie's name written on it. Her face is hot with shame that she concealed it.

I am a monster.

The kettle clicks off. Both of them start.

At the same time, there is a swish as the patio door is pulled open. Ruth is first through it, her face an equal measure of concern and cheer when she sees who is sitting at the table.

Jackie has turned her head, noted the three figures at the door. She snaps back to stare ahead, her hands balling into fists.

What she had planned is happening, a forced meeting, but now it has come to fruition, Vivacia hesitates.

Jackie glares at her. Ruth remains in the doorway, effectively blocking Dallas and Rose from entering.

It is Ruth who breaks the deadlock.

'Shall I make tea?' she asks.

She strides in, embracing Jackie as she passes her. 'I'm so sorry, Jackie,' she says.

Jackie remains motionless. She does not return Ruth's embrace.

Long moments of silence. Vivacia watches as Jackie straightens in her chair.

'Coffee,' she says – snaps, really. 'I have coffee.'

Vivacia exhales.

Tenterhooks now. Everything – the children's future – rests on what happens next.

'Come in, children,' she says, and is pleased that her voice sounds semi-normal.

It would be natural to introduce them; she needs to do so, to project a sense of normality into this little scenario. But there is nothing normal about this.

Ruth, once again, seems to know exactly what to do.

'Kids, come and help me with all this stuff,' she calls. 'First one to carry the biscuit tin to the table gets an extra one.'

They move like lightning, so far from the sluggish, malnourished children they were when they arrived here. They've been with her for long enough for Vivacia to know that it's not starvation driving them now, but simply being children who have been offered a challenge with a food-based reward.

Rose is quicker, the leader, the determined one, skidding to a stop in her socked feet on the tiled floor. She misjudges the distance, barging into Ruth's leg. She does a comedy skit, pretending that she's been knocked off balance. Rose breathes out a giggle that is barely audible as she reaches for the biscuit jar and carries it carefully to the table, Dallas in her wake.

Vivacia slides into a chair and looks at Jackie. Jackie's eyes are fixed on Rose, but the expression on her face is impossible to discern.

Dallas comes over, leans against his sister's leg. Carefully, Rose takes three biscuits out of the jar. She slides one over to Dallas. She breaks her extra, 'winner' biscuit in half and passes that to him too.

Vivacia hears Jackie sigh.

She pounces on it.

'Children,' she says, 'this is Jackie. This,' she turns to face their grandmother, 'is Rose, and Dallas.'

Jackie sighs again, her eyes on the tabletop now.

Ruth comes, the aroma of the coffee strong in the air. She places the mug down in front of Jackie.

Jackie hooks a finger into the handle and raises her eyes to look at the children. 'Hi,' she says.

Her voice cracks, and the single word is almost as inaudible as Rose's laugh.

The children don't answer her, but they shoot her a single, curious look.

Vivacia doesn't want to overdo it. If she pushes, if she keeps them in Jackie's sight long enough, will Jackie remember not who their mother was, but instead concentrate on their paternity?

The anxiety is palpable. She imagines it spreading like a virus, floating on the air across to smother Jackie. Vivacia flicks her eyes to Ruth. The older woman must know what Jackie is feeling. How hard it is for her to see her girl's children, who are also the children of the man who effectively killed Cally.

Vivacia feels tears spring to her eyes.

No, she reminds herself, silently. *He didn't do that. I did.*

Ruth locks on her gaze and pinches her lips together.

'Hey, kids, we've only watered half the garden,' she says. 'Are you going to help me finish the rest?'

They turn as one, biscuits finished, moving to the patio and out into the garden.

Vivacia shoots Ruth a grateful look.

'It's hard to believe how dry it is out there now, after all that rain. How quick the weather turns,' Ruth says, conversationally, as she follows the children. Just outside the patio she picks up a watering can, an old-fashioned metal one that used to belong to Kay.

Vivacia hasn't seen it for years. She wonders where Ruth found it.

Jackie stands abruptly, her chair scraping on the floor. 'I have to go,' she says. 'I have to speak to the police.'

'Oh.' Vivacia's heart lurches in her chest as she stands up. Jackie's coffee is barely touched, still steaming on the tabletop. 'You could stay,' she says. 'Have something to eat…' she trails off helplessly, looking into the garden.

Rose is standing at the fence. Her usual sentry point, staring up the unseen hill to the place they came from.

Vivacia's throat tightens. Will Rose stand there forever? What does she see? Will it always be imprinted on her memory – those last days in the caravan, what she saw yesterday – or will it fade over time?

'I hated you.' Jackie's voice, when she speaks, is low and brittle.

Vivacia starts and turns back to face the woman she's known all her life.

'If you could have kept your husband happy, he wouldn't have been interested in Cally,' Jackie says.

Vivacia lowers her head as her eyes fill with tears.

She doesn't realise Jackie has gone, until she hears the click of the front door as she closes it softly behind her.

Vivacia sinks back down to sit at the table.

–

Ruth has rallied today. Vivacia can't help but think of Charles: how, when Kay and Stephanie died, he didn't comfort her, but instead saw it as an opportunity for coercion.

Ruth has stayed here, making herself useful, getting food together, interacting with the children, giving them things to do, dressing it up as a game.

Just like Kay, just like Stephanie would have.

Later, they are all in the lounge. The children are there, surrounded by toys; a deck of playing cards is scattered on the carpet. The television is on, background noise. Ruth seems to have settled herself in for the evening. For once, Vivacia is grateful.

Vivacia tries to rally herself. She had thought last night would be her last night here, but tonight definitely is. She wants this sense of family, something to hold on to when she's serving a life sentence.

She sits on the sofa, legs folded underneath her. The curtains are open. She watches Jackie's house, not even trying to stay hidden.

The lights are on in Jackie's kitchen. Every so often, a shadow passes the windows, as though Jackie is in there, pacing.

What is she thinking, as she walks up and down in there? That Vivacia, essentially, though inadvertently, took the life away from her daughter, and needs to pay in a court of law? Or are Rose and Dallas on her mind, that fleeting glimpse into the lives they have here, in this cottage, with Vivacia?

Vivacia flicks her gaze from Jackie's house to the road, keenly listening for the sound of a car engine and sirens snaking up the hill, or the sight of headlights or flashing blues.

Her mobile phone pings, announcing a text message. Vivacia glances at where it sits on the table. She's left it on since Charles's body was found, and after, once the children were officially in her care.

She reaches for it, sees it is a text message.

> Hi, V. Just wondering if Rose and Dallas would like a play date tomorrow? Oliver, Cooper and Baker have been enjoying the pool since the weather got better.
> Let me know, Aster xoxoxo

Wordlessly, Vivacia passes the phone to Ruth.

She ponders as Ruth reads it. Aster's older kids are in Rose and Dallas's age range. Oliver is eight, Cooper is six. The youngest, the only girl, Baker, is five.

She looks at the children, heads bent close together. They are playing some intricate game with the deck of cards that now snakes along the carpet towards the fireplace.

Have they interacted with children in the past? Were there other kids in what she's starting to think of as a commune?

Regardless, Rose and Dallas are not in the commune now. They are here, in the real world, and no matter what happens to Vivacia, they will never be returned to the awful, barren place at the top of the hill.

Her mind ticks on, reaching further forward. It's up to Vivacia to secure that future for the children. The more people see them here, and get to know them, the more likely they will be to fall in love with them, just like Vivacia has.

She thinks of Aster, of what she knows about her. Admittedly, it's not much. She does know that Aster has three children, has the money and the time and the initiative to give them everything they could ever want.

Things that Vivacia has scoffed at in the past; the fact that Aster is a seemingly overprotective, helicopter mum. But she includes her kids in everything she does: her daily walks, baking those awful-but-healthy things like vegan banana nut scones. Although she's got the finances, she doesn't hand them over to a paid nanny or an au pair.

'I've seen their pool, it's very nice!' Ruth has finished reading the text and hands back her phone.

Vivacia takes it, her mind wandering from Aster to the woman across the street.

She twists in her chair again to peer out of the window. The lights are still on over there, Jackie is still inside.

Why isn't she calling the police? Why didn't she call them the instant she walked out earlier? Why has Vivacia not been arrested yet?

Vivacia slips from the chair to her knees, beside Rose.

Rose turns to face her. Large, green eyes, golden flecks like marble.

Vivacia holds back a gasp at how beautiful the little girl is. A memory flashes to her, clear as day, of this girl when she came here. The green skin, the eyes, red as the morning sky that announced the incoming rain of biblical proportions. The stick-thin arms, the belly, grossly swollen.

Now, with love, care, food, air, exercise, she looks normal.

Vivacia strokes Rose's cheek. Externally, they are perfect. They could give Aster Gould's kids a run for their money. But what lies inside?

Rose pulls away from Vivacia's touch and turns to Dallas. Though she doesn't touch him, he starts, looks to her, as though she has called his name.

An unseen, unheard conversation, Vivacia is certain of it. The tells are there: Dallas pursing his lips as if deep in thought, a response to whatever Rose has 'said' to him.

Finally, as one, they nod. A single, identical, jerk of their heads.

Rose turns back to Vivacia. 'We're staying here,' she says, clear as day.

Vivacia gasps, shoots a look at Ruth, who is smiling through tears that freely fall.

Rose hasn't spoken much at all, but each time she has, she's been in distress.

This is the first time that they have heard Rose speak in a manner that doesn't come from trauma.

We're staying here.

Belatedly, the full impact of Rose's statement hits Vivacia like a physical blow.

God, she wants this. She wants these children in this home, amongst these people. It's all she's ever wanted, and it's always been denied to her.

Now, on the periphery of having it all, it's being snatched away once more. She deserves that, she knows, but she doesn't want to lose this.

Vivacia pushes her hands into the carpet and stands up.

'Ruth, are you okay if I pop over the road?'

The older woman swipes at her face. 'Of course, lovely girl. We're fine here, right, kids?'

They look at her, this woman they've known only a day, and return to their game.

—

On the walk over the road to Jackie's house, the hope swirls and dances inside. Briefly, as she steps off the kerb, it switches to anger. She is furious at the unfairness of everything.

But then *his* voice is in her ear.

You killed her, because you killed me. I told you not to mess with me.

And then the heaviness is back, dragging down her heart, tightening and squeezing a fist around her lungs.

By the time she reaches Jackie's door, she's almost in tears.

The door, she sees, is ajar. Vivacia pushes it open, and all those years come screaming back. Her coming in here, going straight up the stairs to Cally's bedroom where her friend would

264

inevitably be in bed. Cally coming over to hers, letting herself in. The whole village left their doors unlocked, as though it were 1950s England.

The thought runs through her mind now, and for the first time she wonders how the old-timers felt when they saw the gates going up, and the fences.

Everyone locks their door these days.

Which is why it's given Vivacia a little kick of fear that Jackie's door is ajar.

She takes a deep breath and barrels through.

'Hello?' she calls, and her voice sounds nothing like her own.

'Yeah, here.' There's a shuffling sound coming from the kitchen. 'Thanks for coming out, I realise it's... Oh.' Jackie stops talking when she sees who her visitor is. 'It's you.'

Vivacia's heart drums a beat in her chest. 'W-who did you think it was?' she asks.

Jackie shrugs and leans against the doorframe of the kitchen. 'That officer, Diminski.'

Vivacia doesn't correct her on DI Demoski's name.

'Oh,' she says. 'I-I'd hoped to talk to you. First, before you... Before you talked to the police.'

Jackie sniffs out a little huff. 'You'd better come in, then. I suppose it does concern you, after all.'

Vivacia hurries down the hallway and into the brightly lit kitchen. Now she's here, now that Jackie is in front of her, she's lost for words. All the intent she had back at her own home has vanished. All that is on her mind now is how long she's got to change Jackie's mind before Detective Inspector Demoski arrives.

Vivacia stands awkwardly opposite Jackie in the kitchen, the place where she's stood hundreds of times before. There's a scent in here, notes of coconut, the tropical aroma hitting Vivacia hard.

It's Cally's smell.

Underneath the fags and the booze, this scent was the one that defined Cally.

Vivacia inhales as she looks around to identify it.

There it is, a Jo Malone candle, burning on the windowsill. Vivacia stares at it. Jackie follows her gaze.

'She bought the perfume, do you remember? A hundred quid. She didn't work, did she? I asked her where she got the money. She never told me.'

Vivacia nods. She knows where Cally got the money. From Jackie's own purse. But she'll never tell her that. She promised back then, and now, it's the least Vivacia can do.

'After she went, the house was... It started to smell like a normal house. I–I couldn't stand it. So I bought that.' Jackie raises her chin defiantly, as though Vivacia is going to scoff or laugh at her.

For Vivacia, it's the softest side of Jackie she's ever seen.

'I suppose you want a coffee?' Jackie asks. 'The kettle just boiled.'

Vivacia draws a breath. She hadn't expected to be offered anything by Jackie.

'Yes, please,' she says.

Jackie stares at her for a long moment before turning her back and busying herself at the worktop. She moves deftly, opening drawers and cupboards, pulling out spoons and sugar, the paper rustling as she opens a new packet of ground coffee.

'Get the milk out if you want some,' instructs Jackie.

Vivacia does as she's told and waits in an excruciating silence as Jackie sets about pouring the two mugs. Jackie flicks her a look as she opens the drawer in front of her a crack and slides something back in. Vivacia can't gauge what Jackie is thinking tonight. She's so aware that her whole future hinges on this impromptu coffee date that she's scared to even open the conversation.

She swallows past the lump in her throat and forces herself to speak. 'I'd give anything to have her back,' Vivacia says. 'For him to have never come here, and Cally to be here instead.'

Jackie utters a dry laugh. 'But then you wouldn't have their kids, would you?'

It's the perfect opener. And time is running out. 'Dallas and Rose need me,' says Vivacia, bolder than she feels. 'They need love and stability. I can give that to them.'

Jackie draws a breath to speak but Vivacia cuts her off. 'And they need you, too. Family, blood family, Jackie.'

Jackie stares out of the window. 'Too late for all that,' she says.

Frustration wells inside Vivacia, burning and twisting up her throat. Never does she shout, but right now, she feels on the verge of throwing a Cally-style tantrum of epic force.

'It's not too late!' she cries. 'You can stop this, you can let me stay here, let me love them, and you can love them too. I know if you just give them a chance—'

'What are you talking about, "let you stay here"?' Jackie snaps.

'Don't turn me in, don't tell the police what I did. Please.' The moment the words leave Vivacia's mouth, she covers her face with her hands.

She hadn't come here to beg for her freedom. She'd come to implore Jackie to step up and stay in the children's lives.

Or maybe that's simply what she told herself, and this was what she'd subconsciously planned all along, the moment she walked out of her own home.

Jackie comes at her around the table. Vivacia steps back.

'Diminski isn't coming here for you, you idiot.'

'W-what?' Vivacia frowns. 'What do you mean?'

As though all the breath and fight have left her body, Jackie slumps into a chair.

Jackie's eyes pierce through Vivacia. Her face is granite, her gaze ice. Only her mouth, trembling uncontrollably, betrays her.

'You didn't kill Charles,' Jackie whispers. 'I did.'

34

VIVACIA – NOW

Fury dashes Vivacia's fear and pain away like flood water. She's at the well again, watching as all the feelings that have stayed with her for over a year, intensifying since Charles burst free of his watery grave, are washed clean until the only thing that is left is scorching, fiery rage.

'Why?' Vivacia's voice is husky, raw, and she's shocked that she sounds nothing like herself.

Jackie's mouth is clenched into an ugly twist. 'Because I knew no good would come of it. Because I knew from the first time that I saw him that he was bad news.' Jackie laughs, but it is bitter and cold. 'Her head was so easily turned. She was like a magpie, saw something new and shiny and didn't look any deeper than the surface.'

'But why did you *kill* him?' Vivacia is genuinely perplexed.

'Because if he was no longer around, I thought she'd come home.' Jackie's jaw is still hard, but her eyes betray her emotion.

'Oh, Jackie,' Vivacia closes her eyes.

'She always came home!' Jackie cries, shrilly. 'Always, after a bender, after an adventure, she'd come tripping down that road.' Jackie presses her fingers to her lips. 'She always came home.'

And she would have this time, if she hadn't been locked in that stinking, decaying caravan along with her two children.

Vivacia knows this. Jackie does too. Vivacia's rage spikes again regardless.

'How?' Vivacia spits. 'How did you kill him?'

By her sides, she can feel her hands curling into fists, the nails digging into her palms.

As if sleepwalking, Jackie moves over to the kitchen sink. She's unsteady, using the dining table as support, banging her hip against the chair back.

She pulls open a drawer beside the sink and withdraws something that she holds in her closed hand.

'What is it?' Vivacia hisses.

When Jackie doesn't reply, Vivacia lurches forward and grabs hold of her wrist.

Jackie keeps her hand closed, and Vivacia grips her fingers, curling them back one by one until Jackie utters a sharp cry and something tumbles to the floor.

Vivacia stoops to pick it up.

'Careful,' cries Jackie, fearfully.

At Jackie's tone, Vivacia lets it tumble onto the tabletop. She can't even see what it is. It's wrapped in cling film, the contents indistinguishable.

'What is it?' Vivacia asks again.

'Foxglove, hemlock, belladonna.' Jackie's voice is so quiet that Vivacia has to strain to hear her.

Vivacia shakes her head, dazed. 'You don't know which one?'

Jackie looks at her, dead in the eye. In the single glance, Vivacia realises what Jackie is saying.

'All of them?' she gasps.

Jackie shrugs.

'You poisoned him.' Vivacia grips the edge of the table. Her mind goes back in time, to when Kay taught her all about the wildflowers that grow in Wolf's Pit. Medicinal herbs, rare plants, poisonous, silent killers.

She remembers Charles that night. How at first he had appeared drunk and then, when he looked at her with those huge, wide pupils, she had thought he was on something.

269

Without warning, Vivacia becomes aware that her face is wet. She dabs at her cheeks angrily.

'You let me believe that I was responsible for his death?' Her tone is low, angry again, her voice breaking. 'I thought I was going to prison. All this time, for a whole year, I thought at the very least I was going to hell!'

'Purgatory!' Jackie shouts, suddenly, making Vivacia jump. 'That's where I'll be, after I've served my time.' Then, all the fight leaves Jackie's body. She leans over the sink, knuckles white as she grips it. Her back, already stooped from years of angst and worry for the child who will now never come home, is even more hunched tonight.

'Get out, anyway,' Jackie rasps. 'You don't need to be here.'

All is lost. Not for Vivacia, not like she imagined, but for Jackie.

It doesn't feel like a win for Vivacia.

She has failed. Failed in connecting a grandmother with her rightful grandchildren.

Vivacia remembers how important Kay was to her. All that wisdom, shared. All the things she'd taught her. Sometimes, she bypassed her own mother entirely to go to Kay.

Rose and Dallas won't have anyone like that now.

She opens her mouth to implore Jackie one more time, but before she can speak, there is a tap at the door.

'Hi, Mrs Jenkins?'

Jackie stills at the sound of DI Demoski's voice. Seconds later, the woman has pushed the door open and appears in the kitchen.

'Ah, good evening, Ms Lomax.' She greets Vivacia.

'It's Williams.' Jackie and Vivacia speak in unison.

Their eyes meet. A strange bonding moment over an inconsequential detail.

'I understand you wanted to talk with me?' Ola Demoski turns her full attention to Jackie.

'She had some questions, about Cally, when she will be able to make arrangements,' Vivacia breaks in. Her words are nonsense. Jackie will have been fully informed, just like she was about Charles's corpse. Her thoughts twist and settle as she improvises. 'Jackie was understandably shocked when you broke the news to her. She needs reminding of some of the details.' She lowers her eyes respectfully and wrings her hands, playing a role.

So sorry to be a bother but we're not the sort of people this happens to, you'll have to forgive us.

Ola softens. 'Of course,' she says. 'Anything you want to know, I'll help you where I can.'

Jackie stands motionless, a deer in headlights, her eyes flicking from Vivacia to Ola.

'Sit down, Inspector. Would you like a drink?'

Ola shakes her head and utters her gratitude. Businesslike but kindly, she draws Jackie to sit also.

Vivacia passes behind Jackie and lays a hand on her shoulder. 'It's all right,' she says, sweetly. 'DI Demoski will remind us of everything. Do you want me to ask her your questions?'

Jackie looks up at Vivacia, who sends her a silent message.

Just think of some questions. If you don't, I will. You're not turning yourself in, Jackie.

A snap decision. It isn't hard. If Jackie really needed to confess her sin, she would have called the police first thing this morning. She would have told them last night.

She won't spill her awful truth.

Life will go on.

Dallas and Rose will have their grandmother.

Won't they?

Vivacia breaks eye contact. On the table is the wadded parcel containing Jackie's awful secret. In one, fluid motion, as Jackie watches on, Vivacia scoops it up and puts it in the bin. She turns to the window and stares outside.

It's pitch-black out there now. Everything is under cover. Even the moon is swathed in heavy clouds. Vivacia's house, its occupants, Lady Well – all of them are hidden tonight.

She hears Jackie draw a breath, preparing to speak.

'My girl,' she says. Her voice cracks. 'When can I lay my girl to rest?'

–

'What did you do that for?' asks Jackie, once Ola has left.

'Purgatory,' says Vivacia.

Jackie cocks her head to one side, confused.

'You're going to be punished, just like me,' says Vivacia. 'A self-punishment, living with what happened. I'm doing the same time behind bars as you are. Because I should have stood up for myself, I should have kicked Charles out the first time he put me down. I should have paid more attention to Cally, instead of thinking about myself, and my own problems. If I had, this might never have happened.

'But instead of punishment, we've been given a second chance. At happiness, Jackie! In return for the gift of those children, we can give Rose and Dallas the best life they could ever have in the hope that when it all ends, and we leave this life, Cally will be waiting for us, and she'll forgive us, and she'll know we did our very best to raise her children.'

Jackie makes a sound deep in her throat as Vivacia advances towards her.

'And you're going to do this with me. You're going to be a grandmother to those beautiful children. You're going to tell them all about Cally, all about you and this place, and you're going to make them know how loved they are. And when your life is done, you'll have paid your penance, and Cally will know that.'

Jackie dissolves in front of her. She shakes her head violently, tears blending into the deep lines etched into her face. Her arms are out in front of her, reaching blindly.

Vivacia takes a deep breath and steps into them.

There is no more talk. No need for any further words. There might be, soon, in the future, in years to come. For now, both women are equal.

For Vivacia, it's a strange, new feeling.

She feels an ache across her back. Absently, she rubs at her shoulders. She knows this pain. She's had it before, after Charles had gone for the final time. Her body has been fraught for so long; this ache is the feeling of trauma leaving her body. Right now, she is suddenly exhausted.

She reaches for her coffee, as yet untouched but still steaming on the table.

'No.' Jackie is alert now, eyes wide, reaching for Vivacia's cup. She gets her own too, marches over to the sink and places the cups in it. From the cupboard to her left she pulls a cream liquor, crusty around the lid, probably left over from a Christmas years in the past, when Jackie actually had things to celebrate.

Vivacia laughs, a sound almost foreign to her ears. 'Just a small one,' she says. 'Because we've got responsibilities now, haven't we?'

Jackie nods as she pours a measure into tiny glasses and passes one to Vivacia.

Jackie holds hers aloft. 'To new beginnings?' she phrases it as a question, her voice hesitant.

The fact that Jackie falters, that she looks to Vivacia for guidance now, lends Vivacia a strength that she never knew she could possess. The tables have turned. Vivacia is in charge now; Jackie will follow her lead.

The knowledge is powerful.

'New beginnings,' she confirms, and clinks glasses with Jackie.

The postcard is on Jackie's fridge now. Vivacia can't stop staring at it.

'Do you think she actually went to Barcelona?' she asks now.

273

Jackie looks up, startled. 'I don't know,' she replies. 'I hope so. I really hope she went somewhere in all that time she was away.'

Grief hangs heavy in the room, cloaking them as they stare at the card, both lost in their own wonderings.

'That man who died,' Jackie says, breaking the silence. 'He liked you.'

Vivacia shrugs. 'I really didn't know him all that well.'

It's not true, she realises. She *did* know him. And suddenly the parallels are awfully clear. He was like Charles. An outsider, coming in here, chumming up with the locals, charming her.

Had he spotted her weaknesses, that very first time they met?

What had been his endgame?

She shakes her head. She will never know now.

And she's glad of that.

It is late when Vivacia takes the glasses from where they have settled, in the lounge, through to the kitchen. She's been here for hours now, and she wishes she'd brought her mobile phone with her to text Ruth. It's something she will need to do now, carry it with her. Now she's got children to take care of, and family in the form of Jackie, and friends who want to arrange play dates, like Aster.

'Aster invited the children to use her pool,' Vivacia calls through to Jackie. 'Maybe you'd like to come along?'

'Pfft!' Vivacia smiles as she hears Jackie's response from the next room. 'Can you imagine me sitting there, in amongst that lot?'

'I can,' Vivacia says quietly. 'They're good people. Decent, kind.'

'Maybe,' Jackie replies, grudgingly.

It's going to be about bridging the gap, she sees now. Not just herself and Jackie, but between the old-timers and the new blood. It can be done. Ruth has already done it. Vivacia is getting there.

She rinses out the glasses, drying them thoughtfully as she dares to look to the future. She picks up the coffee cups and is about to put them under the running water when she falters. Peering at the rim, she sees a piece of white, like a minuscule petal. She grabs the other mug, bringing it close to her face, squinting at the same remnants that float in amongst the coffee bits at the bottom.

She remembers earlier, her own surprise when Jackie offered her a beverage, how furtively Jackie made the drinks, the glance over her shoulder. Vivacia averting her gaze. How Jackie had slid that drawer open ever so slightly, reaching in, the sound of what she'd thought was a packet of coffee being opened. Something which sounded very much like cling film being unwrapped.

Her mouth is dry, suddenly. She abandons the mugs and looks into the cupboard to see the coffee that Jackie actually used. Half-full. Not new. Not just opened.

'All right in here?' Jackie is in the doorway, arms crossed, leaning against the frame.

Vivacia forces a smile. 'Yep, just washing up, then I'll be on my way.'

Before Jackie can object, Vivacia rinses the mugs, squirts some washing-up liquid in them and scrubs them thoroughly.

Behind her, she can feel Jackie's eyes on her.

Jackie faltered earlier. Vivacia remembers the zing of power she'd felt. She draws on it now, pulls out this new woman, the one who is a mother, the one who isn't frightened to be herself.

She opens the door of the cupboard below the sink. Pulling out the bottle of bleach, she unscrews the cap and pours a hefty dose into each mug.

Behind her, she hears Jackie's sharp intake of breath.

Straightening up, Vivacia turns around and fixes her stare on Jackie.

'Best let them soak a little while,' she says. She smiles, cool and steely, just to let Jackie know that *she knows*. 'See you tomorrow. Goodnight, Jackie.'

She can see Ruth's face at her window as she makes her way back to her cottage.

She is free now, she reminds herself as she walks up the path to her own home. Really free, with no worries of arrests or imprisonment hovering around her like a shadowy ghost. She can start anew, making ties and bonds in a community that she'd all but given up on.

She shivers. Enjoying this newfound excitement and strength, instead of the apprehension she so often feels.

Ruth envelopes her as she enters the house. She tells her that Rose and Dallas are in bed, sleeping soundly the last time she checked on them – and does Vivacia know that Dallas sleeps with his eyes partially open?

Vivacia smiles at the older woman. 'I noticed,' she says as she bids Ruth goodnight.

She sits down after checking on the children, relishing the knowledge that she can sit here until she decides to go to bed. That she won't have to move quietly around her home, peering between the curtains for police cars coming up the road, or unwanted visitors knocking on her door.

She thinks about Jackie, and her confession, and those coffee mugs, the remnants inside them.

The fact that they were not in just one mug, but both.

It's chilling. If Jackie was going down, she was taking Vivacia with her.

But she didn't.

They are both free now.

It's been days, weeks, months, *years* of trauma. It's nearing an end now. There's a light at the end of what has been a very dark tunnel.

She takes a bath, luxuriating in it, no longer feeling the need to have a rushed shower in preparation for those who might come knocking. With the water that swirls down the drain, so does the expectation that this would be her last night of freedom.

Clean, cleansed, feeling renewed, she wraps herself in a towel and picks up her jeans from the floor. Rooting in the back pocket, she pulls out a bundled wad wrapped in tissue.

Jackie's poison.

Vivacia wonders if Jackie will check that it is still in her kitchen bin.

Vivacia imagines the older woman, peering into the bin, pulling out all the trash and rifling through.

She tells herself she doesn't want to leave it in Jackie's house. Doesn't want to think of the other woman having a bad day, or a down day, and making herself that one, final drink.

Really, Vivacia acknowledges, to have it here is a kind of insurance policy.

Charles is gone. Rob is gone. There is nobody else in Wolf's Pit she can imagine would ever deserve a similar justice.

Vivacia pulls herself up onto the edge of the bath and hooks her arms over the wide ceiling beam that runs the width of the bathroom. The wood is old, with deep grooves and notches, born of a hundred years of being. To the far right of the beam there is a hole. It was once a knot in the wood, she reckons, but time has hollowed it out. It is a perfect hiding place.

Vivacia pokes the wadded ball of wrapped poison deep into the hole.

Her smile in the mirror is the last thing she sees before she turns out the light.

35

THE CHILDREN

Home.

Rose knew what Dallas was thinking. He didn't want to go back up the hill to the only home they'd ever known. He got jittery, fidgety, but Rose realised they were not going up the hill and shot a glance at him. Immediately, he quietened, compliant with a look from her.

Sometimes it took all her energy to still him. Sometimes, he reminded her of Father. Quiet, until he wasn't.

The house that the woman took them to was nothing like the home they'd come from. It was bigger, for a start. Clean and roomy, like the big houses Rose had seen when Father used to take them out driving. The walls were lined with books. Books! Crayons and pens and paper, as if this woman cared nothing for the rules of living.

Doubt crept into Rose's mind.

She glanced at Dallas.

Maybe things are different in this world.

His eyes danced around, landing on a small knife that glinted on the worktop.

Rose caught his attention.

Maybe you need to be different here, too.

He lowered his head, docile.

For now. But he kept looking at the blade anyway.

There was a garden here, too, Rose could see as she looked out of the large glass doors. A proper one, not just land with old car parts and patchy, bare grass. There was a fence beyond it, so that part wasn't much different. The fence was actually very similar to the one at the top of the hill, with its iron railings.

They must have walked in a loop, because Rose could see the small pile of bricks they'd been sitting on when the woman found them.

This house stood by itself back here, but from her earlier walk, Rose knew there were other homes nearby. Places where people wore nice clothes and dressed their children according to the weather. Gardens which had pools in them. Houses where people could read what they wanted and write stuff down and speak out loud and use phones without having to hide them. Filled with people like the mother and her three children that Rose had seen earlier. Where kids shouted and the adults talked in confident, snappy tones.

The kindly lady who led them in out of the damp and wet told them her name was Vivacia.

Rose blinked, the name a vague memory in her very distant past.

Rose looked around carefully. Another memory, older than all the ones she'd had before, came back to her. Another house, one they used to live in.

–

Before the beginning, when they were really little, there was another place. Walls, and ceilings which were higher even than father could reach. Slippery floors that gleamed orange, with swirling, black pieces.

'Knots,' said Mother. 'That's what they're called.'

Rose looked down at her shoelaces. She couldn't tie them herself. Mother did that for her. 'A double knot,' Rose said, but she knew confusion was draped on her face like a silken cover.

'Also called knots.' Mother nodded and trailed her hand across a floorboard.

Her finger moved in a smooth sweep, stuttering when it reached the roughness of the flawed material.

There were parties in the place with knotted wood floors and tall, tall ceilings. Rose and Dallas were allowed to attend but had to be on their best behaviour. Invariably, the parties would begin with glitter, glamour, beautiful ladies who smelled like a thousand different flowers. The gentlemen wore suits, and music would play gently and softly.

Rose always swore to Dallas that she would stay awake until every guest had left, but she never did.

As the music was turned up higher, Rose's eyelids would begin to droop. Mother would carry her up to the bedroom. The bed was covered in coats. Dallas would be there already, snuggled deep in fur and leather.

Dead to the world, laughed Mother.

Rose would wait until Mother had left before leaning over Dallas to check. Not dead, just sleeping.

Sometimes, in the summer, the sunshine would wake Rose after a party. She would leave Dallas sleeping, and wander downstairs. The house was different on those mornings after. The knotty wooden floor would be coloured in dark red puddles, and dusty with white flakes like flour. Bitter, pungent tobacco smoke hung heavy, and some partygoers remained, sprawled out on the sofas, legs draped over the armchairs.

It was on one of these party weekends when everything changed. It was still early, before the *debauchery* came, as Mother called it.

The three-storey house was filled to bursting. The music was on. Rose swayed in time to the song, the glasses a clinking cymbal, the women's laughter tambourines, the men's a booming base.

A new man, one Rose didn't recognise, stood in the open doorway, four suitcases surrounding him.

'What the…' he blustered, taking in the scene. 'What the… What the *fuck*!'

Confusion on the partygoers' faces, frowns from the women, the alpha men squaring up to the intruder.

Father, dodging around the people who had begun to argue with the stranger, coming towards Rose. He swept up Dallas effortlessly, held him under one arm. With his free hand he jabbed at Mother's waist, poking her until she cried out, herding her towards the back door.

'My things!' Mother cried.

'Leave them,' muttered Father.

He reached Rose and she raised her arms, a smile on her face as she waited to be swooped up into the air like Dallas had been.

Instead, Father grabbed the back of her neck in a vice-like grip. 'Out,' he said, and she'd never heard his voice like that before.

In the street, Father shepherded them all down the passageway and to the bus stop on the corner. A misty rain had begun, and Dallas started to grizzle.

Mother stamped her foot and slapped at Father's arm. 'Always, you do this!' she cried. 'This was never our home, was it? It never belonged to us, did it?'

They all looked back at the house, lights blazing in every room. At the front, men poured out of the door. Rose saw the man with the suitcases, still blustering, his face red and ugly.

Mother curled her hand into a fist and punched Father in his chest. 'Why can't you be a normal man?' she asked, and her voice was sharp and shrill. 'Why can't you just work for things, like a normal man?'

Father gripped her wrist and shoved her. She staggered backwards, slipping off the pavement into the gutter. 'Shut up! You've never worked a day in your *life*!' he hissed. His finger came close to her face, almost touching her nose. 'Just shut up, or I'll leave all of you right here.'

Mother covered her face with her hands. 'I should have listened to them. They were right. You're just a shit. A real shit.

281

All those things you said about Vivacia. There's nothing wrong with her. It was you all along. You're a bully. A useless, hopeless, nasty, lying bully. That poor girl.' Her shoulders juddered with sobs. 'That poor, poor woman.'

Dallas looked on. He had stopped grizzling and was watching, seemingly shocked at Mother's animation.

Mother sat on the kerb. Her tears stopped, and to Rose she seemed very, very tired.

'Now I'm Vivacia,' she said. 'Now I'm in her shoes.'

Rose peered at Mother's feet, her brow wrinkled in confusion. She didn't know the woman Mother was talking about, but she was definitely wearing her own shoes. Silver ones, sparkly and pretty, if a little worn.

Father closed his eyes and passed a hand across his face. 'Shut up,' he said again. 'Just keep quiet and wait here.' Father forcefully arranged them in a huddle. 'Don't move.'

He took off, walking fast back the way they'd come. 'My things!' called Mother. 'You get my fucking things, Charles!'

Rose watched as he vanished into the darkness of the night. She wondered if he would come back. She imagined life with just Mother and Dallas if he didn't come back.

She could call Mother Mummy again.

The misty rain stopped. The grey clouds parted. Something shone in the sky, a glittering trail across the black night.

A falling star.

Rose wished on it.

–

Father came back, a bag over his shoulder. His pockets bulged. The night bus arrived; he lifted Dallas onto it. Blue lights flashed as the police chased down the road. Rose, the last to board, watched as they braked sharply. The suitcase man was there, hands twisted into his hair, his face still red.

282

'…my house!' she heard him say. He shrieked the words, his face changing from red to purple. 'All those strangers, in *my house*! Like they've been *living* here!'

Rose sat next to Father. He stared out of the window. She looked at his pockets, at the silver candlesticks that poked obscenely out, the gold chains that wrapped around them, the blood-red ruby ring, balanced precariously on folds of silken handkerchiefs. Other things, too: a curly strip of stamps and some postcards, with photographs of places she had never been to. They had Mother's name on the other side, and a single kiss. It wasn't Mother's writing, though.

After the long journey of bus, train, bus again and then a lot of walking, they reached the caravan. Rose surveyed it, inside first; then, she stood outside and looked at the small structure, wondering where the other two floors were.

Father stood tall and proud. 'We tried it your way,' he said to Mother. 'Your partying, social lifestyle. It didn't work. So now we'll do it my way.'

There were no knotted wooden floors inside. Rose asked Mother in a whisper about it.

'Vinyl,' said Mother. She sniffed and her mouth turned down. 'Cheap,' she said.

She looked towards the door, the hill and fields beyond, and looked at Charles. She raised her chin, proud and defiant. 'Maybe I'll go back home,' she said. 'Maybe I'll visit Mum, take the kids to meet her.' She hesitated, faltering in a way Rose had never seen. 'Just for a visit.'

Father carried on as though Mother hadn't spoken. 'We'll build this place up,' he said. 'Build our own community with like-minded people. Where everyone is equal.' He smiled, and to Rose it looked a little like the grin of the shark in the book that she'd left in the big house that was never their own.

Father's shadow fell to block the light as he closed the door firmly, shutting out the blue sky.

36

EPILOGUE

It's been years since they've held a harvest festival in Wolf's Pit.
The last one she remembers is the one when she had her very
first foster child, Alfie.

It's nice that they are making an effort again. A new start
for a new community. Vivacia comments upon this to Ruth as
they stroll the paths arm in arm, stopping at Mr Bastille's apple-
bobbing stand.

One of Aster's boys is there, and so is Mr Bastille's new dog,
and Mr Bastille himself.

He looks amazing, thinks Vivacia as she glances at him. He
looks like he did years ago, when Serafina was alive, before she
got ill, before he hit the bottle.

Aster and Chloe-Joy have their own stall, which is selling
Chloe-Joy's green smoothies, and Aster's vegan cakes and
cookies. Vivacia watches as some of the older residents eye their
wares with suspicion.

As if the new bloods are looking to poison them.

Vivacia smothers a smile with her hand. If only they knew.

Ruth squeezes her arm and nods across the green at Jackie,
coming towards them, Rose on one arm, Dallas clinging to the
other.

'It's a good sight, yeah?' comments Ruth. 'I didn't think I'd
see it, to be honest.'

'V!' This from Dallas, along with a smile that lights up his
face.

Like it always does when Dallas produces any noise or speech, Vivacia's heart melts.

It was his idea to call her V. Or maybe Rose's. They got it from Rob, and it doesn't trouble her as much as she thought it would.

'Hi guys,' she says, opening her arms to allow the children to tumble into them. 'Did you have fun?'

Rose nods and shoves a biscuit into Vivacia's hand. Vivacia studies it, the chocolate chips oozing out of the still-warm dough and the sprinkles of crystalised sugar. Definitely not one of Aster's. Vivacia bites into it.

'Mmm, sō good, thank you so much, sweetie.'

Chloe-Joy sidles up to them. 'Beer tent?' she asks. She looks at each of the adults in turn, putting a hand on Jackie's arm so she knows she is included.

A small gesture, to some, but huge to Jackie. Her face flushes with pleasure.

'Vivacia!' Baker, Aster's youngest child, trips up to them and grabs Rose's hand. 'Can Rose and Dallas come and play with us?'

'Yes!' shouts Dallas.

Vivacia smiles and turns to Rose, crouching down so she is on the same level. 'You want to go play?'

Rose narrows her eyes, glances at Dallas, who says, 'Yes, we do.'

Rose turns back to Vivacia and nods. Vivacia pulls her in for a hug and breathes in. Beneath her hands she can feel how much fleshier Rose is now, and as she looks down and catches sight of Rose's tanned arms, with not a hint of green, she holds the girl harder.

'Off you go, then,' she says.

Dallas takes Rose's hand and leads her off towards the bouncy castle.

They sit in a semicircle, Chloe-Joy, Jackie, Vivacia and Ruth.

Chloe-Joy, bless her, is talking to Jackie. Jackie, still not entirely comfortable with being in a group after so long living as a hermit, is trying to reciprocate.

But it's not Jackie that Vivacia is watching.

'What's up?' asks Ruth.

'I'm fine,' she replies. 'It's just... I'm thinking about Rose.'

She looks over to the bouncy castle, where Dallas is hurling himself from wall to wall in a frenzy, his shrieks of excitement matching those of Aster's kids.

Neither of them can quite believe he is the same boy that arrived in Wolf's Pit all those months ago.

'They've swapped personalities,' remarks Ruth.

Vivacia gasps and turns to face her. 'You noticed it too? It's not just me being...'

'Overprotective? Needlessly worried?' Ruth teases her for a second before her face turns serious once more. 'No, I've noticed it too. He's found his feet. This is a good thing, darling. Dallas no longer needs the protection of his sister. Now, he's conforming to the stereotypes of society.'

She tilts her head. 'What do you mean?'

Ruth gestures to Aster's kids. 'Look at Oliver and Cooper. They rag their little sister mercilessly, but they still look out for her. Look, look!'

Vivacia watches. The boys have been ribbing Baker all morning; Vivacia has witnessed it. They told her she was too slow, too young to keep up with them. Baker had gone off crying, but she's back now, trailed by Iris's grandson, Evan. Evan is older than the little ones, eleven or twelve, full of pre-teenage angst. Little Baker has something he wants: a toffee apple. Something ridiculous, something Blind Iris would buy him in an instant. But he doesn't want it bought. He wants to take it.

Vivacia bristles. She knows boys like this. She remembers Alfie, the foster child, how he was moulded into something entirely different by Charles. She wonders who has shaped Evan.

286

Baker's high whines reach her ears. Cooper, the middle child, is by her side in an instant, Oliver close behind him. Oliver zooms past his siblings, raising his chest and puffing himself up as he barges into Evan, who is a good two feet taller than him.

Evan backs off. The toffee apple is returned to its rightful owner by Baker's big brother. Drama over, Aster's kids scatter. Dallas and Rose remain, hand in hand, watching the disturbance with an apparent lack of interest.

'See. I've seen that countless times since Evan has been here. And so has Dallas. He's *learning*.'

Vivacia nods her agreement. She knows what Ruth is saying is right. Big brother. How Rose and Dallas's roles seem to have switched.

Only… there's something more. She thinks of all those times at the beginning, when she would find Dallas wrapped in Rose's arms in bed. She'd thought he was seeking protection. Sometimes, like a whisper, an unwelcome thought creeps in.

What if Dallas wasn't seeking comfort in his sister's arms, but rather, she was holding him back.

She shakes her head, chases the thought away and turns back to the group.

Vivacia leans towards Chloe-Joy, who has engaged Jackie in conversation about the benefits of something called a 12:12 diet.

'…eat for twelve hours, then fast for the remaining twelve,' Chloe-Joy says.

Jackie blanches. 'You eat solidly for twelve hours?'

Vivacia tenses as Chloe-Joy laughs. Slowly, she realises it's not the laughter that would have come from a place of cruelty, not like Charles's mirth.

She is still healing. So is Jackie. So are the children.

They will heal, tend to their own wellbeing, they will go on. Sadly, so will the next group of those who have been traumatised – like Evan, like Alfie – who will follow the examples of their parents and enablers.

All Vivacia can do is her best.

Aster's boys are back now, sliding over the bouncy castle, Rose in their midst. Vivacia winces; she seems so small compared to them. But she's plucky, unafraid of getting hurt. She laughs freely, through a mouthful of hair that has escaped the ribbons that Vivacia so carefully tied this morning.

Dallas is not there anymore, and Baker hasn't returned.

Vivacia stands. Ruth looks at her inquisitively.

'Bathroom break,' she lies. 'Back soon.'

The cottage is empty when she walks in. Not only silent, but deafening with the absence of those who have made this place a home in the last few months. It jars Vivacia at moments like this.

The children leave a trail of themselves as they meander through the house. Coats and shoes and leaves and soil.

She loves it.

But there are moments, such as this one right now, when there are no shoes in the hallway, no coats, no abandoned picture books or random playing cards to litter her path.

The house is pristine, like it was during those lost years, after Charles and Cally had gone, before the children arrived. Like Lady Well, deep and dark and black. Vivacia's breath catches in her throat as she wonders if it were a dream. What if none of it actually happened, and she'll wake up and there will be no Rose and no Dallas, and she's alone.

Or worse, she may wake up and find Charles looming over her, tucking the sheets in around her, his dark eyes regarding her, his wallet on the side, as he whispers to her.

You don't mess with me. You never mess with me.

Frantically, Vivacia shoulders open the living-room door and falls through it. She walks quickly to the armchair over the far side of the room. Planting her hands around it, she pulls it forward and leans in the gap to scrutinise the wall.

There, a smear of red, orange and yellow, and a dot of green. A partial rainbow, drawn by little Baker three months ago while Rose and Dallas looked on, open-mouthed.

Satisfied, Vivacia pushes the chair back into position. It wasn't a dream. The rainbow is her mark of proof. If Rose and Dallas didn't exist, Baker wouldn't have been in her house with crayons in her sticky, podgy fingers.

She had thought about painting over it, but decided it wasn't necessary.

She hasn't told anyone how often she comes in here when the place is empty, and the fear overtakes her, and she rushes to the wall for confirmation that she's not living some nightmare on a continuous, Groundhog Day loop.

She puts a hand on her chest and attempts to calm her breathing.

She works through a list to aid her.

The children are real.

Rose is on the bouncy castle, with the children of Vivacia's good friend.

Their grandmother is there, sipping wine, trying to pretend she's not uncomfortable.

Ruth, the stable, sound, kind voice of reason in Vivacia's life, keeps an eye on them.

It's just Dallas.

Where is Dallas?

She hears his voice as she slides the patio door open. He is chatting incessantly, and still now, after months of him talking, it makes her heart leap with joy.

It falls, though, as she scans the garden. He is not there.

No panic, she can hear him, follow the voice.

But she doesn't need to. That fence panel is shifted to one side, leaving a clear gap for two small bodies to pass through.

He is on Lady Well.

Again.

It draws him, that damn place.

She doesn't know why; it doesn't even look like anything of interest. Just a raised patch of earth, bordered by rickety old house bricks and a lid that looks like a drain cover.

The children whisper about it, she knows that much. The original legend was that it was a hole in the ground to catch the predatory wolves that roamed this land. It is where the village got its name from.

But now, rather than the old urban myth, the children whisper a modern legend from which present-day monsters burst free when the rain falls. Snippets of conversation overheard from their parents, who actually witnessed the monster.

The kids dare each other to sit atop it, and, as she peers around the fence, she sees that's exactly what Baker and Dallas are doing now.

Dallas's voice is low, quiet, rasping, so unlike his little-boy excited cry, and sounding more like a fully grown man – Vivacia's hair rises on the back of her neck.

'Evan was wrong to take your belonging,' he is saying. 'But you were also wrong to keep it from him. Everything must be equally shared. Nobody should own this, or that. Don't you agree, Baker?'

Vivacia hears the little girl whisper an obedient, 'Yes.'

'And so, on the seventh day we will march around this city seven times, and the walls of the city will collapse, and everyone will be free.'

It is vaguely familiar. It is the sort of rhetoric she imagines Charles would often speak, after he'd been shut out of this community. And Vivacia knows that Dallas is talking about the walls of Jericho, the Book of Joshua. It is the extent of her knowledge. She doesn't know what chapter it is, and she's 100 per cent sure that Dallas wouldn't have learned the story from anyone inside Wolf's Pit.

After all, the churchgoers were whittled away to nothing years ago.

They are all sinners here now, and none of them care a jot.

It is muscle memory. She knows plenty about that. Knows that the sight of a red wallet causes bile to rise in her throat.

The memories remain, along with all the speeches, all the lessons Charles tried to teach her.

Dallas remembers them too.

Dallas is carrying on his father's legacy.

Learned behaviour, or DNA?

Despite the unseasonably warm day, Vivacia feels ice-cold.

She wants to drift back through the house, return to the festival where she can sit with the ladies and sip cold, crisp white wine. She will hear the joyous squeals of the kids enjoying themselves instead of a madman's religious rantings.

Alternatively, she can draw on her relatively newfound power and nip this in the bud.

She straightens her shoulders, pulls the fence panel open wider and stamps her way through the gap.

'V!' Dallas, who only seconds prior reminded her of an evangelist, transforms instantly into the eight-year-old boy that he is.

He rushes at her, and she wraps her arms around him, feeling the love pass between them as surely and as physically as a bolt of lightning.

'Kids, you need to stay inside the fences, you both know that.'

Baker clambers to her feet and shuffles past Vivacia into the garden. Vivacia herds Dallas through after her.

'I'm not kidding, guys. Baker, if your mum knew you were outside what do you reckon she'd say?'

Baker, all wide eyes and blonde ringlets, stares up at her. 'She'd say I couldn't come play here anymore,' she whispers.

Vivacia pauses and studies the little girl. Is it her imagination or does Baker sound *hopeful* at the mention of the potential punishment?

She sighs. 'Back to the festival, you two. Dallas, find your grandmother. I'll be right behind you.'

She watches as they slope off towards the house. At the door, Dallas puts a hand on Baker's arm and leans close to her.

Vivacia ups her pace and has just about reached the pair when she hears Dallas whisper.

'Don't worry, Baker, someday, there will be no fences keeping us in at all.' He puts his hand around her upper arm and pinches it. 'They won't mess with us.'

Vivacia closes her eyes.

There is work to be done here.

Much work, to unravel the constraints that Charles has so cleverly woven around her boy.

She drifts around the empty cottage, hating the silence, but not wanting to step back into the forced frivolity of the festival.

She finds herself upstairs, closing the door behind her as she slips into the bathroom. She balances on the bath, resting one hand lightly on the beam above her head. With her other hand she spider-walks her fingers across the old wood until they dip into the hole. The padded parcel crinkles at her touch and she breathes with relief, pulling it out so she can confirm its presence.

Jackie's poison. The same sort that killed Charles. The one she took that night when all the truths came out from Jackie's house.

The parcel of poison that Vivacia now keeps safe, hidden in her own bathroom, high up in the beam where nobody apart from herself would ever look.

Her safety net.

Should things become untenable.

Should certain people become unmanageable.

She brushes the dust off her hands and climbs back down to stand on the floor.

She will never use what is hidden up there on Dallas. There will be no need to. He is still so young. He is pliable, malleable. She can fix him of the warped ideas of his father that have infected him like a virus.

She will fix her most cherished boy. It is her life's work and she's ready for it.

But it is good to know it is up there, her secret in the beam.

Just in case.

AUTHOR'S NOTE

The Green Children of Woolpit

I am so lucky to live in the UK county of Suffolk, a place rich with a tapestry of history, folklore and legend.

Wolf's Pit, or Wulf-pytt, to use the medieval name of the ancient village, is not far from my home. Today it is called Woolpit. As the name suggests, the location was a large pit, used for trapping and catching wolves.

In the twelfth century, around the year 1150, during the harvest, a group of villagers came across two young children – a girl and a boy – with green skin, next to, or crawling out of, one of the wolf pits. They did not speak English, or any discernible language. They were dressed in strange clothing, and they acted very nervously.

They were taken to the home of Sir Richard de Calne. He offered them food, but they refused to eat. After a few days, they discovered green beans growing in de Calne's garden, and they eagerly gobbled them up. Soon, they were eating the food that the other villagers offered them, and the green tinge of their skin returned to normal colour. Sadly, the little boy grew sick and died, but the girl, who took the name Agnes, flourished under the care of the Wolf's Pit residents.

Eventually, Agnes told the villagers that she and her brother had come from a place called St Martin Land. She said it was a place that exists in perpetual twilight, though, according to Agnes, from their homeland they could see a 'luminous' country. The divide between the two places was a considerably sized river.

According to Agnes, they were feeding their father's flock in the fields when they heard a noise that they had never encountered before. Here, in Wolf's Pit, the sound was a common one, the chimes of the bells of St Edmunds. From their father's field, they listened to the church bells with great delight, and then quite suddenly found themselves in Wolf's Pit. They were stunned by the bright sunlight, and the change in temperature.

It is not clear whether the green children existed, or if it is a myth. The story, however, does appear in at least two historical accounts by chronicler and twelfth-century abbot Ralph of Coggeshall, and historian William of Newburgh. If you go to Woolpit today, you will see the village sign which shows a church spire, a wolf, and two children hand in hand.

There are many theories about the green children of Woolpit.

One of them is they came across the sea from Holland and were the offspring of Flemish immigrants. Their parents may have been persecuted and killed by King Stephen or Henry II. Lost and wandering for a time, the green colouring of their skin could have been the result of malnutrition. Another argument put forth is that the children were poisoned by arsenic and left to die in a forest near the Norfolk border. They survived and made their way to Wolf's Pit.

Or possibly, they were not only from another town or country, but another world altogether.

They claimed to have come from St Martin, a word that is close to Martian...

Of course, here in England, and especially in the south-east, there are many villages which incorporate the name St Martin.

Nestling next to the theory that the children came from another world entirely is the similar legend of Agartha, which describes an ancient lore that a world the like that we have never seen exists in the earth's core. An inner earth world that is linked to every continent by an extensive network of tunnels. This myth can be traced back to a French occultist, who, in 1910, republished a detailed account originally from 1886. According to the legends, there are several entrances to Agartha, in Kentucky, the Bermuda Triangle, the Soviet Union and the Himalayas. Could there be another, undocumented entrance, in the English county of Suffolk?

Taking a piece of the past, whether it be myth or fact, and finding out where that information will lead in a fictional account, is, readers, the spellbinding beauty of storytelling.

I hope you have enjoyed my incorporation of the Green Children of Woolpit into *The Perfect Village*.

Acknowledgements

Firstly, I am so appreciative for my family, all the generations (two of which have a starring role in *The Perfect Village*). Thank you to Darren and Cat and of course for my parents, Janet and Keith Hewitt. All the strange little historical facts that are embedded in my brain from my childhood were learned from these two.

To Marley, my constant writing companion, who reminds me with increasingly regular frequency when it is time to take a break and step away from the laptop.

Thank you to my agent, Laetitia Rutherford, and everyone at Watson, Little. The whole team at Canelo publishing; my editor, Siân Heap, thank you for your continued support and enthusiasm, for seemingly reading my mind on some sticking points and suggesting bold moves that made the story all the better. Kate Shepherd and Thanhmai Bui-Van who work incredibly hard to get authors and their books out into the world. Thanks to Iain Miller, as a fellow Suffolker, who may know the history of the Green Children.

Copyeditor Daniela, who did a wonderful job picking up those things that slip through the net and require clarification or attention, and for leaving me a lovely note in the margin saying how much she loved *The Perfect Village*, and also Alicia. Thanks to proofreader, Miranda and Head Design for their fantastic cover.

The writing community – those special groups of wonderful writers of all genres who I am so thankful to call my friends.

The bloggers, publishers, and book clubs; everything you do is appreciated.

My crime writing support system, Marion Todd, Sarah Ward, Sheila Bugler and Rachel Lynch. We are literally scattered from one end of the UK to the other, but we are in each other's hearts and inboxes every day.

Finally, a huge thanks to you, the reader, and as always, as long as you keep on enjoying my books, I'll keep on writing them.